P1

MW01048158

TRUMPED! Sex, Money, Real Estate: a love story

"Compelling, hilarious, and—sadly—utterly believeable."
—The Petter Times

"I feel like one of the 'chosen ones' to be among the first to discover this book. It's sure to become a cult favorite."
—Victor Howlin, comedian

"Witty, sharp, and yet compassionate for its hapless hero, TRUMPED! sucks you into its world, and then leaves you crying for more."
—Morten Gaie, Best Books Reviewed

"I am repelled by the satire…"
—Ronald Ace, motivational speaker

Praise again for TRUMPED! The juxtaposition of an honest sewer plant worker, a conniving mortgage broker, and a sexy blond looking out for her own best interests makes for a hilarious take on America in the 21st Century. Once you start reading, it's hard to stop.
—K. Hays, Practicing Virtues

"So good, you have to ask yourself, how did I live without it?"
—US Tomorrow

"I can't wait for the movie."
—Anonymous

TRUMPED!
Sex, Money, Real Estate

a love story

S. Pareto Rose

WingSpan Press

www.TRUMPEDthenovel.com

Cover photograph ©iStockphoto.com/2HotBrazil.

This is a work of fiction. All characters in this book are
fictitious, as are the places and incidents, and any resemblance
to actual persons, living or dead, business, companies, events,
or locales is entirely coincidental. Except Mickey, you know
who you are. Oh, and Ed, he knows who he is. But everybody
else is a product of an over-active imagination.

Special thanks to Mike Maley, Kim Hays, Christina Suter, and James
Salter for their encouragement, wise comments, and willingness to
read. Also thanks to Nat Quick, Jane White, Greg Harning and Bob
Carberry.

For information about the screenplay adaptation, go to
www.trumpedthemovie.com.

Printed in the United States of America

Published by WingSpan Press, Livermore, CA
www.wingspanpress.com

The WingSpan name, logo and colophon are the trademarks of
WingSpan Publishing.

ISBN 978-1-59594-349-1

First edition 2010

Library of Congress Control Number 2010925516

This book is dedicated to our parents, who taught us that rare is the piece of wrapping paper that cannot be reused. And to our children, Juliano, Claire, and Emily.

TRUMPED!
Sex, Money, Real Estate

a love story

"SAN FRANCISCO (MUNY Magazine) - The verdict is out: real estate is the new deal. Home values are like balloons on nitrous oxide- they just keep getting higher. If you've got a house, you've got more than profit on paper. You've got equity under your roof, cash in your pocket, and credit cards galore. Keep on spending."
Dick Holler, MUNY Magazine, Nov. 15, 2005

Prologue

Sump Valley Sewage Treatment Plant, California, a Bright Spring Day

"My mortgage broker got me a hell of a deal," says Robert, biting into a salami-turkey-Mozzarella sandwich with gusto. *Chomp, mumph, chew.*

The maintenance crew and the operators are sitting around the control console in the sunshine eating their lunches to the sound of blackbirds vying for seeds in the drying sludge and the faint whiff of processing waste. Spirits are high: It's the aftermath of the .com boom and money is flowing like waste water.

He continues, his jaw intermittently chewing while he talks. "We owe 75,000 on our place but it's..." *chomp, chew* "...worth at least a half a million dollars. So I go to this mortgage broker and say I want to refinance." Robert takes a long slug of his soft drink. "No problem, says the guy. And he gets me 150,000 dollars in cash. 2.5% adjustable, sign here and *wala!* New truck and lux RV."

"Oh yeah?" says Doug, washing his double beef bean burrito down with Lime Jarana soda. "My mortgage broker got me 200 K and I owe more than you on my house. I've already paid for a customized Vet. Cash."

Frank guffaws loudly. "How the hell are you gonna fit in a Corvette, Doug?"

"None of your business, dickhead."

"Hey, well guess what my mortgage broker got me?" says Mike who's been dying to cut in. "A negative amt loan. And we don't pay on the house. We don't even have to pay all of the interest. Brand new house."

"Whoa," says Frank, impressed. Frank is the youngest and doesn't own anything except his vehicle. "Do you think your guy could do something for me?"

"If you look on the internet," interrupts Robert, "you can find companies that'll give you a loan with nothing down. My broker is helping me buy a second house now with nothing down, just the equity in our first one. Then I'll sell it. That's the way to make money now: real estate. Jump in before prices go so high you can't afford it."

"Yeah," says Jack, eating the last of his chips. "Real estate is the only way for guys like us to get rich. You gotta have money for the stock market. You don't need nothing for real estate."

"Hey, about being on a reality show?" jokes Ed, crumpling up his sandwich paper and tossing it into the can. "You don't need a buy-in for that."

*"Real estate is the most beautiful thing in the world. It's real, it's
solid, and it gives me a hard-on every time. I love it."*
Ronald Ace, The Great Dream

1

Golf is a beautiful game. Everywhere you look on a golf course,
it's spacious, clean, and beautiful. Everybody is healthy and well-
groomed. They wear nice pastel shirts and speak in confident
voices. There's no empty lots, no homeless talking to themselves.
No garbage bins or junky cars. No rat-infested ivy or untamed
junipers marring the greens. No potholes or traffic jams. No dead
trees. And no electrical lines or telephone poles to wreck your
view. Only calm expanses of rolling green grass dotted with pale
moons of sand here and there and the leafy silhouettes of trees.
Even the sky above your head is separate from everybody else's
sky. It's a world unto itself. And when you get tired, you just drive
your cart over those smooth green pastures to the club house.
Hello, you say, to some associates and the president of the bank
you met at the seventh tee. How about joining us for a bourbon
on the rocks? No? How about a whiskey sour? Lunch? Shall we
have lobster or prime rib? Lovely day, isn't it? How's your 401 K
doing? It could be better. Mine only gained a quarter of a million
this year...

Ed chuckles to himself, and goes back to fixing his dad's old
lawnmower for the umpteenth time. It's a Saturday morning and
he wishes the mower would just completely die so he could feel
justified in throwing it away and buying a new one. But it lives
on, his father's spirit incarnate.

Ed Fasouli lives on the family homestead, a neighborhood eyesore ever since developers put in one of the best golf courses in the area right behind the house. To begin with, the homestead was a generous, stone-clad house, one-story, three bedrooms, double lot, big old trees, on a pot-holed county road. Then came the golf course. Then came the improved golf course. And then came the fancy gated community with country club houses and landscaped yards. Now his place is the inner city of Country Club Estates. Between the recurring drought, the cost of water, and all the broken sprinkler heads his lawn looks like mange, and his house, now dwarfed by the others, looks like the maintenance shed. But one day he's going to make a lot of money. He's just waiting for the right opportunity.

Now, unbeknownst to him, an arrogant investor named Keaton Brown is out on the fairway behind Ed's house arguing with his father, Harry Brown, founder of Pacific Realty. They have just pulled up to the seventh tee and Keaton is trying to hurry things along because he has to be back at the office in two hours.

"Jeez, Dad. Haven't you read The Ronald by now? 'Home.' What is that? Would you hang on to an old washing machine just because your parents had it?"

"You shouldn't treat someone's home as an investment, Keaton!" says Harry. He's been in the business a long time. He's seen the town quadruple over the past twenty years and he's proud to have been a significant part of that growth. But he doesn't like what's happening now. "What if people suddenly can't make their payments? Who's left holding the bag?"

"What does it matter, Dad? In the end, you've cleared the deal. That's all that counts." Keaton purposely sticks out his elbows as he bends down to tee up the ball, to push his dad away. His old man and all his 'scruples,' as he calls them. What's the purpose of being in real estate if it isn't to make money? He takes his stance, pulls the club up high, rotating the way his golf instructor taught him. Then a thought pops into his mind and he drops his arms. "You are being sentimental about something that is just a product. A product that can be used as a vehicle to create wealth."

"What do you know?" grumbles his dad as Keaton brings the club up for a second time, rotates back into position and, in one smooth motion, brings it down solidly behind the ball. A satisfying 'thwack!' rings out and the ball sails up into the cloudless sky before it does a banana slice to the right.

"Shit," says Keaton.

"Frikin piece of junk," says Ed, losing his patience with the lawnmower. He throws down the wrench on the cement. It bounces off the driveway and lands in the dirt. The head of the bolt he is trying to loosen drops to the ground in a sprinkle of rust. He sits back on his heels and glares at the lawnmower.

Now if he could afford a gardener like two-thirds of the homes in his neighborhood, it'd be different. Like Mickey Schulz across the street. Then he wouldn't even have to worry about a lawnmower. He'd just tell the gardeners what to do, and they'd do it. In fact, if he had a gardener, he'd have a housekeeper too. Then he wouldn't have to worry about cleaning the house or getting the kids to clean the house. Now that would be good. Imagine being a single dad with two kids and every morning at seven a.m. the housekeeper shows up. Makes the coffee, prepares the breakfast. All he has to do is show up in the kitchen. The newspaper would be waiting on the table for him. If the kids didn't like the breakfast, well, tell Juanita to make them something else. He wouldn't have to make dinners anymore either! Juanita, I feel like fried chicken tonight, he'd say. Do you think you could take care of it? Oh, si senor Fasouli, she'd say. And all he'd have to do is go off to work and when he came home: Fried chicken waiting for him for dinner. It'd be better than being married! Of course, if she was attractive, maybe a dark-haired beauty, with lovely breasts…

Ed's ruminations are suddenly truncated by a piercing

scream. His heart feels like an explosion. He jumps up to a standing position. It's Meledy! Where is she? He looks wildly around, waiting for a second sound to come, to tell him where he should look. And then he hears it: Meledy sobbing wildly.

"Daddy, Daddy," she cries. His fifteen-year-old daughter comes running from the back yard, blood everywhere. On her face, on her hands, on her hair, on her chest. Tears streaming down her face.

Ed runs toward her, his arms around her before he even knows he's reached her. "Oh, my baby! What happened?"

"My tooth," she cries, holding out her bloodied, quivering hand. And there, like a little pearl, is the lower half of her left front tooth. "I was just in the backyard listening to music when a golf ball hit it."

"Oh, jeez," says Ed. "Don't worry, honey. We'll get it fixed. It'll be alright."

"Wow…" says eleven-year-old Buddy running up to them with his friend Sam. Buddy is Meledy's eleven-year old brother and Sam lives across the street and is his best friend.

"Awesome," says Sam.

This makes Meledy cry even louder.

"Buddy!" commands Ed. "Go into the kitchen and bring me a clean glass from the cupboard with a little milk in the bottom. Hurry up! Sam, you go with him and look for a bag of frozen peas in the freezer." The boys start running towards the house. "And bring me the car keys!" shouts Ed.

"Come on, honey." He leads her into the garage where he grabs a roll of paper towels to soak up the blood and assess the damage. "Don't you worry," he tells his whimpering daughter, "they can reattach things like that now. It'll be fine."

Buddy and Sam reappear with the milk, a bag of frozen peas and the car keys.

"Can we go with you?" asks Buddy, "Please?"

"All right," says Ed. "Push the lawnmower out of the way." He leads Meledy to the twenty-year-old, dark blue Mercedes station wagon (a really solid car even if it has the sex appeal of a tortoise) parked in the garage and opens the front passenger door for her. "Hold the peas on your mouth," he says and gets in behind the wheel. Buddy and Sammy climb in the back and Ed starts up the motor. Ed puts the car in reverse, steps on the accelerator pedal and the wagon shoots out of the garage.

Honk!!

Ed jams on the brakes and looks in the rearview mirror. A brand new black Escalade fills up his view. It's Mickey Schulz, Sammy's dad, who has just backed out of the Schulz driveway across the street.

Mickey rolls down the tinted glass of his car, leans out the window and shouts, "Hey Eddie! What's the hurry? Sell me your house and I'll throw in a moving truck so you have someplace to sleep!" He laughs manically, and, without waiting for any response from Ed, he speeds off down the tree-lined street.

"I guess he's late," says Sammy, face red.

Your dad is such an asshole, you poor kid, thinks Ed. He waits for Mickey to reach the end of the street, and then he continues on his way.

Sam is a good kid because Michelle is a good mother. Nobody can be blamed for who their father is. Look at Ed's father. The tightest, stingiest, most negative old Greek in town. He was so tight with money that you could hear his fingers squeak every time he had to pay for something. The only big thing he believed in was his home. A man's home is more than a castle, he used to say, a man's home is his family. It's the only thing in life that gets passed on from generation to generation. Which is why Ed still lives in the family home. His dad would have disowned him if he would have gone to live somewhere else.

By the time Ed pulls up to the dentist office, Meledy has stopped whimpering. Dr. Vasarin's office, Ed knows this from passing by it on his way to work, is open 24 hours a day, 7 days a week, and is the "Home of the Xtreme Tooth Makeover." The front door opens silently as he pulls it towards him and they all file in.

"Hello there," says the receptionist solicitously. "What can we do for you today? Oh you poor thing!" she exclaims, noticing Meledy. "It must hurt terribly."

Meledy, holding the bag of frozen peas to her mouth, looks at her like a dog that has just been punished. She shakes her head and mumbles, "No, it doesn't hurt too bad."

"A golf ball hit her," explains Ed. "Can you believe it? My daughter's just had her a front tooth broken by a golf ball," as if he can barely believe it himself. The receptionist coos sympathetically again and hands Ed a clipboard with a form to fill out.

"Do you need a pen?" she asks, offering him a black one with a giant tooth attached. "You can fill this out while I notify Dr. Vasarin."

Ed takes the clipboard and pen and goes over to the waiting area. "Take a seat, kids," he says.

The waiting room has many chairs lining the three walls. It's as if Dr. Vasarin anticipates twenty patients at a time. He sits down in the nearest chair and looks down at the questions on the clipboard. He pauses at the address for a second to steal a glance at the gorgeous woman sitting opposite him. Luckily, she's reading a book and doesn't notice him. Ed looks back at the form and fills in the address, checks 'no' to previous medical conditions. Then he glances up again, as if he's considering what he will write next. She could have been a model. She has beautiful blond hair, and she's wearing a deep-cut blouse that indicates lovely breasts underneath. He glances at her shapely, tanned legs. Then he looks at the book she is so engrossed in. "The Dream," by Ronald Ace. Ronald Ace? Isn't he that big real estate guy who's on TV all the time? Ed finishes the form and takes it back to the receptionist. He waits while she scans the form.

"Meledy Fasouli, okay. And Dr. Vasarin has never seen you. Okay. And is that 1200 or 1700 Country Club?" she asks.

The lovely blond casually looks up from her book.

"1200," answers Ed. "1200 Country Club Estates."

The receptionist makes a note. "And what's your wife's name and phone number?"

"There is no wife," says Ed dryly.

The receptionist, slightly embarrassed, coughs and asks, "Would you like to pay with credit card or personal check?"

"Check," says Ed. He hasn't bothered with credit cards, as strange as that may sound, ever since Jayne took him to the cleaners. At least, that's how he sees it.

"Okay, it'll be just another few minutes," says the receptionist.

The blond turns her curious glance from the exchange at the reception window to the children. Meledy, noticing her, glares back. Ed, oblivious, sits back down in the chair and glances at Meledy to see how she's holding up. Meledy tries to smile and he gives her a thumbs-up. Then he turns to look straight ahead, the way any normal person would do, and is met by a smile so white and flirtatious, that it practically blinds him. Mesmerized, he just stares.

"Meledy? Dr. Vasarin is ready for you now," says a voice from a hereto closed door. Ed turns. It's a tall, bulky assistant in white pants and smock.

Thank god! thinks Ed. He rises and walks with Meledy to the door of the examining rooms, but the assistant pushes him back.

"They do better without their parents hanging onto them," she says crisply. She takes the bag of frozen peas from Meledy and dumps them in his hand. "Come on, honey. We'll call you if we need you, Mr....," she looks at the clipboard, "Fuceoli."

"Fasouli," says Ed in irritation.

He settles back down in his chair and there she is again, looking straight at him, beaming, book in hand. Ed is starting to feel unnerved. Is she some kind of religious fanatic? Or, is she just showing off her teeth? He decides to smile back and then his gaze

9

slides automatically downwards to her chest. She doesn't have lovely cleavage, she has fabulous cleavage. Deep and inviting. He clenches the bag of peas a little tighter.

The woman takes his smile as an invitation. "Poor girl!" she exclaims softly. Her voice has a foreign accent and is melodic and warm. "Teeth are such important accessory for woman!"

Embarrassed to be caught looking at her chest, Ed quickly looks at her nose. "Well, she doesn't know much about stuff like that." What kind of stupid answer is that?

"Must be very difficult, raising girl with no mother. You have girlfriend who can teach her?"

"Uh, no," he stammers in surprise. How does she know there's no mother?

"You live in nice neighborhood. Must be nice women there to help. All woman want to help girls be beautiful!" She says this with such conviction, such warmth, such compassion that Ed finds himself curiously drawn in. He shifts the bag of peas to his other hand.

"What country do you come from?" he asks.

"I come from little Astonia," she pouts. She looks lovely when she pouts. Those sweet lips. "Nobody hears of that country. Very little, very poor." She looks at him hopefully, and at that moment the ugly dental assistant appears.

"Mr. Fuceoli," she barks.

Ed bolts upright, forgetting about the frozen peas, and they fall to the floor with a plop. He looks down at them in horror. If he bends down to pick them up, he will be at eye-level with the woman's skirt. This won't do at all.

"Mr. Fuceoli?" The assistant's voice takes on an audible note of impatience.

"Fasouli!" says Ed. "Just a moment." He looks at the assistant and then at Buddy and Sammy who are hunched behind an old "Sports Illustrated" magazine from November 2004.

"Buddy!" says Ed, moving in the direction of the assistant. "Grab the bag of balls, the peas! I mean, the peas!" Humiliated by this slip of the tongue, he hurries to speak to the dental assistant.

The foreign woman turns her amused gaze at Buddy and Sam who have been peeking at her from behind the magazine. The two of them take in her inviting smile, simultaneously drop the magazine and lunge for the lumpy bag of no-longer frozen peas. In a scene that only a comedy duo would have attempted, they actually butt shoulders and break into loud giggles. Then they hurry back to their safe seats, leaving the peas in the middle of the floor.

The woman laughs at them. Then she rips out the last page in her book, grabs a pencil from her Coach purse on the floor beside her, and scribbles something down. She folds the paper in half, and in half again. And in half again, until it is a neat, small packet.

"Tatiana Talliin?" announces the ugly dental assistant, opening the door.

Tatiana collects her book and purse, and then gracefully bends down and picks up the bag of peas. The boys watch her.

"Bye-bye, boys," she says. "Mr. Fasouli?" She proffers the bag of peas to Ed who is writing a check at the counter. The little white folded piece of paper sits clearly on top of the peas. She gives him her most gorgeous come-on smile and looks him straight in the eyes. "Call me."

Ed takes the peas and the note. No one has come onto him like this in ages. He's the middle-aged, single dad at the school events who the committee moms all feel sorry for. He's the dad who's always alone at the sidelines of the baseball game because the husbands don't feel comfortable around him. And he's the one the waitress are all so kind to when he takes the kids to Applebits for dinner. And now he is totally at a loss.

"Thank you," he mutters, wondering what he should say. The thought of a 'date' scares him to death. Luckily, Meledy comes out the door at that moment and Tatiana disappears into the examining room.

Ed finishes writing his check, gets an appointment card, and breaths a sigh of relief. He shepherds his kids to the door and holds it open as they file past. Then, just before he exits himself, he surreptitiously unfolds the paper and sees…a name and a phone number. He stares at it. He thinks of those full breasts, those gorgeous legs. What the hell does a woman like that want with me, he thinks? He crumples it up and tosses it in the umbrella stand next to the door and pulls the door firmly behind him.

"What do you say kids," he says once they are all in the car. "Shall we go to Applebits for lunch?"

"I want pizza!"

"I can't eat. Let's go to Smoothie Palace."

"That's too expensive."

"Taco King! Taco King!"

What a headache.

That night, after work, Tatiana Talliin unbuttons her slightly too-tight blouse (she really needs to stop eating those peanut butter cups but they are so creamy and salty/sweet; she adores them) and slips on a silky camisole. On second thought, she decides to take off her bra as well and trades her skirt for a skimpy pair of sleep shorts. There. That feels better.

She looks around her small studio apartment and imagines that one day, this will just be her dressing room. She saw a photo of Lada Ace's dressing room in a magazine once. It wasn't just a room—it was a ROOM. A whole room with wall-to-wall shoe cupboards and chests of drawers and rack after rack of clothes; beautiful, colorful, elegant clothes.

For a studio, her apartment isn't bad. The price is certainly right. Her salary as a manicurist at the Golden Toe Spa is not very much. But she is sure that one day she will be rich. She is studying The Ronald's works, and she is convinced it can work for everyone. You just need enough ambition (she certainly has that; after all, she's braved the immigration officers in San Francisco) and, what's that word? Per-ser-ver-ance. If one thing doesn't work out, another will. She looks in the mirror and smiles at herself. She is the maker of her own destiny and she is sure her destiny is here, in this country brimming with real estate potential.

She walks over to an ivory-painted chest of drawer and pulls out a pack of matches from the top drawer. Then she proceeds to light all ten candles arranged on both sides of the altar she has made there. She checks the water level in the vase of flowers next to the photo. The flowers are white Lily of the Valley and Balinese Jasmine, and they smell heavenly. She breathes in the fragrance deeply and happily. Lada's favorite kind. She lowers her eyes and tries to still her mind and focus her attention, and then she looks up. There, in the center of her alter, is the gold framed photo of Lada looking regal and all-knowing.

"Oh, wise and beautiful one," she murmurs, "help me to be more like you. To follow in your footsteps." She pauses thoughtfully. "Today I met a man who doesn't look like much, but he has perhaps much potential. You made The Ronald into what he is today. Even though maybe he doesn't know it. I am thinking, this man, he owns house on golf course and he has no wife. Land is beginning of all wealth. This is beginning. He hasn't called me. But I got his number."

She reverently picks up the photo and kisses it and gently puts it down.

"I am the maker of my destiny," she intones to herself. Seize the moment. She came here to make her destiny. Good-bye crummy Astonia.

She still remembers the day she walked off the plane and into the San Francisco International Airport. She felt exhausted and exhilarated at the same time! All those people! Like a river flowing to the flood gates of the immigration officers. Everyone pushing and moving ahead towards one place: United States Homeland Security!

When she got to the Immigration officers, the crowd divided. U.S. citizens to the left, non-U.S. citizens to the right. She filed along between the ropes and began the slow march forward to the agents who could grant you entry or turn you back.

Finally, she was at the head of the line. She could feel the eyes of the guard watching her. She pulled back her shoulders, and gave him one of her blinding smiles.

"How are you?" she asked.

He mumbled in return, stripping her with his eyes. She laughed. Such a homely man. Like one of the farmers back home.

Then it was her turn. She strutted up, passport in hand and looked straight at the agent behind the window with her most disarming smile and pushed out her chest.

"I'm here religious visa," she cooed innocently, handing over her already opened passport. She watched in pleasure as the officer's gaze lingered long on her cleavage before looking down at the passport.

"Tatiana Talliin?" he said, feeling the t's roll off the tip of his tongue. He looked up again and smiled at her. God she had beautiful breasts, he thought. He quickly passed her passport over the scanner without lowering his eyes and grabbed his entry stamp. "Welcome to the U.S., Miss Talliin," he said, banging the stamp down on his hand instead of her passport without even noticing. "Where are you going to be staying?"

She smiled coyly. "I have old auntie in Santa Rosa," she said.

"Lucky her," said Officer Smith, licking his lips wetly, and still not moving his eyes. "You take care of yourself now."

He never once looked at her visa. Tatiana reclines leisurely on her fake satin sheets. Almost a year has gone by—something has to come her way! She is not going to accept failure. She believes! But time is ticking. She won't be young forever.

"Life is about taking chances and if your foot slips through a hole in the safety net, the point is—you've taken a risk. I'm huge because I take risks—every day."
Ronald Ace, The Magic of Business

2

As the morning sunlight hits his face, Ed stands in his front door and has his usual split-second fantasy. His is the most beautiful house on the street and everything around him is simply an extension of his own property. In fact, he's so rich that it's actually his own private golf course he is looking at. But then a car goes by down the street and he is once again just looking at the overly-manicured yard and ostentatious portico of the Schulz house across the street.

He takes a deep breath of the mild spring air and shuffles out into the morning and down the walkway. He passes the sagging cardboard box he keeps besides the garage for all the golf balls that fly over the fence, and stops at the sidewalk. There it is, his morning newspaper. Lying in the gutter as always. Why can't that guy in the ratty Toyota ever make it as far as the driveway? He bends down and picks up the paper, and shuffles back towards the house, humming to himself, ready to get on with another day. Might as well.

"Meledy! Buddy!" he shouts as he passes through the living room on his way to the kitchen at the back of the house. The aroma of freshly brewed coffee fills the room. The first cup of coffee. His favorite time of day, when anything is still possible. Who knows what today will bring?

He chooses his "Worker of the Month" cup and pours himself a cup coffee. Sets it on the counter and as he does, he sees he

15

forgot to go through the mail from yesterday. There it is, still in a pile. He picks it up and quickly shuffles through it: A credit card offer ("You have been pre-approved!"), a real estate flyer ("I've got a buyer for your house!"), a car dealership ad ("Get a new Chevy and pay nothing for a whole year!"), the dentist reminder (need that), another credit card application, another shiny real estate card and a free house appraisal coupon (what's that for?). Junk, thinks Ed, and dumps it all in the recycling bag at the end of the counter. He pulls the carton of milk out of the fridge, and grabs three bowls from the cupboard, three spoons from the drawer. These he sets on the table, and then scoops up the various cereal boxes with their various contents from the counter and sets them on the table too.

"C'mon guys!! We've got to leave in twenty-five minutes!" he calls.

"I'm coming," yells Meledy in a totally annoyed tone of voice from another part of the house. "Buddy is hogging the bathroom."

Ed pours a splash of milk into his coffee and sits down at the table to glance at the morning's headlines. At that moment, Buddy half-falls, half-runs into the kitchen, throws his backpack near the kitchen door and grabs the Marshmallow Peewees. Meledy is in hot pursuit behind him.

"I dibbed those, you butt-head," she snaps and neatly snatches them out of his hands.

"Dad!" wails Buddy.

Meledy grabs one of the cereal bowls as she sits down at the table and pours the bag of cereal into her bowl, but all that's left is a half of a cup of cereal dust.

Buddy starts laughing. He's planned this all along. He's the one who put it back empty yesterday. He quickly snatches the Sugar Loops, Meledy's second favorite, before she realized what happened.

"I hate you," she snarls. "I'm going to have English muffins."

16

By the time Ed drops the kids off at their respective schools and drives through the curved wrought iron gates of the Sump Valley Sewage Plant where he works as an operations engineer (a 'soft wares' engineer, as he likes to joke), it's past eight-thirty.

The Swamp Valley Sewage Treatment Plant was constructed decades ago next to an estuary leading to the river. Originally, it was supposed to have had a pond system to naturally filter the effluence before it was released into the river. But the town council sold off a chunk of the land to a developer for a good price and put in a traditional system with huge sediment tanks and processors which relied on a lot of mechanical parts to move sludge and water during the various stages of filtering. There were constant breakdowns and the whole place was seriously in need of upgrading because the district population had more than doubled in the past twenty years. More people, more shit. Everybody knows that.

One day we are going to have a huge mess, thinks Ed, stepping out into the pungent smelling air. He's parked in his usual spot upwind from the settling tanks. It's a longer walk to the maintenance building, but the car loses the smell of the plant faster in the evening. Plus, he gets a chance to listen to the birds as he walks in. He likes that about where he works–all the birds from the estuary hang around the plant picking at the seeds and bugs. It's a peaceful sound that helps drown out the drone of the machinery. The sewer plant wasn't his first choice of a job, but it is safe, secure, and the regular guys are loyal to him. If he has to leave early for a school function, or can't make it in because one of the kids is sick, they always cover for him.

He shoves his cell phone into its holder and heads towards the maintenance building. Halfway there, he passes three Mexican guys hired to paint the rusty diverting valves and pipes and he glances at their work. They have about seven cans of paint with them and seem to be painting according to a sketch taped to one of the pipes, like a paint-by-numbers picture.

"What are you guys doing?" he stops to ask. "Are you color-coding the pipes according to that sketch?"

"Yeah," answers one of the guys as he puts the finishing touch on a peacock blue pipe.

"But those two pipes shouldn't be the same color," exclaims Ed. "One goes to the estuary and the other goes to the first sediment tank. They're two totally different systems!"

"Oh, well," shrugs the guy with the baggy jeans, boxers showing. "Mr. Steward think it look better, and he's boss. He pay. So if you don like it, you go talk to HIM."

"Steward?" asks Ed incredulously. "What does he know about the system?" Steward is the plant's new director, hired by his uncle, a city manager. It was pure nepotism. You don't need an MBA to manage a sewer treatment plant, you need an engineering degree so you can understand what's at stake. Maybe Ed didn't finish his degree, but he sure understands what's at stake.

Disgusted, he turns away and strides across the rest of the forty feet to the maintenance building, muttering to himself. "All this for a picnic. Hey guys!" he greets Dave and Big Doug as he enters the building.

Big Doug has a long face. "Boss," he says, "we got a stuck valve. The release valve in settling tank number two is frozen solid."

"*Ohshit*," says Ed, like it's one word, and they all laugh. "You already did the usual, right?"

Big Doug nods his head.

"I knew this was going to happen," says Ed. "It's going to keep happening more and more. Tell Frank to get his ass over there. He can help me."

Ed dons his overalls and then locates his rubberized hip boots hanging on a peg. Gloves, a large hammer, and a humongous box wrench finish his gear. He checks the messages on his desk, pops his cell phone in his shirt pocket, grabs the over-sized rubber gloves, and heads for the door. By the time he gets to settling tank number two, Big Doug and Frank are already on the catwalk circling the upper edge of the tank. Frank cinches the last clasp on his safety harness while BD watches Ed climb the ladder. BD is already sweating profusely in the mid-morning sun.

"You all set to go down?" he jokes as he hands Ed the second safety harness. BD was hired as the plant welder, but he's constantly got back problems and can't weld. No one dares to say it's because he's so fat, but they all think it. And they've got to outsource their welding every time something breaks, while BD amuses himself with overseeing others. Today he's the spotter. He's a nice guy, just totally useless.

Ed nods and hands BD the tools in exchange for the harness. He looks down into the tank. Luckily it drained fairly completely. He pulls on a pair of surgical gloves and then the big rubber gloves and follows Frank down the iron-rung ladder on the inside of the tank and joins him in the muck. It stinks, no two ways about it. He blocks his sinuses and breathes from his mouth while they study the large, rusted, crud-covered valve at the end of the pipe which protrudes about a foot out from the side and two feet up from the bottom. A tiny brown trickle clings to the bottom of the pipe. The last time this happened, it took them all day. Today he wants time to go home before he goes to Buddy and Sam's baseball game.

"Lez ged dis sucker loose and ged ouda here," he says in his nasally, congested sounding voice. He awkwardly fits the box wrench onto the valve and the two of them start pressing downward.

He hands Frank the wrench. Frank is twenty-two and his MP3 player has become a growth on his head. He bounces his body in time to some rhythm that only he can hear. Ed thinks it's dangerous but Frank swears that the goofy earphones he hooks backwards onto his ears so that the sound is behind them allow him to hear just perfectly.

"What?" shouts Frank pushing down hard on the wrench.

"We just don't want to break it," says Ed loudly. The thing is really stuck. But if they don't get it unstuck, they'll have to have it replaced, which means even more lost time, and in the meanwhile, they are running out of settling tanks and the sludge eventually has to go somewhere.

"You boys let me know if you need anything," calls BD from the catwalk. His fat belly presses against the railing like rising dough. "You wouldn't want to slow down preparations for the pic-y-nic, now would you?" Ed and Frank both laugh. Everybody is talking about the picnic.

At that moment, Ed's cell phone starts vibrating in his pocket. Should he answer it? It might be one of the kids.

"Here, try this," he says. He hands Frank the hammer and hastily pulls pulls off one of the gloves so he can grab his cell phone. "'ello?" he says, sounding like a three-day cold.

"Eddie?" says a woman's voice hesitantly.

Ed is dumbstruck. Of all times. He quickly opens his nasal passages. "Yes, hello. This is Ed."

"Oh. Remember me? We met at Dentist Office?"

"Uh, hi. Sure. I remember you." What was her name again?

"Then I'm so happy!" Tatiana says now. "Imagine how embarrassing if you don't remember me. You didn't call me."

She makes a little sound through her pouty mouth. She is taking the morning off and working the evening shift. She luxuriously stretches her slender legs on the rose-colored sheets and runs the fingers of her right hand lightly across the narrow strap of her camisole, and then casually pulls her hair up from the back of her neck.

"Uh, listen," says Ed, blushing as if he were in the room with her. "I'm kinda busy right now."

"Everything okay, boss?" shouts BD from up above. Ed turns his body away for a little privacy.

"I just calling to go on date," says Tatiana. "Maybe Saturday you're not busy." She has an incredible voice. It's like the titillating feel of a stream of pure cool water streaming down your back on a hot day. "You could pick me up downtown at streets Third and

Hastings, say around five o'clock, and we could have some fun. What do you think?"

"What?" says Ed loudly. He can't hear well over Frank's hammering. He glances in that direction and notices with a certain amount of alarm that Frank is getting the valve loose and that the trickle of effluence under the valve is getting bigger. "I can't hear you very well..." says Ed.

"A date," shouts Tatiana into the phone. "Do you want to meet me at five of the clock Saturday at Third Street and Hastings? Where I work?"

"Third and Hastings? Sure." Ed looks over his shoulder at Frank and sees that the trickle is now a steady full stream. "But I really have to go now." He is about to hang up when he realizes... "What was your name again?"

"Tatiana. But call me Tat. Is much more friendly. Bye-bye!"

"I got it, boss!" shouts Frank. "Let's get out of here!"

Ed looks over and sure enough, it is flowing. He grabs his wrench and hammer from Frank and the two head for the ladder. Franks gets there first. He grabs hold of a rung and starts the ascent. "Sounds like you've got some mud coming for your turtle..." he says.

"Oh, shut up," says Ed following close behind him. "Where did you learn that one?!" He's planning on calling to cancel later when he has a free moment. He'll think up some excuse.

"Well, at least you'll have a date for the picnic. Who wants to come to a company picnic all alone? Especially one honoring our new director. What a douche."

"Who cares about that," says Ed. "But if we ever have a major emergency here, I swear to God it'll be all his fault for buying paint instead of parts."

The two reach the catwalk and catch their breath. Frank looks down.

"Whoa, dude!" he says. "That was close.

Ed is still thinking about what's going on at the plant when he drives up to the baseball field that evening. The parking lot is filled those giganto new SUV trucks, which honestly do not fit into normal parking spaces, and he needs to either park in the dirt somewhere or take the risk of parking next to one of them and getting his car scratched or even dented. He chooses the dirt, and has a longer walk to the field. As he walks up to the bleachers, he hears the parents discussing loans and refinancing and the current trend of buying houses for nothing down. What ever happened to just talking about baseball? He says hi and nods to a few faces, but then takes up his usual spot behind the backstop so he can watch the pitches come in. It's a home game and Buddy's team needs to win this game if they're going to make it to the championship this year. As he stands and looks out at the field, waiting for the game to begin, he notices that the back field fence is lined solid with real estate, bank, and car dealership banners. It used to be the lone tire dealership or the local dairy banners so you could concentrate on the game.

In the parking lot behind him, a beige SUV pulls up, circles around, and then parks in the dirt under a tree next to his car. An attractive, dark-haired woman gets out and opens the back passenger door. A fat little Corgi hops down onto the pavement. The woman leashes it and hurries towards the field, dog in tow.

"Ed!" she says warmly, coming up to stand next to him.

Ed turns towards the voice and his face lights up with pleasure.

"Michelle!"

Michelle gives him an innocent peck on the cheek and Ed feels his cheeks go warm for a split second. "What's the score?"

'They're just starting. You haven't missed anything."

"Good. So, how's our heroine doing? You must have been terrified," she says, touching his arm in lightly.

"If only you knew," says Ed. He steps back ever so slightly. He hates to admit how attractive he still finds Michelle after all these years. He tries to rationalize it by telling himself he's just horny as hell. And he is. It's been too long—way too long—since he's had sex with a woman. But he hates dating because they always want to know what happened to 'the mom' and he does not like to talk about that. Plus, when it comes down to it, he hates spending money on a date because it usually doesn't amount to anything. He'll shell out for an occasional porn movie to watch after the kids have gone to bed, but that's about it.

"I bet you thought about your dad, didn't you," asks Michelle.

"Well, I suppose it crossed my mind," Ed admits.

Ed's dad, John—may he rest in peace—was killed by a golf ball in the middle of his own driveway one fine day. What a shock that had been. Michelle had first met the man, and Ed too, at John's restaurant. Her dad had a law office next door. One day, after high school got out, she went downtown to deliver some papers for her dad. But it turned out, her dad was having a late lunch at John's. The two were talking and Ed was there, bussing tables, his after-school job.

"Here's my son," said John proudly to Michelle's father, while Michelle sat next to him. "I'm teaching him to work for a living. Not like you lawyers," he joked, patting Ed on the back.

Michelle still remembers to this day the way Ed rolled his eyes and mouthed 'not like you lawyers' behind his dad's back. She'd always liked his sense of humor. Kind of dry and a little wacky once you got to know him. He had been the fastest pitcher on the high school team but his father never went to more than one game a season. When Ed was offered a baseball scholarship for UC, all his dad had to say was, 'Baseball? You idiot! How you going to earn money playing baseball? You go to the JC and learn business! That's what you're going to do.' Maybe that's why he really joined the Navy, she thought. Not because of her, like Mickey said.

"That's what you get for owning the best lot on the golf course," she teases him. "So, is she feeling better?"

"She's fine now. She's tough. She soaked up all the attention and missed a day of school. That's all."

"Anything I can do to help?" Michelle has helped care for Meledy ever since Jayne left. In fact, once Jayne left, Michelle became like a second mother to the kids.

"How about bringing Daisy over to visit? That's usually good for a laugh," says Ed. He and Michelle look down at Daisy simultaneously and Daisy, on cue, gets up and sniffs the puddle of pee she just noticed she was sitting in.

"This dog," says Michelle shaking her head in exasperation. "Maybe you'd rather not..."

"Want a professional opinion on how to clean it up? Friend rate," says Ed. How could anyone love a dog like that?

Buddy is first to bat. He steps up to the plate and takes a few practice swings.

"Thataboy, Buddy!" shouts Ed. "Fast hands!" The first pitch comes in and Buddy hits it hard, straight out to left field. A loud cheer goes up from the team parents. It's a home run! First hit, first inning. It bodes well.

"Too bad Sam doesn't get up to bat very much," says Ed. "He's improving, but there's a lot of talented kids on the team. If Mickey ever spent a little time with him..." He might play better, thinks Ed. But Mickey is too busy gallivanting around. Real estate seminars, broker meetings, affairs. Ed glances sideways at Michelle. He wonders if she knows about Mickey's infidelities. He can't believe she's that stupid.

"You know that's not going to happen. You're just being nice because Buddy is so good. He takes after you."

"It is tough having to live up to a gifted father," says Ed, reaching up and smoothing his hair back like an old time movie star.

"You were good, that's for sure," says Michelle. "You should play again! You like it."

"Na, it's over. But, hey, would you mind if the kids came over for dinner Saturday? I have ..." here he stops. What should he say he has? An appointment? A meeting? Call it like it is... "I have a date with a woman." With a woman I don't even know, he thinks.

"You have a date? Why Ed! I thought you didn't date. You never go out with me!"

"You're married!" says Ed.

"So? I'm never with my husband."

"Well, you're with his dog all the time and that's just as bad."

"Daisy? But I feel sorry for her. And she's so irresistible."

Ed looks down at Daisy with a mixture of distaste and compassion.

"Yeah, just like Mickey, irresistible."

"Oh, Ed."

Daisy looks at Ed and burps. Dogs. "They're worse than five year olds," says Michelle, shaking her head. "So where did you meet her?" she asks.

"The dentist's."

"Oooo," winks Michelle. "White teeth."

"It's a pain to become who you are meant to be, believe me. But it's more of a pain if you end up being somebody else. Don't ever stop goaling yourself! "
Ronald Ace, My Life!

3

Saturday afternoon, after six hours of other women's nails, Tatiana hurries home to get ready for her date with Ed. Life is so full of promise! She loves this great country where dreams and fantasies and real life come together. Who cares if it doesn't last long? She's an optimist. She knows that nothing lasts forever and if it's bad, hopefully it won't last too long, and if it's great, hopefully you can draw it out for a long time.

What should she wear for this important first date with a man from the country club? She studies the clothing options and decides on a tight, coral-colored, v-neck tee-shirt and her jeans from an upscale department store she hardly ever visits. She redoes her make-up, then brushes her hair and shakes it out to give it that slightly wild look. She considers her footwear and decides on the Nuekis. Then she gives herself an assessing look in the full-length mirror on the closet door. No! She needs a skirt. In a flurry she reselects, redresses and stands before the mirror once again. Much better. The coral tee-shirt, short cotton skirt and pumps look just like an outfit she saw in the Come Mo' Magazine at work. A necklace. She needs a necklace. In another minute she's out the door and steering her Toyota Camry downtown.

She parks in the lot behind the Golden Toenail Spa and walks to the corner of Hastings Street which is where the spa is, right next door to Pacific Realty. She has butterflies in her stomach. Dear Lada, she prays as she waits, help this go well. She sees an old, dark blue Mercedes station wagon round the corner. It pulls up to the curb, parks and the driver's door opens. Out steps Ed wearing a faded Hawaiian shirt and jeans. Tatiana's spirits fall like a rotten tomato hitting the ground.

"Ta..Tat..iana?" says Ed, coming towards her. She is just as gorgeous as he remembers from the dentist office. And the coral color really sets off her skin tone and hair. "Hi. How are you?"

"Hi, Eddie," says Tatiana with a sour note in her voice she can't hide. "This is old Mercedes. Is only car you have?"

Ed looks at the family car in surprise. "Actually, yes," he answers. He loves this car.

"Humph," says Tatiana. She stands there in a cloud of disapproval. But then her better self takes control, the self that has been raised on good old-fashioned, Old World fatalism and opportunism. "Well, is Mercedes." She smiles. "Okay, let's go."

She gives him a peck on the cheek and he lets out an audible sigh of relief. He'd had visions of the date ending right now. She steps over to the passenger side and looks expectantly at him. Oops, he thinks. He does a little awkward side-step to the door and opens. He's forgotten date protocol. He suddenly notices a half-eaten banana and a dirty kleenex tucked into the door pocket and a game boy and pencil on the seat. He quickly reaches in and throws them on the floor behind the seat and holds out his hand to her.

"Thank you," she says primly, ignoring his hand as she sits in. Then she looks straight ahead. Old car. She sighs.

"So," says Ed brightly as he gets into the car, "where would you like to go?"

"You decide. Isn't it man who takes woman on date in America?"

"But you called me!" he laughs.

"So?" she waves her hand dismissively. "Now we're together

on date. You decide. Take me somewhere nice. There's many places I don't know here."

"How long have you been in this country?"

"Oh, I don't know," she answers vaguely. "Maybe a half a year. Maybe a year."

"You speak very good English for only being here such a short time."

"I come from little tiny country," snaps Tatiana. "That means nobody speak my language. We have to learn other language. It's not so hard. Let's go." She doesn't want to sit here forever.

Ed looks at her in astonishment. She is not like other women, that's for sure. He starts driving. "I know," he says as he pulls the car into traffic. "Let's go visit a winery in Sonoma."

"I'm not much wine drinker," she says. "I like water."

"Okay," he says. "Let's drive out along the river and then I'll take you to one of my favorite restaurants for dinner. How does that sound?"

"Perfect."

They don't talk much as they drive through the rolling countryside, but the silence isn't uncomfortable. Once in a while he points something out—a particularly large spreading ranch surrounded by miles of white wooden fence, or a villa surrounded by vineyards high on a hill. "How do they get a house all the way up there?" she asks, looking in wonder. Later, when they pass an abandoned farmstead near the road, she muses, "Why is nobody live there? Is so beautiful."

When they approach the river, the fields turn into open wetlands. Here Ed turns and drives down a broad peninsula. It's so broad, in fact, that you think the river is just making a bend westward. "You know, there used to be farms here too," he tells her. "The soil was very rich. But they were too small to compete. So people left and now it's open space. The local environmentalists want to pass a bond to make a completely ecological sewage treatment plant, with natural ponds and reeds doing the filtering rather than tanks and chemicals. But it's an uphill battle."

"Humph," she says skeptically. "Who wants to live here? Too damp."

At last they come to an old Victorian house set right on the edge of the river. Ed parks in the gravel parking area and they get out of the car.

"Oh!" Tatiana exclaims. There is an expansive view of the river and across it are the lights of the town that are just beginning to twinkle in the twilight. The horizon is red behind it. "Red at night, good for sailors," she laughs. "Is old saying in Astonia."

"Wait till you see the view from inside," says Ed, leading her to the restaurant. "And they have a great wine selection." He's already forgotten she doesn't drink.

Tatiana looks at the restaurant's sign. A large wooden carving of a cormorant hunches next to 'The Cormorant'—Fine Family Dining.' "Is bird place?" she asks. It's a little more rustic than she had in mind.

"Believe me. It's great food," he reassures her as he holds open the front door. "I'm Greek. We like food. We used to come here when I was a kid. Before they built the golf course behind my house, the land belonged to the family that owns this restaurant. I grew up playing with their kids. And after my mom died, my dad and I came here every Sunday."

"Ah! So you even grew up in Country Club?" says Tatiana, reminded of her quest. "You must have old family." They step into the restaurant. It's actually quite stylish inside and the view from the window, as the waiter shows them to their table, is spectacular this time of day, just like Ed said.

"Well, we're not exactly an 'old' country club family," says Ed, chuckling at the thought of his dad being called 'old country club family.' He pauses while he looks at the menu.

"Madam?" questions the waiter, pad and pen in hand.

"I like chicken breast with savory lemon sauce, please," she answers.

"And I'll have the fish with roasted potatoes," says Ed. "And," he looks at Tatiana, "what kind of wine?"

She looks at him and rolls her eyes, then shrugs. "Whatever."

"Okay, we'll take a bottle of Chardonnay," says Ed.

"Which one would you like? We have a Plated Sterling Vineyards, a Cuttola Select, or Igor Lake?"

"The Igor Lake will be fine," answers Ed. No point in ordering something expensive if Tatiana is not into wine.

"I like sparkling water, please" she says to the waiter.

"Of course," says the waiter.

"So, how you come to country club?" asks Tatiana after the waiter leaves.

"My grandfather bought our house back in the 40's before anyone had even thought about putting in a golf course. But when the Rodman Developing Corporation came in to buy up all the land, my dad was the only one who refused to sell so we still have a couple of acres that aren't part of the development."

"Acres. What is this?" she asks. That sounds useful to know.

"About four house lots by today's standard, I guess."

"Hmm, that pretty big," she says approvingly.

"Not really. But nowadays, people don't want a lot of land. They don't have time to take care of it. And frankly," Ed pauses while the waiter puts plates of nicely arranged food down in front of them, "I don't seem to have time either. I'm always behind. I have these big idea about what I'd like to do one day, but, you know, it all costs money."

But Tatiana isn't listening. Her food has arrived and she smiles at it in approval. It looks very appetizing. She looks over at Ed's plate. Fish. Well, fish is okay. She takes a first bite. "Mmm. Very good," she says with contentment. Then her mind goes back to the topic at hand. "A couple is two, like you and me, so that is eight houses. Not bad," she says between mouthfuls. "Land is beginning of all wealth. Astonian proverb. You look more like

Astonian farmer, not like important man from old family. But I think that is American. Very…what do you call it? …low-key?"

Ed laughs self-consciously. "This is my best Hawaiian shirt, I'll have you know!" But even he knows that it's pretty faded.

"So now you tell me. How did you come to America?" he asks.

"I come on religious visa," she says demurely. She's been waiting for this question.

"Religious visa?"

"Yes," she says. "I am Aceist." She pauses briefly. Ed's head is slightly cocked and he looks at her expectantly, waiting for her to continue. Tatiana knows it's a stretch, but it is the truth. She found a copy of "The Art of the Resurrection," left on one of the plastic chairs in the lobby of the central train station, and her destiny has been cut ever since. She read The Ronald, then she learned everything about Lada, and that led her to leave Astonia and that bull-headed Eduardo. She is a believer! And it wasn't that hard to convince the embassy worker that she was deserving of an EB-4 visa.

"But I run out of money and so now it is work, work, work." She heaves a huge sigh and Ed notices how her chest rises and settles underneath that breath-taking cleavage. He quickly jabs his fork into a piece of fish and brings it to his mouth. "But now I am thinking real estate. Do you think people buy houses from me?" She looks at him coyly.

Ed gulps down the last of his roasted potatoes. "Absolutely!" he says enthusiastically. And washes them down with a long swallow of wine. He notices that she's hardly touched hers. Why won't she eat potatoes?

"What about you?" she asks. "What profession do you practice?"

"Me? Oh, I'm in engineering of sorts. You could say."

"You mean like software engineering?"

"Yes! You could say I deal in soft wares."

Tatiana smiles happily and takes a tiny sip of wine. She

stretches out her legs under the table and accidentally-on-purpose brushes against Ed's leg. Ed feels an electrical current shoot up his body from the spot where she touched him.

"Do you like your food?" he asks, and presses his leg lightly back against hers.

"Mmm." she murmurs. And then she is reaching out her hand across the table. "I think we are make for each other."

A warning bell goes off in Ed's head and he pulls back. This is too quick! He likes her straightforwardness but... "I haven't had a date like this in years," he says. "You can't imagine how my kids reacted when I told them I was going out with you. You'd think I was going to sell the house or something drastic."

Tatiana's face falls. She does not want to invite him to her apartment, that's for sure. What to do now?

"You mean you don't want to sleep with me?" she pouts.

"No! No! You're gorgeous. It's just my kids aren't used to it."

Tatiana considers for a moment and then she says, "You invite me to your house for dinner. You will see. I think the children will like me. Underneath you are very dynamic man who needs woman."

"Really?" Ed is trying to ignore the heat he's feeling in his groin. But, whew. The thought of burying his face between her gorgeous breasts. He's getting a hard-on. Think of something! Think about baseball statistics!

"*Absolutely*," says Tatiana. She spears a big piece of chicken and leans across the table towards him. She pops the bite into his surprised mouth. "We are meant for love. I can tell."

"Thoreau said: 'I know of no more encouraging fact than the unquestioned ability of a man to elevate his life by conscious endeavor.' This means, to reach your full potential, you need to ride the elevator to the top floor."
Ronald Ace, My Life!

4

"I can't believe you're making us do this," complains Meledy the next Saturday.

"Come on, Mel," pleads Ed. "It's the first time I've invited a woman over in a long time. She's from a foreign country and doesn't know a lot of people here yet. Maybe you'll even like her."

"I liked her," says Buddy coming into the kitchen. He cups his hands and holds them out in front of his chest. "Vavavavooom," he says wickedly and starts cracking up.

"Buddy!" says Ed sharply.

"Well, this place will really impress her," Meledy snickers.

"What do you know?" asks Ed defensively. "All you do is hang out with your friends. You're not even here half the time anymore."

"There's nothing to do here."

"Aw come on, Mel. It's not that bad."

"You're right. It could be worse." Here I go again, thinks Meledy, being a brat. "Sorry, Dad."

Ed has done everything he could think of to make this clean-up fun. He even played one of his old rock CD's really loud. Right now it's playing "Crazy Little Thing Called Lust." He grabs Meledy's hand and swings her around in time to the music. "I'll take you and your friends anywhere you want to go within ten miles, roundtrip, okay? All you have to do is help me with the kitchen and check that the bathroom is clean. And that Buddy actually vacuums the living room and doesn't just turn it on and off. Please?"

"Oh, all right," she agrees. He throws her for one last swing, and sees satisfaction that she smiles.

"I'll do the counter while you do the table, okay? Just get the stickiness off. Come on, Buddy! You too. Go vacuum the living room." He gives him a playful push and starts on the kitchen.

Ed is nervous. It's different when Michelle drops by. And she never stay long. But now, a total stranger! Well, Tatiana can't expect too much, Ed reassures himself, seeing as she knows he's a 'bachelor' dad and all. But a little cleanliness is in order. The table and counter are the worst. They have a way of self-generating junk and mess. He doesn't know how it happens, but every time he cleans, it propagates more junk. He sorts through another stack of old mail, files the bills in the rectangular bill basket and circular-files the rest. The remaining counter junk he dumps into a plastic grocery bag and throws into the broom closet. By the time he rediscovers this bag, he knows, so much time will have passed that he won't remember a thing about it. It's happened before.

By the time Ed has showered and changed, picked Tat up at her apartment and driven back, it's almost five p.m. He pulls up into their driveway in the Mercedes station wagon and Tatiana, who has been chatting animatedly since he picked her up, falls abruptly silent.

"Here we are!" he exclaims, hoping to put her at ease. He hops out of the car and opens her door. She steps out. Her sandals make a little click as the heels hit the pavement and he notices how her knit dress nicely shows her lovely ass. She clutches her bag and stands stiffly looking at the house. Then she turns a hundred and sixty degrees and looks with great exaggeration at the house across the street. Then at the house next door on the right. And then at the house next door on the left.

"Now, I know it's not much.." says Ed, starting to divine what is going through her head.

"Much?" she interjects with rising inflection. "Much?" she repeats. "Is dump."

The finality in her voice makes his heart sink. He didn't think much of her apartment, but that was just it: He didn't think much of it either way. So why was she so upset?

"Look at other houses," she says. She sounds downright surly. She is about to say something else when she suddenly feels the barest breeze brush across her cheek. She feels a luminous presence and then a voice in her head says, 'Think potential for value, Tatiana! Everyone starts somewhere. What matters is how far you go from where you start.' It is Lada, smiling and encouraging her! Oh, how Tatiana loves that voice. It soothes and gives her courage.

"But there is much potential for value," she says, looking at Ed firmly. "*Laebiotsimisordeneneitd paeeval*, we say in Astonia. Pull the day! This is still fab'lous address." She heaves a sigh and turns towards the front door, heels clicking.

"I've been planning to do a remodel, you know," says Ed, hurrying after her. "I just…"

But Tatiana isn't listening. She's following her own train of thought. "Many people want live here. You can be rich man with little effort! Just borrow money to fix house and when house looks nice, all other houses look nicer too. Then you sell house for big profit and…" They have reached the front door and Tatiana turns to Ed and grabs his hands and pulls him close in a burst of new emotion.

"You can be successful, rich man, Eddie!"

Ed looks into her eyes and for the first time, he sees the reflection of some very faint flicker of hope for something he never thought he would obtain. He turns and leads her into the house.

Walking into Ed's house is like going back to the late seventies. It's not because he chose it to be that way, it just is that way. It's the way it was when his mother passed on. And his dad never changed anything after that. And then, when his dad passed on and Ed took over the house, he didn't have the inclination to change it. And after Jayne left, what was the point? He's used to it and so are the kids. They'd probably complain if he changed anything.

"Hey kids! We're here!" he calls brightly. "This is Tatiana. You remember her from the dentist's office?"

He and Tatiana stand at the entry looking expectantly at Meledy and Buddy, who are watching TV. It's commercial time and the large screen TV is flickering with the sunlit image of a semi-naked, short, paunchy man with a couple of gold chains around his neck and a large gold watch reclining on a lounge chair. 'The number again, folks,' urges the man who is encircled by four women in bright, scanty bikinis pushing their bulging cleavages into his face, 'is 1-800-55-MONEY for a free trial copy of How to Make a Million in Real Estate. Yours for just $19.99, plus shipping and handling. Don't wait. It's better than Ronald Ace's!' At this, the women scream in delight and jump the paunchy man and the screen goes to black.

Buddy howls in laughter, while Meledy snickers in derision. It is funny. Even Ed has to suppress a laugh.

"Kids! Turn it off!" he admonishes them. They look at him as if they've just noticed that someone is in the room. They stand and shut off the TV.

"Hi, Tatiana," says Meledy without smiling.

"I'm Buddy!," says Buddy, sticking out his hand. "I remember you. Do you want to play a game?"

Tatiana looks amused. "Hi, Buddy," she says. "Hi, Meledy. How is tooth?"

"It's okay," she says. "I have a cap on it now."

"Let's see," says Tatiana. "And you call me Tat. Is easier than Tatiana. All my friends do."

Meledy obligingly flashes a brief smile while Tatiana looks at her tooth.

"Don't even notice difference," proclaims Tatiana, even though the split second smile wasn't enough to see anything.

"She's doing great," says Ed. "What did you ask, Buddy?" Ed feels like he's had too much coffee even though he hasn't had any.

"I said, let's play a game," answers Buddy.

"Sure! Why not? What do you think," says Ed, turning to Tatiana. "What do you want to play?"

But before she can answer, Buddy grabs a game out of the cupboard from under the TV. "Let's play Twister!" he says.

"Are you crazy?" says Meledy.

"Oh, is okay. I play games," says Tatiana reassuringly. "In my home we play chest very often. What is this 'Twister' game?"

"Chest?" says Meledy.

"Wait a minute…" says Ed, trying to remember how Twister goes and if it's an appropriate choice.

"It's fun!" answers Buddy. "It goes like this." He spreads the large plastic sheet covered with the blue, red and green and yellow circles on it on the floor. Then he holds up the spinner and looks directly at Tatiana.

"The referee spins the spinner and then they call out a color. Like, 'Red!' Then, they call out a foot or a hand. See? Like this. 'Red hand!' So now I put my hand," Buddy places his feet squarely at the side of the plastic sheet that functions as the game board, and flops his right hand down on a red circle with great exaggeration. Then he looks up at her and smiles the way only eleven year old boys can do. "You have to do it fast because you want to be the first one to put your hand on the circle. It's easy!"

He flips himself back up right and looks at Tatiana. Tatiana looks skeptically at the plastic sheet. She always won when they played games at home when she was a child, but she's not sure she understands how you win at this one. What happens if you get on a square first? Is the goal to be the one with all hands and feet on the ground first? But then what? Don't you get all tangled up?

"I'll be the referee!" calls Meledy.

Tatiana glances at Ed. Did he plan this? She is determined to get through this evening with grace. She slips off her sandals.

"Okay, I try," she says. "Is something new."

Meledy spins the spinner and they all wait expectantly. Around and around it goes. Then it slows and stops.

"Green! Foot!" calls Meledy.

That was easy, thinks Ed as he steps onto the nearest green circle. He looks at Tatiana across the mat and smiles. She steps onto a green circle and looks at him.

"Blue! Hand!" shouts Meledy.

With lightening speed, Buddy flops one hand down on a blue circle. Ed and Tatiana both bend down and reach for the same circle.

"Hey!" says Ed playfully.

"I put my hand first!"

Meledy spins the spinner again. It lands on Green/Foot. That's too easy. She nudges the spinner a little further on.

"Yellow! Hand!" she says.

Buddy puts his hand down on the yellow circle right next to the blue one where Tatiana's hand is. He now has a clear view into the cleavage of her dress. He grins. Ed reaches for another yellow circle and Tatiana sees that the closest one for her is crossing his arm.

"I quit!" she says standing up. "I'm hungry." What a stupid game!

Meledy starts laughing and Buddy joins in. Ed playfully whacks him and he collapses easily onto the floor. Ed looks at Tatiana and smiles apologetically, but she is obviously not finding it funny.

"Okay kids," says Ed. "Knock it off. Time to get the pizza going." He holds his hand out to Tatiana to steady herself while she puts on her sandals. "I hope you like pizza."

Tatiana shrugs as he leads her into the kitchen. She follows along, her sharp eyes missing nothing: the old furniture, the family photos, the ugly drapes, even the avocado-colored kitchen cabinets. But, at the same time, she sees that the house has potential. Out of the sliding kitchen windows she sees, beyond the ratty backyard, the fabulous green lawns and leafy trees of the golf course. The family room, next to the kitchen, with its strange double door, reveals a small lake in the distance, pink with the glow of the setting sun.

"Eddie, why you never put money into fixing up this house? I don't understand."

Ed pops the pizza into the oven, gets out the plates, stalling for time. He clears his throat. Shrugs his shoulders. "Well," he finally says, "you know, when the kids' mother left, I could barely keep up with things. It just didn't seem important."

"Life has hard times," she pronounces matter-of-factly. "But is past. Now, you must fix up your house. Look," she points to the family room. "Here you make sun room with glass doors that go to deck and hot tube."

"Tube?" Ed is surprised. "Oh, you mean tub."

"Tub?"

"Hot tub."

Tatiana waves the words away with her hand. "Whatever," she says.

She wanders to the other side of the kitchen where the laundry room is and opens the door. A washer and dryer in avocado green stand side-by-side next to a narrow back door with a small window. She smiles. Her father was a washing machine repair man. He used to pretend to fix old washers and dryers, only he would tell the customers he couldn't fix their machines. He'd sell them a new pair and then, after some time had passed, repair and resell the old ones in another town. It was pretty good business in those days.

"Here is where should be entry hall and stairs!" she exclaims to Ed who is dressing the salad. "You need second floor, like other houses. Imagine master bedroom upstairs the size of whole house! Big closets, one for you, one for me, dressing room, bathroom with big double jets. Just like in Xtreme Makeover!"

Buddy and Meledy have just walked into the kitchen. Buddy hears that last bit. "We watch Xtreme Makeover!" he says enthusiastically.

"I love that show!" says Tatiana, coming out of the laundry room.

"Takes a lot of money to do what they do," says Ed.

"But anybody can get money, Eddie! You can get money. You just have to think big."

"Yeah, Dad," says Meledy. "Think big! All my friends have their own computer and cells phones now."

Tatiana looks at Ed in surprise. "Even I have smart phone now!" She pulls a cell phone out of her purse and holds it up. "Look. With six upps!"

"Upps?" says Meledy? "What are those?"

"Address Book, Date Maker, GPS, Around Town, Money Tracker. I even have special English Dictionary ups."

"You mean apps," says Meledy. She rolls her eyes and take the milk out of the refrigerator. "Dad! The pizza's burning!"

Sure enough, the steam coming out of the oven is starting to thicken. Ed hurries over and pulls out the pizza which is not burning at all. It's fine. "Do you have to exaggerate everything so much?" he asks Meledy in exasperation. "Buddy, get the plates. Tat, what do you want to drink? A little wine?" The minute he says it, he remembers she doesn't drink wine.

"Sparkling water," she answers. "That's best for skin, for body, for everything!"

"I'm so sorry. I forgot to get you something at the store," says Ed. He feels like a fool. "How about ginger ale?" he asks hopefully. He remembers sighting a can at the back of the fridge two days ago.

"Pipe water fine."

"Pipe water?" says Buddy, holding the plates in midair.

"She means tap water," says Ed.

"Duh," says Meledy.

Ed puts the pizza on the table. He pulls out a chair for Tatiana and they all sit down around the table. Tatiana looks at the pizza like it's a wet dog that has just been served up. The melted cheese is bubbling in its own grease, the slices of pepperoni are slick with fat, little grey balls of some kind of meat float in shiny tomato sauce.

"It's Wild West Cowboy pizza, our favorite," he explains hopefully. He hands the pizza wheel to Meledy.

Meledy takes the wheel and, glancing at Tatiana, rolls into the pizza with gusto, cutting it into huge quarter size pieces. She grabs a piece and doesn't even make it to her plate before she's tearing a huge bite off into her mouth. So huge it doesn't even fit. "I just LOVE pizza!!" she exclaims.

"Me too!" says Buddy, grabbing the piece closest to him. He turns and smiles directly at Tatiana's breasts. "It's better than hot dogs or chicken!"

Ed serves Tatiana a piece. It flops over the edge of her plate and she daintily edges it away from her dress. She picks up her fork and slowly begins cutting it into bite-sized pieces. This is not what she had in mind. Not at all.

Ed pulls up in front of Tatiana's apartment. "I think they liked you, I really do. I'm sorry you can't spend the night." Tatiana turns towards him and glares. She is so tired of the whole fiasco. If she had wanted children, she would have had children with her first husband. Or maybe even with no husband. But the fact is, she doesn't want children and she never did want children. And this Ed. He unnerves her. It's too hard.

"Spend night!?" she spits. "You have Mercedes, but look how old! You say you have country club, but is just house. Then, you have house, but in fact is dump. What else you lie about? A girl like me needs man who wants make something with his life!"

Ed is speechless. He didn't think it had gone that badly. He looks at her and the way she is glaring at him, accusing him. Has he not made something of his life? He does have two children, a job and a house. And he has big dreams. Doesn't that count for something?

"But, at least I'm not lying to you," he defends himself. "I really like you. You have...spirit," he says. He pauses. "What can I do better?" To make you like me. To make you want to have sex with me, he thinks. Because actually, he knows she wouldn't have slept over even if he had asked.

Tatiana's face softens. She decides he is hopeless but sincere. "Fix up your house, Eddie! Make it look nicer! Make yourself look nicer! Get white teeth. Look like you have money, and then you can get money!" She shakes her head as if this should all be so evident. And then she leans over and gives him what every man dreads: a quick, unenthusiastic smooch. The precursor to the pity fuck. Ed looks at her sadly. Oh, all right, she seems to say. And she leans in and gives him a second, more promising kiss. Her lips are warm and sensual, and she lingers this time.

"Bye-bye, Eddie," she says, opening the car door. She wishes he wasn't so cute.

That night, in her studio apartment alone, Tatiana thoughtfully meditates on her photo of Lada while she tries to understand how she could possibly have made such a wrong judgment. Even if he did kiss nicely. Even if he does live next to the country club. Her mind is running two tracks simultaneously. One track is trying to remember all that she can of Lada's early biography and how she got from one step to the next for comparison, while the other is trying to take out the wrong pieces she had in the puzzle of Ed Fasouli and put the correct ones in.

"I think he has no backbone," she decides. But then she reminds herself that many people are not what they seem to be on the surface. It is the potential of a thing that is the real nature of that thing. The potential of a person, the potential of a house, the potential of a relationship. Even the potential of a country. That is what matters in greatness. And selling is realizing potential. No potential, no sale, she practices. And to be honest, she doesn't have any other potential on the horizon at the moment.

"I tell him to get money," she tells Lada earnestly, taking a deep sniff of the jasmine. "We will see." She picks the photo up by its gold frame and brings it close to her face. She looks deeply into Lada's eyes and plants a light kiss on her lips. "One man can solve many problems, if right man."

Meanwhile, Ed sits alone at the computer in the family room. The kids have gone to bed and he is dreaming about his life. Maybe he really could get rich. At least richer than he is now. Just because his father hated the idea of owing money for anything—hated spending money for anything—was not a good enough reason for him to live such a frugal life. So what if his income isn't that big? 'You've got to spend money to get money.' Isn't that what they say? How's he ever going to get ahead if he doesn't….risk something? And he has less to risk than other people because he doesn't have any payments yet except the usual bills. If he fixed up the house, Meledy could bring her friends around and not be embarrassed. He could put in a pool and a baseball practice area for Buddy. And, of course it would be nice to have a relationship again. What woman wants to hang out in a house like this? People live in huge houses nowadays, and he hasn't spent any money since Jayne left. He could borrow money and upgrade his life. Increase his value. Tatiana is right. The guys at the plant are right. Now's the time. Time to start a new era, the post-AJ era: After Jayne.

BJ—Before Jayne—he had had the usual youthful dreams of getting rich and making an estate of the house. Then Michelle dumped him. He met Jayne at a stupid, boring, beer-drinking party. She was tall and athletic with straight brown hair. The only thing that said 'homemaker' about her, was that she thought it would be 'cute' to have kids. But she had a sense of humor, and they were both fans of the shortstop, Jaguar Glasston. They had sex together, and decided that was good enough to go to baseball games together. And things just developed from there. What a great reason to get married. He took the job at the treatment plant, she had Meledy and took up boxing. Then she got pregnant with Buddy. She quit boxing and took up auto mechanics. She even bought an old Mustang to work on. It was pretty funny to see her under the car with her belly fitted tightly up against the chassis. She was replacing the muffler when her water broke.

Ed hurried home and took her to the hospital. And who does she meet there? Aside from Michelle, who was having Sammy two rooms down, she meets another man. But no, not another man like that. That would be too simple for Jayne. Jayne meets another gay man. A nurse, working at the hospital. She extends her stay, and when the hospital finally kicks her out and she comes home, she makes her big announcement. Timing had always been one of her specialties. Ed had been trying to work and take care of four-year old Meledy, and Jayne comes in and says, "This is it, Ed. The real thing. The thing called love that only comes once in our lives, and I'm not going to let it get away from me." Ed couldn't believe his ears. "And guess what?"

"I can't imagine," said Ed, still reeling with the implications.

"I am done with tampax! Done with childbirth, and done with vaginas! I've already got an appointment for a sex change. I've been a man all my life."

"Jayne, you are clinically depressed. You have postpartum depression. Every woman gets that. It'll pass. Talk to your doctor. Get help."

"I have talked to my doctor. I'm not a woman. I'm a man, and I'm not depressed. I'm happy! I'm in love!"

How is it possible to have a wife, and then two children and no wife? Worst period in his life. Worse than when he joined the Navy and found out Michelle had left him.

He pulls himself back to the computer screen and the present. So how do I get a loan? Money is cheap right now, everybody is saying it, everybody's doing it. Where is it? He types in 'Refinance loans' and hits the enter button. Thousands of hits appear on the screen. He clicks on one of the links, but you need Flash and his

computer doesn't support it because he hasn't upgraded. He tries
another. It's the Barried and Daet National Mortgage Company,
advertising free refinancing. That sounds good. He clicks on the
box "Apply for a loan." An online form appears that says, "Please
fill in your name and address." He types in 'Ed Fasouli, 1200
Country Club Estates' and hits enter. The program prompts
him: "Please fill in the information for your employer." He types:
'Sump Valley Sewage Treatment Plant,' and hits enter. A new
prompt comes up: "Please tell us your current income." He enters
'$60,000' and hits enter.

This is easy, he thinks. Is that what it's like now to borrow
money? He's feeling rather good about this. A new prompt
appears on the screen: "Please enter the current value of your
house." What should he enter here? He hasn't had it appraised in
years; it never really mattered to him because he had no intention
of selling. He decides on '$500,000' as a ballpark figure and hits
enter. A new screen shows: "Please enter the value of your current
mortgage. Be sure to include your current monthly payments."

Now this is a hard one, thinks Ed. He scratches his head
and finally enters '$0.00.' A loud yellow screen pops up: "You
have entered an invalid amount. Please reenter the value of
your current mortgage. Be sure to include your current monthly
payments."

Ed tries again. How can he have monthly payments if his
house is paid off? He enters '$0.00' and hits enter. But the same
invalid screen comes up. He decides to click a button at the bottom
that says "Skip this menu." That's always a good tactic. A pink
window pops up. "Skipping this information is not an option."
Ed tries to hit the 'go back' button, but he gets an error message.
The session is no longer valid. Furious that he apparently has no
value, Ed hits the ESC key over and over.

"Your computer does not have Flash," says the computer.
Whomp!Whomp!Whomp!

Ed hits the control shift button over and over, but he's in a
loop. A loop is that terrible place known as computer purgatory

where all bad computer users are sent for losing their patience and for trying to do things they should never have attempted in the first place. Also, for not respecting the laws of computerdom. So why does he keep hitting the same button over and over when obviously he's in a loop and nothing is going to happen? Because he feels helpless. Ah, but he's not. In one smooth motion, Ed bends down, grabs the main plug and yanks on it as hard as he can.

"Die you piece of junk," he hisses. And feels like a total idiot.

He strides into the kitchen, opens the fridge and grabs a beer. He walks out to the front of the house and sits on the stoop in the cool night air. As he sips his beer he contemplates Mickey's house across the street. Big bucks Mickey Schulz. Mr. One-Upmanship. They competed in baseball (Mickey was worse), they fought at school (Mickey was bigger), he took Ed's girlfriend (Mickey was more dashing), and then he moved in across the street. How does he do it? He has this way of staying close and yet always making Ed feel kind of bad. Because his mother befriended Mickey's mother, it was like he was stuck with Mickey for life. Like computer purgatory, an inescapable loop.

Down at the end of the block, headlights appear. Slowly the circles of light grow larger. The soft purring of an expensive engine becomes louder until the car is right in front of his house. The high beams switch on and the light opens wide to include Ed sitting on his porch. Then the engine cuts out, the lights disappear and a door slams. Footsteps approach. And, there he is, standing in front of Ed.

"Ed!" says Mickey, with a slur. "Isn't it past your bedtime? Don't you usually turn in with the kids?"

"Very funny," says Ed. "What are you doing out so late?"

"Business, business."

"Yeah, right," says Ed. Mickey sits down on the porch next to Ed.

"Something's up," says Mickey. "You don't usually sit here.

Let's see…" Mickey pauses for dramatic effect. "What could it be? Love? Money? What else is important in this world?"

Ed debates. Should he talk to Mickey or not? It'd be nice to talk to someone. Money is Mickey's business. And drunks don't usually remember much. "I just tried to get an online loan and I can't even get a credit card because I haven't borrowed any money in so long. Can you believe it?"

Mickey laughs at Ed. "You are sucha …waddtheycall it?… luderite?" he slurs. "Go to a bank! Better yet, come to me." Mickey perks up hearing what he's just said. "What do you need money for?" He has picked up a scent. It's his nature. That's why he went into real estate instead of banking—he likes money, but with a thrill. Maybe Ed has finally gotten the real estate bug and wants to buy something. That would be good, very good. Mickey has several properties he needs to unload. He's on the pulse of things, he knows the big days are over. He and Keaton were just talking about it over dinner.

"I was thinking about finally fixing up the house," answers Ed.

"Oh, you aren't going to sell it on me…" jokes Mickey.

"As if. My dad would turn in his grave."

"So it is love!" Ed wants something because of a woman! And any man who wants a woman, thinks Mickey, will usually do pretty stupid things to get her. Mickey intuits the beginning of a potential deal here. Nothing wrong with helping a friend and making a little commission. "What are you thinking about doing? Tell your old friend Mickey."

"Oh, stuff like remodel the kitchen and bathrooms. Put in a pool. Landscape the backyard. Fix up the living room and bedrooms." Ed shrugs. "I mean, not major-major, but you know, definitely an upgrade."

"Well, hey. Let me help you with a little loan. How much you thinking about?" asks Mickey, firing up his internal calculator.

"I don't know. Something in the ballpark of $150,000?" says Ed.

"That's nothing! I could get you that tomorrow, at a really sweet interest rate. Too much money floating around now anyways. Might as well put it to good use. After all, we go way back."

"Yeah, that we do," says Ed, more than a little ironically.

"Tell you what," says Mickey, not even noticing the ironic tone. "Seriously. Let me help you out. I'll even give you the first three months almost free. If you go to a bank, they're going to give you the royal run-around."

Ed looks at Mickey curiously. "You are serious, aren't you?" He takes a long swig from his beer, and then drains the bottle. This is an unforeseen, but actually, when he thinks about it, easy way to get money. Really easy. Get the money and then fix up his house fast, before Tatiana totally walks out of his life.

"I am serious," says Mickey. "How many times do we have a chance to really make a difference in someone's life?" That's a fair thing to say, he thinks. I can help Ed out and make a little money in the process.

"Okay, you asshole, if you want to lend me money through your business—mind you, through your business—I'll consider borrowing money from you. How long would it take?"

"You can have it Monday."

"That's not necessary," says Ed. And then the image of Tatiana pops up in his mind. Her body standing close to his in front of his house. Her saying, 'You can be successful man, Eddie.' What harm could there be in borrowing a little money? Look at all those credit card and home mortgage ads that come in the mail every day! Everybody's doing it! This is his chance to take a risk. And let's face it, he can always sell the house for a handsome profit.

"Okay. Sure," says Ed. "But from your business. Not privately, okay? I don't want Michelle to know about this."

"Monday," promises Mickey, throwing his arm around Ed's shoulders, his alcoholized breath enveloping Ed's face. "Starting Monday, your life's going to be different!"

"You don't want to get stuck looking at some woman's rack, even if it's awesome, and forget to close the deal, because if you don't get them to sign on the dotted line, you haven't made a deal. You've just thought about making a deal. And there's a big difference. It's like the difference between thinking about sex and having sex."
Ronald Ace, The Magic of Business

5

Mickey goes to his brokerage office early on Monday. He wants to have everything prepared before Ed arrives. He fires up his computer and opens his forms generator application. He chooses a loan agreement template and starts creating an estimated borrowers statement:

FASOULI   Edward
1200 Country Club Estates   California
Item: new 1st loan from MD LLC.

And here he stops.

Ed's an idiot, he thinks. To think he can do anything worthwhile with only $150,000.00. He's totally out of touch. It costs that much just to put in a new kitchen nowadays. And to think that Michelle almost married him. Mickey shakes his head. Plus, Mickey continues his train of thought, from a business point of view, it's just not interesting to lend Ed such a small amount. Why doesn't Mickey get him...Mickey pauses to look out the window at the early morning traffic...a half a mill. That's a good, solid amount. Ed's property would cover the debt easily, if he ever ran into problems, because it's clear. Mickey is sure of that because he knew Ed's dad. Plus, 500 K will yield a healthy commission for Mickey, not to mention the interest if he puts all the fees into the amount he loans.

There's so much to consider in a deal like this. The bottom line is, he's doing Ed a favor, getting him the money so fast. Ed won't argue about reasonable fees, reasonable being the operative word here. He could offer him say, a 1.4% adjustable, the 1.4% being the first three months. Then he could bump it up to say 5.7%—that's not so bad—and let it float there for a while. But how much should he charge him for the broker fee? 1%, 1.5%, 3%? It's so tempting. He's even charged 6% before. Well, he'll think on it as he goes. So he starts typing in the form, line by line:

    Item: new 1st loan from MD LLC   500,000.00
    Type: home equity loan
    Title search:

He pauses. Ordinarily, he would order a title search, but there's no way he can get it done in time, and anyways, he personally knows who owns the property, so it's not really essential. But he can't leave the fee out—it's standard procedure to charge for one. So Mickey types in $2,300.00.

    Appraisal fee:

That's another obvious. Mickey knows what the property is worth because he knows what his own property is worth—he lives across the street. No need to contact Jim, his appraiser buddy (he loves that guy; he can come up with some of the most outrageous values for really marginal property), but it is standard to charge for one. He types in $400.00.

    Escrow fees:

They don't need to call it escrow because it's just between the two of them, but he should include some closing fees for Country Club Mortgage Company. He types in $400.00.

    Additional charges:

Hmm, how about...$115.00?

    Overnight service fee:

That's good. He types in $125.00, and continues down the list.

    Doc prep fee:
    Notary fees:

Recording fees:
Loan processing fee:

Definitely, a loan processing fee! He types in $600.00.

Loan origination fee:

This one is important, no personal loans here (Mickey smiles to himself). What rate should he give Ed? Hmm... How about a nice low-sounding rate, then he can stiff him with a healthy brokers fee? Poor guy, he knows nothing about borrowing money. There are lenders out there who are worse than Mickey. He'll be a nice guy and keep it at 1.5%. Ah, heck, make it 2%. He's been dying to go to the Port Royal golf course in Bermuda ever since they remodeled it. Keaton told him it was fabulous.

Mickey looks at his handiwork. That about covers it; then he decides to go back up and add a small settlement fee. Why not? He types in $50. What does Ed know?

Mickey tallies up the total closing costs and arrives at a figure of just under fourteen thousand dollars. Just for kicks, he pulls out his HP and punches in the numbers and then lets it calculate the magical effect of compound interest: Nice! That's going to be almost twenty-five thousand dollars ten years from now.

He adds the fourteen grand to the $500 K and then figures the payments. He'll give him a big wad of cash to make it better. He'll give him the first three months at 1.4%. Now that is generous. Then he can go ahead and let it move up to 5.7%. That's a healthy margin but fair.

He looks at it thoughtfully for a moment, then goes back and recalculates the brokers fee at 3%. That's better.

Satisfied with his handiwork, Mickey starts in on the promissory note. He smiles as he types in the information. He can't help it. He just loves this. He's a pro. Fifteen grand out of thin air. Not bad for a morning's work. Mickey prints out two copies, one for him, and one for Ed, detailing how the interest rate will change in small print.

That afternoon, after work, Ed drives his old Mercedes to Mickey's office building. It's a two-story square building with a roof of royal blue tiles. It's framed by a scraggly pine tree on one side and a tall palm tree on the other. A large sign in the window of the lower left office says "Country Club Mortgage Company" in handsome gold letters.

Ed walks in the front door and is greeted by the sounds of the Beatles "Yellow Submarine" being played by string instruments. The lobby feels spacious and bright. Ed stops for a moment to look up at the skylight overhead. A glass door to his left says CCMC. That's the one. He enters the waiting room. It's large and barely decorated. Usually Ed doesn't notice this kind of thing, but this feels almost empty. He steps up to the secretary's desk.

"Hi. I'm Ed Fasouli. I have an appointment with Mickey."

The attractive, red-headed secretary smiles charmingly at him. "Of course," she says in a surprisingly low voice. She looks like she finished high school about a year ago. "I'm Tiffany. Mickey is running late. He sends his apologies. Do you mind waiting? I'll bring you some coffee."

"Okay, sure," says Ed.

She leads him into a windowless conference room right off the lobby furnished with a long walnut table and eight hard wooden chairs. Ed sits down in one of them and tries to think calmly, but he can feel his thoughts jangling around in his head. It's already after five p.m. and he needs to get home. He hates to keep the kids waiting, even though he knows they can handle it alone. But actually, it's the money that's making him nervous. He wants it, he wants what he's going to do with it. But he doesn't quite trust Mickey, although, except for the Navy and Michelle thing, he hasn't had any reason to not trust him. Mickey takes chances and look where it got him. He's rich! Besides, there are laws to protect people from dishonesty, so what could he do to Ed?

Tiffany brings in small tray with a cup of lukewarm instant coffee, two packets of sugar and two packets of fake creamer. He decides to drink it black although usually he doesn't drink coffee at all at this hour. He takes a few sips, then gets up and paces the room. It's suffocating in here. He looks at the framed prints on the wall. Dull monotones. Grey carpet, pale grey walls, bland prints, uncomfortable chairs. Obviously Michelle didn't have any influence in here. She always liked colorful stuff. Where the hell was Mickey?

Ed walks out to the reception

"Excuse me," he says to the secretary.

"The restroom is right down there," she says. "Down the hallway."

"I..."

But at that moment Mickey appears from behind another door.

"Eddie-boy!" he says jovially. "There you are! Ready to..." Mickey is grinning from ear to ear on that red face of his. He does a phony little boxing routine. "... feel rich?"

Mickey never changes, thinks Ed. He must have been born blowing hot air out his mouth. He looks down the hall. Should he go now? Turn and leave? This is his chance. He can go home and be with the kids and everything will be just as it always was. The three of them. But then he hears Tatiana's voice encouraging him to be successful. Take a chance! If you don't try, how are you ever going to know?

"Follow me!" says Mickey, sensing Ed's hesitation. He grabs his stack of papers from the secretary's desk, gives her a pinch and a wink, and then pilots Ed back to the windowless conference room. "Have a seat. I gotta congratulate you here, buddy. You're going from a simple homeowner to someone who's smart enough to," here he pauses for extra effect, "use your equity to increase your wealth!"

Ed sits in the chair next to Mickey and looks in surprise at the stack of papers. "I thought this was..." he trails off. What did he think it was? Going to be simple? Just a matter of signing one piece of paper? What does he know! He's never borrowed a large sum of money in his life.

"I know this looks like a lot of paperwork if you've never done it before," says Mickey, reading Ed's thoughts, "but we'll just blow right through it. I've got another appointment in fifteen minutes anyways. It's basically really simple." He laughs easily and separates the pile neatly into two and then fans them out. "One stack for you, one stack for me." He takes a Mont Blanc pen out of his shirt pocket, clicks it open and proffers it to Ed. "It's all standard stuff for a three-month 1.4% adjustable. Your payments will only be $1,766." He chuckles, "that's nothing! And--that was your disclosure, by the way," he adds and points to a line at the bottom of the first copy on the stack. "Just sign here on yours and here on mine. This is the estimated borrower's statement. Here's your borrower's instructions about the escrow. This is about pro-rations and adjustments. This is the promissory note. I went ahead and put the closing costs into the loan just to keep things simple for you. All you have to do is sign here: Easy money! Before you know it, that crappy house of yours is going to look worthy of that beautiful woman you're dating."

Ed frowns. "You met her?" It's so hot and stuffy in the room. He didn't remember introducing her to Mickey.

"Of course I didn't meet her," says Mickey, concentrating on the documents. "But knowing you, she must be a fine woman. Now this one is your borrower's agreement. Sign here."

Ed just can't shake this uncomfortable feeling. "I dunno, Mick, this is starting to feel like when I signed up for the Navy. You know? Sign here and your life is gone? Maybe I shouldn't do this."

"Now, Eddie," Mickey reassures him. "You're just gun-shy. Let bygones be bygones. I got you... Ready for this?" He's grinning like a kid that just got away with stealing a whole bag of candy. "Five-hundred K!!"

Ed gasps.

"A half a million dollars? No. Tell me you didn't."

"Generous, isn't it," says Mickey with a self-satisfied tone.

"What am I supposed to do with a half a million dollars??"

At that moment, there is a sharp, brief scream from the reception area. It's the secretary. "Oh my god," she cries.

Ed turns in his chair just in time to see the tail end of a rat scurry through the door. He starts to rise from his chair. Mickey, glancing briefly towards the conference room door that is ajar, immediately turns his attention back to the task at hand. He gently grabs Ed's right hand and directs the point of the pen to the signature line. Ed is trying to figure out where the rat disappeared, but Mickey is insistent. Ed signs, dots the last 'i'. And before you can say 'compounded interest,' Mickey has shuffled the papers together.

"I'll shove your copies in the mailbox tomorrow," he says to Ed. "You'll see. A half a million is nothing nowadays. And," Mickey digs into his jacket pocket and pulls out a cashiers check, "look what I've got for you!"

Ed takes the check. It's made out for $470,000 from an 'MD LLC' holding company. "Your money. Is that service or what?? And guess what? I've got…" he reaches into his other jacket pocket and pulls out a wad of cash. "How 'bout a little walk-around cash for you? Is this trust or what?"

Ed looks at Mickey speechless. This is all happening much too quickly for Ed. Like a somnambulant, he takes the wad of cash in his hand and looks it. Wow. He has never seen, let alone touched, that much cash in his life. So this is what it looks like. What it feels like. He breaths in deeply. It even smells. Images of himself with Tatiana start flooding his mind from nowhere. Him and Tat in a fast car. Him and Tat in a fancy restaurant with candlelight and white table cloths. Him and Tat in a beautiful hotel with satin sheets. Exotic vacations in Tahiti.

"Put another story on your house!" says Mickey jovially, interrupting his thoughts. "Buy a decent car! Take a vacation instead of just hanging out in that crappy backyard of yours!"

Yes! thinks Ed, feeling the money in his hand. This is how it starts!

*"Sometimes, when it seems like somebody is winding down, they are
just moving in deeper. Watch and learn."*
Ronald Ace, My Life!

6

"Eddie!!!" squeals Tatiana when she sees all that money. All those
greenbacks! That's a word she learned from one of her favorite
Kingstown Trio songs when she was learning English back
home.

"And, I took the day off so we can go spend some," says Ed,
quite pleased with himself. "Let's go spend some money!"

His spirits are high. He called her at home on Tuesday to ask
if she was free Friday. "I have a surprise…a big surprise," he said
hurriedly before she could say no. "And part of it is because of
you!" How could she resist?

So, off they go to the nearest shopping center, Tatiana
hanging onto his arm. She's put on her black J. Crow skirt and
a red ruffled blouse from Moxie Mora for the occasion because
she likes it when the sales girls look at her with respect. The first
place she leads him, known for its exhilarating prices, is Snootie
Brothers. Ed is about to get a total make-over.

The sales clerk at Snootie Brothers sees Ed enter the store
from where he is arranging stacks of sweaters and dismisses him
as being unworthy of buying anything. But when he sees Tatiana,
he changes his mind. Maybe there's a decent commission in there
for him after all.

"May I help you?" he asks, looking only at Tatiana.

"Yes," she answers graciously. "We need navy blue blazer, five shirts. and." she looks pointedly at Ed's jeans, "three pair new slake."

"Slake?" asks the clerk?

"Slacks," says Ed. "A couple of pairs of slacks."

"Do you know your size?" asks the clerk.

Ed shakes his head. It's been so long since he's purchased new clothes.

Two hours and twenty-two minutes later, although it feels like a day. Ed and Tatiana walk out with two new navy blue blazers, three oxford cloth shirts—one pale yellow, one pale pink (Ed really was against that one. but Tatiana prevailed), and one light blue one—and three new pairs of slacks. He's wearing the khaki-colored ones. Tatiana insisted. Then it's off to Needless Markup. Once there. she leads him straight to the shoe section, pausing only to look at a gorgeous pair of pale green, very expensive high heels.

"Try them on!" says Ed. He wants to watch her legs as she saunters to and fro in front of the mirror.

"No! First you!" she says, ever mindful of the task at hand. "First we find you shoes. Then maybe me."

She picks out a pair of black leather loafers, and a pair of brown men's dress shoes. "Maybe these too," she says to the sales clerk. pointing to a pair of leather loafer style shoes.

"Wow. Aren't those a little expensive?" says Ed, cringing inside when he sees the $460.00 price tag. The most he's ever paid for a pair of shoes is $60.00.

"Pfft!" says Tatiana, waving away his concern. "You have money now! You have to look like you have money!" She gives him her total come-on smile and turns back to the sales clerk.

By the time Ed and Tatiana sink into a booth at the Cupcake Factory for lunch. Ed is exhausted. But Tatiana looks at him approvingly. "Now, you need see my dentist. She can make fab'lous white teeth. Look," and she smiles that brilliant, show-off smile she gave him in the dentist office with Meledy.

Ed can't help smiling at her. She just doesn't quit. He looks at her lovely Nordic blue eyes and thinks how great her breasts must look unrestrained. Whew. He quickly turns his gaze back to the menu. Okay. Menu. He forces his eyes to focus on the menu items. Items. He glances at the lunch specials. Steak Diane. What could that be? How about chicken? Breast of chicken? Breast of Tatiana. No, think about baseball.

"Are you ready to order?" asks their waitress. She's an attractive brunette.

"Tat?" asks Ed, looking up from the menu. "You ready?"

"I'll have lunch chicken special and cheesecake," she answers promptly. "Chocolate cheesecake. With whipped cream."

"Okay. And for you sir?"

Ed has been staring at Tatiana in fascination. How can she eat so much? "Uh, I'll have the breast." A moment of silence falls on the table. "Chicken breast."

"Okay," says the waitress, "you must mean the Orange Chicken?"

"Yes," says Ed quickly so as to leave no doubt that that was what he meant. And a beer."

"I'm sorry, sir. We don't serve beer. Would you like to try one of our mojitos?"

Mojito? What the hell is that? "Sure, why not," says Ed. Why not live it up? Even Tatiana forgoes her sparkling water and drinks mojitos with her meal.

"Eddie, look!" says Tatiana as they tumble happily out of the restaurant. "BMW!"

Sure enough, at the far end of the shopping mall stands a grandiose, fake marble building with the imposing solid block letters announcing a BMW dealership. Strings of colorful triangular flags glisten in the sunlight. Tatiana stops Ed in the middle of the parking lot. She reaches up and sensuously combs his brown hair from the left side up and over the top and to his right temple. "There!" she announces. "Next Ronald Ace!"

Ed laughs like he hasn't in years. She is a number. "Mmm,

and big real estate man likes sexy woman," he says kissing her full on the lips.

She kisses him back deeply. Her eyes light up. "Big real estate man needs sexy car. Let's go look at BMW!"

"Great idea," says Ed. "You are so smart." He's always wanted to drive a BMW. Just for fun. Maybe they'll let them test drive one.

Two hours later, Ed and Tatiana pull out of the BMW lot in a brand new, red Z4. Wow. Nothing like the way cash talks. The sleazy salesman in the olive green shirt made Ed an offer he couldn't resist. He and Tatiana can come back and pick up the station wagon later. They head out of town, going nowhere in particular. Just driving. The car hugs the road—at one with the curves, the asphalt, the hills, the sky. Ed feels like there is no distinction between him and the machine. He is transformed. He isn't Ed Fasouli anymore. He's rich, cool and powerful. Who needs viagra? He has power because he has money!

Tatiana, next to him, is in her own state of bliss. Her hand is rubbing Ed's thigh. She likes the feel of his muscle. Better yet, she likes the sleek, subtle vibration of a real sports car. She reaches higher and starts working his crotch through the slacks and the new silk boxers. "Eddie?" she says in the sweetest little bird voice she can do.

Ed keeps looking at the road, barely noticing where they are going. Tatiana rubs a little harder. "Where are we going Eddie?" There's a teasing note in her voice.

"You know where we're going," he answers hoarsely and does a U-turn in the middle of the road. He shifts back up and heads for the shortest direction home, his hand now working her thigh under her skirt. Oh joy. He's finally going to get to fuck her. He glances at the clock on the dashboard. Barely two hours before the kids come home.

Ed steers the new BMW down the tree-lined streets of Country Club Estates until he sees the rose bushes at the Schulz's. That's his landmark for turning left into his own driveway. He takes his foot off the accelerator, swings the wheel around, and... slams on his brakes. He and Tatiana lurch forward, then fall back against the seats as the car comes to a grinding halt one inch away from a huge, banged up debris box parked in the middle of his driveway.

"What..." gasps Ed, "is going on?" A white construction truck, in not much better shape, with the logo "INePT Construction" painted on the side, is parked on the grass next to it. And casually sitting on the ground leaning against the garage are two strange men, one Asian looking and the other Latino. Ed jumps out of the BMW and strides up to them. "What the hell is going on here?" he demands. "What are you doing in my driveway?"

The Chinese guy, wiry and black, curly hair, looks at Ed and then jumps up and angrily snarls something in Chinese at Ed while wagging his head in the direction of Ed's backyard. Ed steps back, speechless. What in the world is the guy trying to say? Obviously somebody has the wrong address here. He opens his mouth to say something but the other guy—the younger, shaved-headed one—starts jabbering at the Chinese guy in Spanish. The Chinese frowns and holds out his hand. The Latino reaches in his pocket and hands him a walkie-talkie.

The Chinese guy presses the button. A grating sound issues from the walkie-talkie: Clewwaakkkshshshshdxk. He frowns at it, holds it out at arm's length and shouts, "Mahodi!! Ploblem here!!" Then he glares at Ed as if it's Ed's fault. "You wait," he commands Ed.

Ed doesn't wait long. A dark, turbaned East Indian man with a pleasant smile appears from around the corner of the garage.

"Good day to you, fine sir," he says with an Indian accent. "You are being Mr. Vasoori?"

"Fasouli," says Ed, frowning. "The name is Fa-sou-li. It's Greek. What the hell is going on here?"

"Yes sir, that is what I am saying, sir," answers the Indian. "I am being Mahodi and we are here to do your house."

"Do my house?" he snaps angrily, his jaw popping with tension.

At this moment, Tatiana appears. She has jumped out of the car to find out what all the noise is about. "Oh Eddie!" she exclaims, hearing the 'do my house.' "You are already starting home improvement? This is so fab'lous! You are man with gumshun." She really is happy. She never dreamed it would happen so quickly. It just goes to show, you can never judge man by shirt.

Ed looks at her and a wave of frustrated disappointment crashes over him. That's it for sex today. She's just sailed off into home-makeover land and he's stuck with an ache in his groin. He brings his hand up to his forehead and massages his temple. He's seething but he's trying to get his anger under control.

"Here is my card, sir," says Mahodi, poking him with a grubby looking white card. Ed snatches the card. He reads it and snorts.

Mahodi/LiangRong/Carlos
INePT Construction Specialists
We do anything.

"I am seeing from your face that you are not expecting us," says Mahodi with pleasant concern. "It is your good friend Mickey calling us saying you are wanting major home improvement in a hurry. We are very fast, sir. And very reasonable. And we are accepting cash."

"But I have no idea what I'm going to do yet," sputters Ed.

"Oh, no problem. We help with design as well. We can make look very nice. Like all the other houses."

"I don't want it to look like all the other..."

"Oh, Eddie," interrupts Tatiana.

Ed looks at her blankly. From somewhere beyond the quiet street he hears a distant rumbling, as if large equipment is being moved. He opens his mouth to say 'I'll get in touch with you when I'm ready,' when a large trailer truck appears around the corner. In a deafening roar, the truck shifts down and comes to a grinding halt two feet from the back of Ed's new, paid in cash, BMW.

"What is this??" Ed feels like he's going to hyperventilate.

"That is being the delivery of the back hoe, sir. Mickey is informing us that you are in need of a remodel fast, so we are currently having a window of time for back hoe."

Tatiana has been listening to this exchange with open ears. "Backo?" she says now, looking at Ed with a questioning face.

"Back-hoe," says Ed, giving extra emphasis to the 'ho'. He turns back to Mahodi. "Hold on," he says adamantly. "I have no permits. Aside from the fact that I haven't decided what I'm going to do here. You need to work with permits."

"Oh, yes, sir. Naturally. But we are specialists for remodels of fast and easy kind. You are doing small remodel, yes? I have special connections for expressing of permitting services for small remodels."

"Oh, Eddie," says Tatiana, thrilled by the sudden turn of events.

Ed looks at her. She is so hot. He could just do some small stuff now, update, freshen the place up, do the yard if it would please her. "Do you do landscaping too?" he asks Mahodi.

"Absolutely," says Mahodi.

Well, why not get the show on the road, thinks Ed. Like the guy says, just a small remodel. But you need to have permits in this neighborhood, Mickey or not. "So how much?" he asks Mahodi. "I mean, the permits."

Mahodi wobbles his head from side to side, a casual smile on his face. "Certainly not more than if you do it without permit."

*"They say no one can know it all, but they're wrong. If you buy my
books, you'll know how to goal and you'll be a huge success."*
Ronald Ace, *How to Be Great*

7

Inside the Golden Toenail Spa on Third Street, the lunchtime
atmosphere is relaxed or torpid, depending on who you are. The
floor is linoleum, the mauve ('Orchid') colored naugahyde chairs
are covered in additional plastic, and the walls are decorated with
a variety of lucky bamboo and gold-framed prints of Buddha.
Soft, generic relaxation music plays behind the low murmur of
the handful of clients reclining in the station chairs.

Tatiana is wearing a white smock that stretches tightly across
her lush bosom and her blond hair is pulled back into a French
knot. She is massaging the feet of a middle-aged woman wearing
a cherry red suit. The woman, Cyndee, one of Tatiana's regular
customers, closes her eyes in contentment and sighs. "This feels
so good."

She pauses and Tatiana smiles at her. "Good."

"I showed four houses today," says Cyndee, as if she felt a
need to explain why Tatiana's hands on her feet feels so incredibly
satisfying. It just sends relaxation through her whole body.

"Four houses?" says Tatiana, impressed. "Real estate must
be very good business. Many of my clients are making real estate.
Every day I hear now they are making money on houses."

"Darling! Any idiot can make money in this market! All you
have to do is buy a house and flip it and you've made a profit."

Tatiana takes a little more oil in the palm of her hands for

Cyndee's dry heels. "Flip it? What is this?" These Americans. They are constantly coming up with new words.

"Flip it. Buy it, throw a coat of paint on it, and get it back on the market as fast as you can. That's what's called 'flipping' a house."

"Ah. So nothing to do with 'flip off'," says Tatiana. Cyndee laughs. Tatiana pats Cyndee's feet with a towel to get off the excess oil. She reaches for a cuticle stick. She is sensing an opportunity. How can she put it? "Real estate is very good," she says to Cyndee, "but I am not knowing best way to start in this business."

Cyndee regards her for a moment and then reaches over the arm of the chair to her briefcase, on the floor beside her. She rummages inside and pulls out a business card and a flyer. The card, printed in a flourishing style, shows *Cyndee Rohber, Exclusive Agent, Pacific Realty,* along with three phone numbers.

"I'll tell you what," says Cyndee, lowering her voice. "I like you. You have energy and focus. A hot listing came on the market this week. I've already had two calls about it, but I'm not meeting with them till the end of the week." She hands Tatiana the flyer and the card. "I'll give you 10% of my commission if you can sell the house. It's not much, but it's a perfect entry-level home or a flipper. Whoever buys this house will double their money. The address is on the flyer."

Tatiana glances at the flyer, then she smiles and tucks it into her smock pocket. Her brain is afire! Eddie knows a rich real estate man. Maybe it's all going to happen! She tries to hide her excitement as she reaches for the tray of nail polish. "Pink pearl today?" she asks.

"Do you think it goes with the cherry?" replies Cyndee, frowning.

"Maybe red better," says Tatiana. She can't wait to get to the phone.

As soon Cyndee leaves, Tatiana pockets her manicure money and hurries back to her cubicle at the rear of the spa. If the front of the spa is somewhat inelegant, the rear of the spa behind the Japanese screen, where the employees go for a break, is just short of rustic with its wooden plank floor, unpainted door trim and stark light bulb. Along the right wall is a unit of ten wooden cubbyholes, each about the size of a school locker. Tatiana's, as per her special request, is all the way at the end. She pulls the little curtain aside. Inside, taped to the back of the niche is a full-sized, torn-out magazine photo of Ronald and Lada Ace. She puts her book, the same one she was reading at the dentist office, aside and digs her phone out of her purse. She speed dials and presses it to her ear. Then she leans her head into the privacy of the cubbyhole.

"Eddie?" she says when she hears his voice at the other end.

"Tat?" He's standing in the parking lot of the sewer treatment plant next to his new car. He was about to go for an iced grande Latte. "What's up?"

"Oh, Eddie, I have hot real estate tip! Is house for sale, very cheap. But we have to decide quick-quick. I have idea. You call your man with money, see if okay to use money for flip-it house. Then we go see it. Is not too far." She pauses, waiting to sense what kind of effect she has had on Eddie. He doesn't answer right away. The silence feels interminable.

"Oh, all right," he says finally. They have almost had sex three times. But each time they get started, they've been interrupted. The first time was their shopping day, then it was those idiot construction workers showing up unannounced again, and the last time it was a phone call from the school. Meledy was sick. Ed figures that something has to happen soon. He's dying to put his face in between those incredibly voluptuous breasts.

"Where's the house?" he asks.

"In old part of town." Tatiana answers. "Ar-vee Street 4-7," she reads from the flyer.

"That's kind of a low-rent area, isn't it?"

"No matter! Is house for flipping!"

Ed laughs. She sounds like a kid at Christmas. "Okay. I'll

call you back later though. I don't have time now." Just as he disconnects, Frank drives into the lot in his pick-up truck, kicking up a fine cloud of dust, and parks right next to Ed.

"For Pete's sake, Frank," he says to the guy as he climbs down from his truck.

"Dude!" says Frank, ignoring the comment. "What's with the hair?"

"Shut up, Frank. And you're late again." Ed protectively pats his hair. He's not used to this comb-over thing yet, and the hair spray makes his scalp itch.

"Sorry," Frank smirks and walks towards the maintenance building. Ed watches him till he's out of ear shot, then he dials Mickey's number.

Mickey is in his office, sitting at his desk smiling to himself, and watching two blackbirds squabble over a small bunch of dates hanging from the palm tree outside the office window. He's just had sex with Tiffany and sold an option ARM deal. The guy was thrilled to be able to move into a 3,500 square foot house for such incredibly small payments. 'Who cares what tomorrow may bring,' whistles Mickey. What should he do next today?

He doesn't have two seconds to think about it because his intercom buzzes.

"Hey, hot-stuff," says Tiffany sassily. "You've got Ed Fasouli on the phone."

"Tiffany!" admonishes Mickey. "Professional. Always professional. Put him through." He puts his feet up on his desk while he waits for the connection. "Hell-o-Eddie," he answers generously. "How's it going?"

"Fine, fine," answers Ed quickly. "Listen, I just have a quick question. What's the situation on me using some of that half a mill I borrowed to finance a small fixer-upper?"

"What?" exclaims Mickey, sitting upright in his chair. "Why would you want to do that?" He's feeling suddenly even more cheerful—if that's possible—than a minute ago. "Money is so cheap right now! Why don't you keep your home equity loan and get a separate one for the house. I assume you're talking about a flipper, right? What's the address?"

"It's on Arvee Street. Number forty-seven, or something. I haven't seen it yet."

"Arvee Street?" says Mickey with guarded surprise. This has got to be his lucky day. That's the property he's put into one of his holding companies. He bought it really cheap, put very little into it, and has barely managed to keep it rented, but he knows that if he wants to make any money off his investment, now is the time because the value is about to drop through the floor. But if he discloses that he owns it, the agent will probably pull out. On the other hand, it would be quite interesting for him to finance this for Ed…

"You must have a real bargain there!" he congratulates Ed. "Let me give you some advice: you don't want to get your money mixed up. It's a much cleaner deal if you just get another loan. I can offer you a special instrument right now. It's genius. You borrow 110% of what you need for the house at a special 1.7% intro adjustable rate. You use the extra 10% to fix up the house, and then you sell it for anywhere from 130-150% more than you paid for it. You pay back the loan and keep the rest. Your end? Thousands, just for doing a little paperwork."

"That sounds straight-forward enough," says Ed, glancing at his watch. "Thanks, Mickey. I'll let you know. I'm going to look at it tonight." Ed closes his phone as he walks back to the maintenance area. Maybe this is easy, he thinks in surprise. I just didn't know about it. All it takes is a little gum-shun. He smiles, thinking about Tatiana.

That evening, as the commuter traffic is still thick on the main boulevards, Cyndee arrives at the house on Arvee Street. She's always early when she shows a house. She likes to check that it's been prepared, and this one isn't ready at all. She sees that someone pounded in a post, but they didn't put a sign up. Idiots. Inferiors, she thinks. She looks around in her trunk and finds a freshly painted "For Sale by Cyndee" sign and hangs it up. She looks up and down the street of this low-end neighborhood. The driveways and sidewalk parking areas are scattered with RV's in various conditions while cars and motorcycles drip oil on lawns. She did warn them. Sort of.

She marches up to the house and pulls a gadget that looks like a pager out of her purse, types in a code, opens the lock box hanging from the front door handle and takes out the key. It turns easily and she pushes on the door. Except it doesn't open. She pushes harder, but it still doesn't budge. She refuses to put her shoulder against it, it'll dirty her suit. So, leading with her strong leg, she kicks the door as hard as she can, and it opens.

A horrible, musty smell slithers out. It's a mixture of stale mold, animal feces, dust, and who knows what else. Great, she thinks. Nobody came to clean. How in the world is she supposed to make deals when she can't even depend on people to clean their houses? She strides to the kitchen and throws open the back door to get a cross breeze going. Then she looks around at the messed up walls and stained carpet. She told them it was a flipper. What do people expect? Nobody wants such a dump. Maybe this girl will get it sold. She sure has drive.

Cyndee rummages in her real estate bag and pulls out a stack of photocopied flyers and a bunch of slightly worn-looking business cards. Each card is from a different agent. She scatters them across the kitchen counter to make it look like a lot of agents have passed through with buyers simply waiting to snap up this fantastic opportunity. It's amazing how many people fall for this trick, she thinks looking around. Potential, it's all about creating potential where other people fail to do so.

At that moment, Ed's red BMW pulls up behind Cyndee's sedan. Ed and Tatiana get out and pause on the sidewalk for a moment as they take in the run-down appearance of the yard and neighborhood. This is not exactly what they had in mind for their first foray into real estate.

"Potential!" says Tatiana to Ed. "Think potential!"

She links her arm in his, as if to grab his doubts and channel them away, and leads him up the cracked sidewalk to the front door where Cyndee awaits them.

"Hi, there! I'm Cyndee Rohber," she exclaims as they reach her. She pronounces her last name Row-bear. She shoves one of her business cards into Ed's hand. "I'm so glad to meet you. Imagine all this for only two-hundred and fifty thousand dollars! And in two months, with a little TLC, you'll double your value."

Double its value, thinks Ed as he shakes hands with her. That's even more than Mickey said it'd be worth. But, looking around, it's hard to imagine.

"Come in, come in," says Cyndee, interrupting his thoughts. "I'll give you a run-through. Unfortunately, I have to hurry. I've got an offer to present at six, but we can meet again." That ought to inspire them, give them the feeling that things are happening here, she thinks. Honestly, all she really needs to do is clean up her office and submit her quarterly. "But, if this fabulous opportunity seems like it's for you, you can just make an offer. At this price the property is going to go really fast." She turns away from Ed and Tatiana and looks at the living room as if she's just seen it for the first time in her life, and it is the promised land. "Look at this room!" she exclaims. "What charm!"

Ed and Tatiana look around the room. Even Tatiana's enthusiasm is dampened. The carpet is old and stained, the door frames deeply dented, and the walls are peeling in places except where there is some faded wallpaper with hunting scenes still hanging. The small fireplace, the best feature in the room, is overflowing with the last tenant's trash.

Cyndee notices Tatiana's glance and chirps up, "Don't you love the built-in bookshelves framing the fireplace?" She waltzes over and holds up her arms. "Everybody wants these now. This house has so much potential! It is just crying for a make-over. Perfect for a first-time home-buyer, or better yet, for a flipper."

Ed and Tatiana look silently at Cyndee. Cyndee does not miss the effect of the house on them. Now she's worried that her usual charm might not be working. She leads them into the kitchen where she has spread all the cards and flyers on the counter. "As you can see," she says looking ruefully at the cards, "the house is getting a lot of action. It's priced to sell!" She hands Ed one of the photocopied flyers. "Let's go look at the bedrooms and bathroom quickly."

She rapidly opens and closes a coat closet door in the hallway (no fool, she) and shows them the two tiny bedrooms across from each other. "Look at this," she says in the second bedroom. The ten foot by ten foot bedroom has mirrored sliding doors along one wall. "You could combine this walk-in closet with the coat closet to make a third bedroom if you were clever!"

Ed, standing in the hallway, guffaws. This is ridiculous. He pokes his head into the hall door across from the coat closet and quickly withdraws. The large bathroom, tiled in rose and black, probably has as much mold as it has paint.

"Jeez! Didn't anybody ever clean this place?" he exclaims.

"Well, like I said," says Cyndee snippishly, and she shepherds them back towards the kitchen. "The house has just gone on the market and it is going fast, let me tell you. So it's up to you. Some deals are so good you don't need to polish them." She chuckles. "I wouldn't think long about this." She absent-mindedly tidies the cards and flyers on the counter. She's clearly getting ready to leave. "The owner is a hard-nosed LLC investment company and they are not giving any wiggle room on the price. In fact," she reaches up to push a cupboard closed, and it springs back open, almost hitting her in the face, "in fact, they're planning on starting a bidding war. So if you want to avoid one, bite quickly and bid high!" That sounds rather good, she thinks as she glances out the back window one more time. "And don't forget the backyard. It has loads of potential too." She turns and beams at Ed and Tatiana with the look of an expectant mother on her face.

Tatiana looks at Cyndee and feels a wave of confidence seep in. There's that word again. Potential! Yes, that's it! Visionaries have potential! And she can see that this house has potential.

She turns to Ed. "This house has so much possibilities! Think what we can do! Eddie," she leans on him, "what do you think?" This might be her only chance at real estate.

Cyndee, taking Tatiana's cue, shakes her head. "Don't be afraid to act fast!"

Both women stare expectantly at Ed. One of them has fabulous breasts that he is dying to put his mouth around.

"Eddie, you have international construction company already working for you. This is meant to be! You gonna be big millionaire! Just like Ronald Ace. You got to start somewhere."

"Just pull the door closed and drop this key in the lock box." Cyndee tells Tatiana, handing her the key. "Bye-bye! Take your time! But don't be afraid to act fast once you've decided."

Tatiana and Ed stand in the musty silence of the house, listening to Cyndee's car pull away.

"Come. We go see garden," says Tatiana after a moment. She takes his hand and walks to the back door. Ed follows her lead and opens the door. Together, they step out onto the buckled cement slab that serves as a patio. A huge, ugly elm tree leans precariously towards the house. Roots spread like knobby, old knees every which way under the thin layer of dry grass beyond the slab. Some dusty privets form a sort of hedge on either side, shielding them from the neighbors. Tatiana stands there, as if mesmerized. Then she lets out a great, soulful sigh. "I can imagine great things for this house," she says. "We gonna be a team."

At that moment Ed's cell phone rings. Tatiana, quicker than lightening, grabs it from his belt holder and shoves it down between her breasts. "Say yes, Eddie," she giggles, "say yes!!"

"Yes," he says. "Okay, yes, yes." And she lets him kiss her long and deeply.

Later, much later, that evening, Tatiana is standing at her shrine to Lada. Her hands are clasping her cell phone and she looks up at the photo of Lada in gratitude.

"Oh, beautiful one," she says in a hushed and reverent voice.

"Maybe I make judgments too quickly. This Ed, maybe he's okay. He got money, now I think he gonna get real estate. Maybe we even have sex. And look!" She holds up her cell phone with the screen saver photo of her and the new BMW Z4 . "I got new car!"

If only her mother was around to see it. That would show her.

"If you want to be successful, get close to successful people. Sleeping with my books under your pillow is as close to me as you can get."
Ronald Ace, My Life!

8

"Gee, I can't believe you could get this rolling so quickly," says Ed as he walks into Mickey's office. He's taken the day off to take care of business, which includes picking up Tatiana for an early lunch and he's wearing his new navy blue blazer and slacks.

"Aw, come on, buddy," says Mickey, eyeing him up and down, "we go way back. Of course I can make time for an old friend." He leads Ed into the windowless conference room where a slick looking folder sits waiting on the table. A pen lies across the folder in readiness. Ed notices it's the Mont Blanc pen Mickey seems so proud of. Maybe it's his lucky pen, he thinks. "Have a seat, Ed," says Mickey, nudging him towards the chair. "This won't take long at all. It's very similar to the home equity loan we did, only, of course this one involves a few more fees for some of the transaction, since it's a house here you're buying. But it's a great deal, let me tell you. Real estate has never been so good!"

As he talks, Mickey sits down across from Ed and opens the folder, separates the stack of papers into two neat piles, and then starts fanning them out, preparing them for the signature.

"Now, I did it just like I told you I would. I got you 110% financing, so you're actually getting $286. Here are the loan docs and the closing papers on the house. I went ahead and made it simple for you so all the fees are just added into the loan. You don't have to touch any of your own money. It's a 1.7% adjustable rate and your first two payments are only going to be $987 a month. Can you believe that? That'll give you enough time, and the 110% percent gives you enough cash to get that baby fixed up and back on the market. Good thing I put you in touch with that construction crew. By the way, how are they working out?"

Ed glances at the stack of papers. Oh boy, here we go again with the paperwork, he thinks. It's the only part of this that makes him uncomfortable. "I have no idea. They showed up, dumped a bunch of equipment, and haven't been back. Strangest thing. I don't know how you do this stuff," he says, shaking his head as he stares at the papers.

"I love to help people realize their dreams, Eddie! That's all."

"You sure weren't like that when we were young," says Ed reaching for the pen. He glances at his watch. He doesn't want to be late. He has a surprise for Tatiana.

Ed pulls up to the corner in front of the Pacific Realty at five minutes to eleven and Tatiana is already there looking scrumptious in a hot pink, tight-fitting dress. Wow, Ed didn't know he liked the color pink so much. He jumps out of the car to open the passenger door for her.

"I have a surprise for you," he says, sitting behind the wheel and starting up the BMW.

"I love surprises!" she giggles.

He steers into traffic and heads in the direction of Arvee Street. Two blocks before, he drives in the opposite direction, just to throw her off, and then tells her to close her eyes.

"But I can't leave my hand on your leg if I cover my eyes," she exclaims.

"That's a ruse!" he says. "I said 'close' not 'cover'. Now, close your eyes tightly!"

"Russ?" she says, squeezing her eyes tightly.

"Ruse," he repeats. "It means an excuse, a cover."

"But that's just what you told me not to do!"

She can be so infuriating, thinks Ed. He has circled the block by now and takes a right turn to Arvee Street. He stops smoothly in front of number 47. "Don't open them yet," he says. He puts his hands on her shoulders and gently turns her body so that she is facing directly towards the front of the house and the big "SOLD" sign hanging there. "Okay. Now! Open!"

"Eddieeee!!!" she squeals, when she opens her eyes. "You did it! You're big roller now!!" And she turns and throws herself on his neck and smothers him with kisses.

They don't even stop for lunch. Who needs lunch? The day is short enough as it is with kids. He drives up to his house, opens the old wooden garage door, drives the BMW inside and closes the door. He looks at her with so much desire that he can hardly speak. "Come on in," he says.

When they get inside, he puts his favorite Rockin Recalcitrans CD on, not too loud, and leads Tatiana to the sofa. They waste no time. They've exchanged a lot of kisses, but never like this. This kissing had a full-blown future ahead of it.

Tatiana runs her hands up and down Ed's shoulders and forearms, feeling the muscles, then runs her fingers through his hair. He kisses her neck, her ear. Caresses her lovely firm breasts, feels the slenderness of her thighs.

"Finally," she whispers, "The Eddie."

He playfully pushes her down on the sofa and her dress stretches beautifully across her chest. He worships those breasts. He wants to suck them so badly. He pulls the plunging neckline even lower until her breasts are exposed and puts his mouth teasingly on her lacy bra. Her nipples stand erect. He teases her there for a while, then lets his fingers play on her thigh.

"Here comes the little mouse," he whispers.

Tatiana giggles while she unbuttons his shirt. "Oh, you bad boy," she whispers. Ed unzips his slacks, starts to take off his shirt.

"No! No! Leave it on! I love man in button-down shirt," she says. "Put on blazer too."

Ed forgets all about his trousers while he pulls the shirt back over his shoulders and retrieves his blazer from the floor. He slips it on.

"Mmm," she sighs. "Come here, big handsome real estate man." She pulls him to her and smoothes his hair across the top of his head. Then she kisses him passionately. He presses his body against hers and rubs his hard groin against her thigh, moving higher and ...

The home phone rings.

Ed jerks up. It's an ingrained reaction. He's got to answer. It could be his kids.

"No answer!" urges Tatiana, pulling him back.

"There might be trouble."

"No!" says Tatiana. She shoves her breast into his mouth and he obliges. He teases it with his tongue. But one ear is listening for the answering machine to go on. Beep. There it is.

"Hey stranger," says the voice. Oh, shit, thinks Ed, it's Michelle. She's supposed to be volunteering at the school. He listens. "Where have you been? I just left a message on your cell phone, but in case you don't get it, I'm going to take the boys for pizza after the practice and then I'll bring Buddy home. So don't worry." She pauses, as if she hoping that Ed might pick up the phone. "All righty, take care." And the machine beeps and goes silent.

Tatiana suddenly pulls away from Ed and sits up.

"Who's that?"

"That's Michelle. She's my neighbor. She helps me out with the kids."

Tatiana looks at him and frowns for a moment. Then she decides to forget it and goes back to kissing him. She brings her hand down to his limp organ. Ed forces himself to think of sex. Think of breasts. Luscious breasts and curving hips and moist caves. He feels himself start to grow hard again. But right in the middle of his efforts, he hears an insistent but muted electronic melody playing. 'My country 'tis of thee..' It's Tatiana's cell phone, coming from deep inside her purse.

Now she involuntarily pulls towards the source of the ringing.

"Don't answer it!" he laughs and kisses her wetly. "After all… we are made for love!"

Tatiana giggles and slides out from under him. She gracefully leaps over to her purse, which she left sitting on the arm chair. Ed is quick. He takes a big step and reaches to grab her arm playfully. But he forgets that he still has his trousers pooling around his ankles. He almost trips and manages to balances himself on the sofa arm. Tatiana stops and laughs at him, forgetting about her phone. Ed seizes the moment and lunges for her. She's caught! He's got her wrist. He divests himself of the trousers. But she uses that moment to slip out of his grasp again. She runs into the kitchen and towards the laundry room.

Ed follows her. She's so spirited! He loves it.

He finds her perched on the top-loading washing machine, vintage about 1985, waving her white lacy panties.

"My daddy had old washing machine like this!" she says. "He was washing machine fix-it man. And when people buy new washing machines, he install and bring old one home. We had Whirlpool, Hoover, Miele, even crummy old Vyatka Russian washing machine."

"Wow," says Ed, barely listening. Where the hell is the step stool they usually keep in the laundry room? The kids probably took off with it. There's no way he can get high enough with her sitting up on the washing machine. Ah! He spies the faded plastic blue stool. He grabs it, puts in place, and stands in front of Tatiana. He wraps his arms around her and kisses her relentlessly.

"Oh, my God," he moans. Her dress is pulled up above her hips and her little jewel is just there, wet and waiting. He feels her tongue circle his lips then push hard into his mouth. He pulls down on the neckline of her dress again and buries his face in her breasts while he explores other moist places. She moans. He grunts. And suddenly the wash machine is jiggling and shaking.

Ed pulls back, startled. She laughs.

"Spin cycle!"

Oh, jeezes, thinks Ed. The machine is vibrating faster and faster. This is unbelievable!

"We gonna have super house!"

"We're going to have super sex," Ed pants.

"You betcha," she whispers.

Suddenly, there is a sharp rapping at the kitchen door.

Ed slams his palm against the wash machine knob to stop the machine. The knocking repeats. He hurriedly pulls up his boxers, pulls down her dress, smoothes his comb-over.

The rapping continues, polite but firm.

"Oh, hell," says Ed. And he goes to the kitchen door.

"Mr. Fasoline, sir?" says Mahodi very courteously, almost apologetically, yet with a helpful looking twist. "Good day to you, fine Sir." He tactfully stares at Ed's nose to avoid any eye contact with Ed's lack of trousers, his strange new hair style, or what might be going through his mind.

Ed explodes. "What the hell are you doing here now? And the name is Fasouli. Mr. Fa-sou-li!"

"Yes, Sir, excuse me, Sir, but we must be knowing if you are wanting to be starting the pool this week or if you are wanting to be starting it after we remove the wall, sir."

"I don't want you here now!" shouts Ed. "Where have you been, anyway?"

"Oh, we are having many diversities, but now we are at your service."

Exasperated, Ed strides over to the kitchen counter. Get this guy out of here. Where the hell is that flyer? Of course. It's already been swallowed by the mysterious paper matter that propagates during the night on the kitchen counter. He grabs an envelope, pulls out the contents, and scribbles 47 Arvee Street on it.

"Here," he says, handing it to Mahodi. "Go here. Here's a key. Figure out how to take out the wall to the coat closet to make a room and the cheapest way to remodel the kitchen and bathroom. We have one month to do it. If you don't finish by the end of the month, I won't pay you. And use the front door for Pete's sake!"

"Are you meaning this month, or next month," inquires Mahodi.

Ed pauses. Well, it's almost the end of this month. "Next month," he says.

"Absolutely, sir!" says Mahodi, bobbing his head up and down. "Yes, sir, we can do that, sir. Very fine."

"Okay, okay," says Ed. "Get out of here. Goodbye. Just do the work."

He hears Tatiana still in the laundry room and slams the door in Mahodi's face without further ado.

Mahodi stands there for a moment looking at the address on the envelope. Then he shoves it into his jeans pocket and leaves.

"Now, where were we…" says Ed slipping next to Tatiana who apparently hasn't been bored while he was away.

That night, after dropping Buddy off at Ed's house and putting Sammy to bed, Michelle sits in her bedroom looking through the new Nice N' Naughty Parties catalog that came in the mail that afternoon. But she's not enjoying it as much as usual. Something is nagging her, but she can't seem to put her finger on it. It's just a feeling of unease. Or the stars in bad alignment. Ed seems to be so different lately. He doesn't tell her what he's doing like he used to, and he's gone more and more. And all this construction stuff in his driveway. The new car. Now some kind of talk about a flipper house.

She hears Mickey in the bathroom. Water is running. Then the click of the shower door as he steps in.

And Mickey seems particularly self-satisfied lately.

Michelle gets up out of bed and goes to his closet. Sometimes he leaves his BlackBerry in his coat pocket. She pats the pockets of his various suit coats. The third one rewards her. She reaches in and takes it out. She activates it, taps on his Organizer, chooses his Calendar. Keys in Ed's name. Look at that: three appointments with him. She goes to the Tasklist and finds an address on Arvee Street, and the name of a title company. Did Mickey possibly talk Ed into buying that dump he owns on Arvee and he is providing the financing? She goes to his MemoPad and finds some calculations of various interest rates on a quarter of a million dollars. So that what's going on. Ed is borrowing money from Mickey to impress that blond bimbo? She hears Mickey get out of the shower and quickly turns off the BlackBerry and shoves it back into the coat pocket.

When Mickey comes out of the bathroom, he tosses the trade journal he's carrying onto the bed and grabs some clean underwear from his dresser. He feels Michelle's eyes boring into him. "What?" he demands.

Michelle picks up the trade journal and shows him the headline: **When to Get Out of a Souring Market.**

"That's what," she says. "Don't mess with Ed, or I will blow your operation out to heaven."

Mickey looks at her incredulously. "What are you talking about?"

"I think you're lending Ed money. And if you do something dishonest with him, I will divorce you in a heartbeat. I've put up with your shit for eleven years, but I'm telling you, that will be it. And I won't be shy about squeezing you for everything you're worth."

"You're still in love with him, aren't you?" laughs Mickey in disbelief. "You're in love with that loser!"

"He's my friend, and he's had enough trouble already. He doesn't need you messing up his life."

"Mess up his life? Why he can do that all by himself! He doesn't need me!"

"You know exactly what I mean. I'm not as stupid as you think, Mickey Schulz. I know what you're up to."

"Up to? Up to? I'm up to putting food on the table for my

family," says Mickey with his best self-satisfied, arrogant smile. "I don't think you mind the lifestyle you have. Or would you rather live in that dump across the street?"

"Don't cross me, Mickey," says Michelle. She gathers up her catalog and her pillow. "I'm going to sleep in the guest bedroom tonight."

"Do what you want," says Mickey getting into bed.

Michelle pads down the hallway and stops to peek in Sammy's room. He's sound asleep. Through the curtains, she sees the light on in Ed's house and she pauses for a moment. She can just barely see him walk through the living room. What is he up to? She'd wanted to stay and talk earlier when she dropped Buddy off, but he seemed distracted. Men! she thinks. He's playing a dangerous game just to get sex. Maybe she ought to expand her line of wares to include men's interests.

Once Ed gets the kids to bed ("Please can we watch just one more episode of Twilight Zone," they begged), instead of feeling tired, he suddenly feels restless. He's not used to so much happening in one day and signing the papers for that house is a big step. It puts his job at the sewer plant in a different perspective. What if he can really pull this off? Make a couple hundred thousand or so. He wouldn't need to keep his job if it works out. He opens a beer and paces the living room, stops by the window to look out and sees the last light turn off in the Schulz house across the street. Then he drains his beer, shuts off the TV and goes to the kitchen. He pauses in front of the counter staring at the pile of junk on it when, floating on the top, the company flyer about the upcoming family picnic catches his eye.

Please join us in the celebration of the
Swamp Valley Sewage Treatment Plant revitalization.
Sunday afternoon
Music and plenty of food
Bring the whole family!

"Real estate is football: if you're running in the wrong direction, you are shit out of luck. You gotta goal in the right direction."
Ronald Ace, The Magic of Business

9

Michelle can tell it's going to be a hot day. She looks at her watch. It's only eight-twenty a.m. and she's already starting to perspire. She sits on the bottom bleacher with Daisy, as always, wearing her plum colored baseball cap, her black ponytail sticking out behind.

The turn-out for the tournament is good, all things considered. The bleachers are pretty full and there's a healthy clutch of parents sitting in their portable sports events chairs. But where's Ed? Ed never misses Buddy's games. He's probably the only dad with perfect attendance.

"Thatta boy, Buddy!" she screams as Buddy hits the ball out to left field, throws down his bat and high-tails it to first base. Where is he? He was here and now he's gone.

Without her noticing, Ed's red BMW pulls into the parking lot and Ed hustles Tatiana out of the car. He grabs her hand and pulls her along. "I think we've only missed the first inning," he says. Ed is wearing, uncharacteristically, his navy blue blazer over a button-down oxford cloth shirt and new blue jeans. Pressed blue jeans. He feels a little silly, but he's more concerned about getting to the game. He told her he was going to drop Buddy off and then pick her up by seven-fifty, but she wasn't nearly ready.

Tatiana allows herself to be pulled. She's curious as to what this baseball will be about, and who will be there. The heel of her toeless sandals lands in a gopher hole in the field and her ankle turns. "*Owa!*" she says, looking down at the annoyance. "Is like football field in Astonia. Full of holes. Eddie, stop!" she whines.

Ed stops and looks at her impatiently while she rubs her ankle. "Okay?"

"I guess," she answers.

Ed scans the parents in the bleachers until he finds Michelle's cap and ponytail. He pulls Tatiana towards her. Then, when they are just a few feet away, he drops her hand.

"Hey, stranger!" calls Ed, smiling like a fool and waiting for Michelle to turn and look at him. She hesitates, and then turns. She takes in Ed's stupid-looking hair, the jacket, the pressed jeans, then she looks at Tatiana. OMG. It's that woman. The one he snuck into his garage during a work day a couple of weeks ago. She looks back at Ed like he's a piece of gum on the bottom of her shoe.

"Hi," she answers.

"Uh, well. How's life? Seems like I haven't seen you in a month." Why does he feel so nervous?

"Fine," says Michelle, and pointedly turns her face back to the game.

Fine, be that way, thinks Ed. I don't need you to approve of my life. "This is my neighbor, Michelle, from across the street," he says casually to Tatiana. "The one I was telling you about." Actually, he'd barely said two words about Michelle. He sees Tatiana giving him a strange look. "I don't mean it that way... forget it," he says, shaking his head.

"Nice to meet you," says Tatiana, looking down at Michelle. She has not really suspected anything up until now, but maybe that phone message was more than she thought. She glances at Michelle's left hand and sees a gold band studded with diamonds. At least she's married, thinks Tatiana. She decides to make conversation. It is always good to know your enemies. Even if they aren't enemies now, they might be one day.

"I've never been to baseball game before," she says to

Michelle, even though Michelle is not looking in her direction. "In my country we play football." It works. Michelle turns to look at Tatiana evenly.

"You mean soccer," she says.

"Whatever," says Tatiana lightly.

"Do you mind if we sit down?" Ed asks.

"The game's almost over," answers Michelle. She slides over on the aluminum bleacher as far as possible, dragging Daisy along with her, and leaving a wet puddle behind. Ed slides in next to her, and Tatiana sits on the edge.

"No wonder you've been missing games lately," says Michelle to him as she stares stonily at the teams of eleven-year-old boys in their white uniforms with red or blue stripes down the leg. "Buddy mentioned that you were busy spending all that money you borrowed from Mickey."

"I didn't borrow any money from Mickey," says Ed hotly. "I took out a loan. What's gotten into you?"

"Nothing. I'm just so glad you're having a good time." She turns and looks pointedly at Ed's hair, sarcasm dripping from her voice. "But it would've been a lot more honest to say, 'Michelle, I'm going to go act like an ass for a while, would you watch my kids?' I believed you. I thought you had work."

"Now wait a minute, you're the one who's inviting the kids over all the time. And I did take Sam to the batting cages last week, in case you didn't notice."

"Wow, go all out." Michelle listens to her own voice and thinks, this is ridiculous. We're squabbling like an old married couple. Other parents are beginning to slide looks in their direction. "Come on, Daisy." She pulls on the dog's leash as she stands up. "I have some errands to run." Michelle pointedly looks at Tatiana who has been trying not to stare at Ed and Michelle by reapplying her lipstick.

"Enjoy the rest of the game," she says dryly, and walks off towards the parking lot.

A quiet comes over Tatiana and Ed. It's like they're sitting in a silent little bubble all by themselves in the midst of the noise and chatter of the baseball game. Finally, Tatiana breaks the silence. "Is old girlfriend?"

"No!" says Ed vehemently. He pretends like he is concentrating on the game, but in fact he's lost track of the inning.

"Humph," says Tatiana matter-of-factly. "In Astonia we have saying. Love is like war: easy to start, hard to end."

"She's married," insists Ed, as if Tatiana has been arguing otherwise. "And she has kids."

Buddy's team is up at bat again. Buddy hits the ball right down center field. The parents cheer. "Run!" they shout. But the ball drops right into the center fielder's glove. A soft moan of disappointment. "Good try, boys," says one of the parents. "You'll get the next one," says another.

"Hey," says Ed, suddenly turning toward Tatiana. "I am so stupid! I totally forgot to ask you! My company is having a picnic this afternoon and I wanted you to come with us, me and the kids."

Tatiana smiles. "Super!" she says. There's no competition after all.

After the games and the hotdogs, Ed drops Tatiana off at her place.

"I'll pick you up around four-thirty, okay?" he says, squeezing her hand. "And dress casually. You're beautiful no matter what you wear."

She blows him a kiss and disappears into her apartment building.

"Does she have to come?" whines Meledy, when she hears about the change of plans.

"What difference does it make to you," says Ed cheerfully. "You don't stay with me anyway. You'll be off flirting with Frank." He winks at her. Meledy rolls her eyes, but she knows it's certainly more fun to hang around with Frank than the rest of the people. At least he knows what's cool in music.

"But seriously, Dad, this is the LAST time I am going. I don't care if...if...if the Black Eyed Beans show up." She's wearing her low, skinny jeans and tee-shirt uniform and that awkward, sullen look that seems to be part of her 'branding' lately.

"I like going," says Buddy. He looks forward to the picnic because he gets to see Brian and Chris, Doug's kids. And it's way cool to see all those huge pieces of machinery and pipes, and to run around the tanks.

Ed has decided that they will all go in the Mercedes. It would be much too tight in the BMW. He carefully combs his hair the way Tatiana has taught him, and gives it a whiff of hairspray to keep it in place. He's wearing a golf shirt with slacks, in the hopes that Tatiana will approve.

She looks lovely, as always, when he stops to pick her up. She's wearing the peacock blue dress he insisted she buy when they went shopping at Needless Markup and her hair is pulled back into a chignon. She's a little nervous. After all, she wants to make a good impression on Eddie's coworkers.

As they drive through the arched gateway of the Sump Valley Sewage Treatment Plant, Tatiana thinks that she hasn't read the name right. The grounds are neatly planted with trees and bushes arranged in attractive clumps and flower borders around the parking area. The car crunches softly on the gravel as Ed drives to a drooping pepper tree.

Not too far away, a very large gazebo with a small stage has been set up in front of the largest of the sediment tanks. Colorful streamers flap lazily in the wind while an assortment of people mill around what looks like buffet tables, beverages in hand. Children run here and there. And on the stage, a trio of classical musicians play. The scene has an almost idyllic feel to it. And the nicest thing is, it's so colorful! Everything is done in shades of berry—blueberry, blackberry, strawberry, gooseberry, raspberry. Tatiana is actually looking forward to this! And she's feeling rather hungry.

She turns to the backseat. "How about you kids? You hungry?"

Buddy nods vigorously. Meledy mumbles and fidgets with her cell phone.

"It's a perfect afternoon for an outdoor party, that's for sure," exclaims Ed.

He stops the car next to a large family van. Steward's turquoise Jaguar is parked in its usual spot next to the office building. Steward must be feeling happy today, thinks Ed. He got his color-coded paint job, complete with landscaping and custom signs explaining things. As if this was some school exhibit. Well, at least the food should be good. He already sees the smoke from a large barbecue off to the side. Might as well eat, drink, and be merry at the company's expense, since he can't change things.

He hops out of the car and opens Tatiana's door. "Madam," he says with a low bow. Tatiana smiles gorgeously and sets her lovely feet (how Ed would love to run his hands up her legs right now) in their lovely sandals on the gravel. She stands up and out of the car. She takes his proffered hand graciously and steps in the direction of the party. Then, abruptly, she comes to a perfect standstill. What is that smell? Her nostrils flair. What is that faint, but pervasive, thick, garbagey smell? She sniffs again. It's not garbage…it's sewage. The gassy, sweet stink of…sewage! Her face turns to stone.

"Oh. My. God," she says in a deep, guttural voice. "Tell me this is joke."

Ed is taken aback. "What do you mean 'joke'? This is where I work."

"You work in shit plant?" says Tatiana in disbelief.

Meledy slams the car door behind her, suddenly alert. This is great! Dad didn't tell Tat that he works at the sewer plant. What a scene! "Oh," she says sweetly, "didn't you know that dad works at the 'shit' plant?" She looks pointedly at Ed. "Daddy, did you forget to mention that detail to Tat?"

Where did she learn this meanness, thinks Ed. Meledy's face

still has the softness of a little girl, but what is this snottiness? "Of course I told her," he snaps at her.

Buddy slams his car door and looks at the trio in confusion.

"Tat, listen," says Ed, treading water as if his life depended on it.

"No, you listen!" says Tatiana, incensed. "First, you say you have country club. But no, you have house. Then, is not house. Is dump. You tell me you're big engineer. But no. You're not engineer. You're shit plant."

"Now wait a minute," says Ed. "I never told you I was an engineer. Just like I never told you I had a country club for Pete's sake. That was your interpretation!"

"*Inter preshun??*" says Tatiana. Her voice is so tense now that it is starting to sound shrill. You call this inter preshun? Nothing is inter preshun here. Take me home!"

"Now, Tat. Calm down," says Ed firmly. "You never asked where I worked. Come on now. You get used to the smell. And they are really nice people. We don't have to stay long. Look at all the birds. They're nice." He waves his arm in the direction of the estuary.

"Birds!" says Tatiana, her voice dripping with distain. "Eddie. This is not how to be rich man. This is wrong business. You need to think real estate!"

"But how do you think I get money to pay for the real estate?" asks Ed, flabbergasted.

"Investment!" answers Tatiana hotly. "You take risk! No risk, no game. If you work this, you can't focus to make big decisions." At this, she spins around and plops herself back into the car. She folds her arms and looks stonily straight ahead. There will be no more bargaining with her tonight.

Ed sighs deeply. "Okay, kids. Back in the car," he says tiredly. He'd forgotten how exhausting relationships can be. He gives the party one last look before climbing into the driver's seat. They are serving tri-tip steak from the barbecue. That would've tasted so good.

The mood in the car, as they drive Tatiana back to her apartment, is muted, to say the least. Tatiana doesn't say a word, in spite of Ed's efforts to ask her more about her dad's business. So he allows Meledy to tune the car radio to her favorite R&B station and turn it up extra loud. Just to piss Tatiana off. What's that old saying of his dad's? Arguments are like moussaka—baked a lot hotter than eaten?

"Pizza, kids?" he asks loudly before the car door has finished shutting behind Tatiana.

*"If you're sitting around thinking about the implications of what
you're going to do, you are not going to be successful.
Thinking is stupid."
Ronald Ace, Failure Be Gone!*

10

The wrought iron gateway of Sump Valley Sewage Treatment
Plant glints in the morning sunlight as Ed pulls up for work. He's
been feeling lackluster about his job and his life in general ever
since the party. At the plant, he has the sense of being excluded.
Nobody has ribbed him about his brief appearance at the picnic
(which he's sure did not go unnoticed), and he hasn't been able
to participate in the post-party talk, including the fun they had
watching Steward's face when the cellist, a member of the trio
he hired for the event, walked off the stage in a huff, leaving the
violinist and flute player to flounder alone.

On the home front, Mahodi's construction crew has been
bouncing back and forth between Ed's house and the flipper house
on Arvee Street, supposedly making progress. But all Ed can tell
is that most of the back side of his house is now torn up and the
backyard has a gaping hole, which he finds depressing to look at.
As for the other house, honestly, he has no idea what's going on
except that now a huge, battered debris box is parked there as well.
Probably being filled up with junk by the neighbors. And of course
he hasn't heard from Tatiana, in spite of the messages he's left.

Ed parks his car and heads towards the maintenance building,
pausing to glance at the estuary waters glimmering faintly in the
distance between the sediment tanks. The blackbirds trill shrilly
as they forage in the bushes nearby while a couple of crows
complain in the pepper tree. As Ed passes the main splitter, near

the secondary clarifiers, his sharp eyes notices that the raspberry and grape colored paint is already flaking off in large pieces. This is not a good sign. He steps over for closer inspection. The pumps are working hard, he can hear that. But why is it so wet? He wipes his finger along the back side of the joints and feels something like wet mud. He looks at it and shakes his head in dismay. Rust. If the paint is coming off like this, then it's worse than he thought.

He tenses his jaw and makes a decision. He was going to have the guys clean out the scum pumping station today, but first he's going to go give Steward an earful. Maybe now that the picnic is over, that blowhard will finally do something for the plant.

Ed makes an about-face and heads over to the small administrative building overlooking the plant. Inside, he says hi to Mary, the secretary, and heads right on towards Steward's corner office. He throws open the door, a man on a mission, and strides into the office.

Steward, with his boyish MBA face, sits behind his mahogany desk wearing a turquoise golf shirt and khaki Dockers, feet up, nibbling nuts from a bowl. One of the nuts is stale, and he frowns at it just as Ed walks in. Steward looks up.

"Knock, knock," he says curtly, seeing that it's Ed, the troublemaker.

"Do you ever look at the reports I send you?" asks Ed, dispensing with formalities.

"Of course, I do," answers Steward. "And then I plug the information into the equipment repair status matrix I developed." He points to his Super Pro laptop computer.

"Repair matrix?" shoots Ed. "We don't need some color-coded matrix of repairs that you can print out and hang!" He throws his arm in the direction of the wall behind Steward. The wall is tastefully decorated with twelve framed prints of Steward's 'color matrix' hanging in a matrix.

"In fact," continues Ed, "you have totally different systems painted the same color!" He strides over to the matrix in question

and taps so hard on the print that it looks like it's about to fall off
its nail. "Do you know how dangerous that is if something goes
wrong? We need real repairs on real machines to protect a real
environment!" Ed's heart is racing and the adrenalin is flowing
like water. He didn't realize he was so upset about all this.

"I understand that," answers Steward, from his semi-reclining
position. He uncrosses and recrosses his legs. "You see, Ed, you
view only the small picture. My job involves a greater vision. I
need to look at everything in total and the symbiotic relationship
between the plant and the community, now and in the future."

"But we're looking at a future of law suits and fines if we
don't do something," sputters Ed.

"That's your job now, isn't it?" answers Steward coolly.

"I keep sending you the requisition forms," says Ed, "and you
keep sending them back! The flow valve for the primary separator
tank is frozen solid. It's almost ten years older than you! The
valves are leaking. They're so rusted, the paint is flaking off. We
are going to have a major spill right here in our own yard!"

"You know, Ed," says Steward, "People have been
complaining to the district that this place is an eyesore. My uncle
gave me an order to improve the appearance of the facilities. So
I followed orders, and so should you. Next year we can catch up
on repairs."

"Just because your uncle sits on the city council doesn't mean
he knows how to run a sewer treatment plant. We can't wait until
next year! Things are breaking now. We need to replace that
automatic flow valve."

"I don't know what you're talking about," says Steward
vapidly.

"This one," shouts Ed, whacking a different print with his
hand, "we need to replace the blue ones!" And this time the print
really does crash to the ground.

Steward jumps up from his desk to retrieve the fallen print.
"You may leave now!"

"No! You have to take responsibility," shouts Ed. He takes a

S. Pareto Rose

big stride towards Steward's desk. "Now!" He pounds on the desk for emphasis, and cashews and peanuts jump and scatter over the surface. "Or we are going to have a lot of shit on our hands."

Steward looks worried. Not about the shit, about Ed. What if the guy has a gun? He glances out the door towards the secretary and then, propping the print against the wall, scurries over to his desk to scoop up the scattered nuts. "You don't order me around," he says nervously. "I'll give you authorization for new equipment when we have the budget. Meanwhile, you fix the old ones, or you're fired."

"Fired?" laughs Ed hysterically. "You're firing me? Well, guess what? I quit!" And he storms out of the office with a huge grin on his face. "Bye, suckers," he teases the guys as he grabs his stuff from the maintenance building. "I'm going to be flipping real estate while you're dealing with shit!" He floors the BMW, spins once around the gravel parking area to make lots of dust, then hits the road.

As Ed pulls into his driveway that afternoon, there is Mahodi's truck. What is he working on now, thinks Ed. He checks the mail, then walks in through the front door. Just as he sets foot inside, he hears a loud smattering sound, like plaster raining down, and hammering on metal pipes explode from the kitchen. He runs over in time to see that Mahodi and Liang Rong have just managed to rip the washing machine out from the wall.

"Hey! Why are you guys tearing out the washing machine?" he exclaims.

Mahodi and Liang Rong stop and look at him. "Good day, Mr. Fasoline," says Mahodi. He brushes the plaster dust from his face, his turban and then his shoulders. "We are making opening, sir, to approach hot tub area."

"But you never even finished the walls where we knocked them out to expand the master bedroom. Or the sliding door from the family room."

Mahodi and Liang Rong look in unison at the hole they cut

in the wall for the sliding glass door. But the sliding glass door turned out to be 6" too long and so they covered the opening with plastic and simply propped the new door over it.

"You are right, sir. It is not finished. But we are not having enough wood to finish the framing for the bedroom. And you are telling us to work on the other house. So we are working on other house. But we need to buy floor materials for other house as well. So we are thinking, we will buy both at same time. But we are not having enough gas to get to Home Warehouse today, so we are thinking, do we not remain active and take out washing machine today so we have room for wood for tomorrow?"

Ed shakes his head in disbelief. "You guys have a strange logic." It's a wonder anything gets done at all. Well, now that he's not working at the plant, it's time to take charge and get things moving. The most important thing is to get that house on Arvee back on the market.

"I want you to push the washer back in the wall," he says decisively, "and tape up the cracks. Get going on the other house. Pronto. Here's some money for gas." He opens his wallet and peels off seven $20 bills. "Go get what you need, for Pete's sake." He gingerly scratches his scalp and presses his comb-over back in place.

At that moment, a delivery horn starts honking steadily from the front of the house. Now what, thinks Ed. The honking continues. It sounds like a car alarm, only louder. He walks through the living room, and opens the front door. The honking stops as if on cue and a truck motor revs. He hurries outside, but instead of the delivery truck he's expecting to see, he sees a huge double refrigerator box on the street exactly in the middle of the entrance to the driveway, and the tail end of a Home Warehouse truck disappearing around the corner.

"Hey!" shouts Ed, running out to the street. "Those assholes! Mahodi!?!" he yells, stomping into the house. "What the hell is this for?"

Mahodi appears with a caulking gun in his hand.

"Why the hell did they deliver a refrigerator here?"

Mahodi raises his eyebrows. "This I am not knowing." he says politely. "I am only ordering refrigerator and giving address at Arvee Street 47. I am thinking they are making mistake because I am giving your address to bill for refrigerator."

"Oh, hell." says Ed.

He takes out his phone and starts scrounging through the papers in the basket on the kitchen counter for something with the phone number for Home Warehouse. He shuffles through real estate ads and utility bills, grocery ads and letters from the school. Even an envelope with a strange return address from an "MD LLC" that looks vaguely familiar. There it is. A receipt for some paint from Home Warehouse. He locates the phone number among all the other numbers on the receipt and dials. An automatic phone system answers.

"Hi, welcome to the Home Warehouse automatic phone system. Your call is important to us. To continue this message in Spanish, press one. To continue this message in Cantonese, press two. To continue this message in Hmong, press three. To continue in Portuguese, press four. To continue in Hindi, press five. To continue in Yiddish, press six. To continue in all other languages press seven. Please note that our system has been designed to immediately disconnect if you push..." But it's no use, Ed has already pushed '0' five times.

"Mahodi!" he yells. "Get that box out of the street before you leave and get going on that flipper house! You've got to finish it because it goes on the market next month!" He grabs his baseball cap off the counter. "I've had enough of this madhouse," he mutters. "I'm going to Buddy's baseball practice." Luckily the Mercedes is parked under the elm tree out on the street.

By the time Ed arrives at the baseball field, a game is already under way. He hurries to his usual spot, standing behind the fence at home plate with his back to the parking lot. He likes to watch the pitches come in and how the kids swing. It turns out—since it's the last practice—that instead of a practice, the coaches have organized a friendly game against another team.

Shortly after Ed arrives, Mickey pulls up into the parking area. He promised Michelle he'd go to at least one event and he's out of time.

He strolls in the direction of the field, not taking in much, because his mind is on what to do with the property he owns on Mario Drive. The problem is: When the development opened, he, along with everybody else, rushed in to buy, and home prices went sky-high. But now, people want out. They can't afford the payments, and values are falling rapidly. Houses are going up for sale every day. If he doesn't get out pronto, he's going to lose his shirt on it. And he hates that. He starts mulling over the idea of foreclosing on his own property. After all, the property is in a holding company separate from the loan he gave himself. It would be complicated but he might be able to pull it off. Of course, it would be simpler to just find some sucker to buy it.

Mickey rounds the corner of the bleachers and who does he see but Ed.

"Ed!" he calls in a hearty voice.

Ed turns towards the familiar voice. "Well, well. Look who finally decided to show up for one of his kid's baseball practices. What's the matter? Business slow?"

"You've got to be kidding?" answers Mickey. "It couldn't be better! Michelle swore she would key my car and lipstick the seats if I didn't come watch Sammy today, seeing as it's the last of the season. She says you've improved his batting a lot. Hair suits you, by the way," he adds with the slightest hint of mockery.

"I'm glad you chose to protect your car. It'd be a shame to mess it up," says Ed sardonically. "So how are things with you and Michelle?"

Mickey shrugs. "Same as always. So how's the remodel?"

"Which one?"

"The flipper. You ready to get it back on the market? I have somebody I can recommend to you, when you're ready for an agent."

"I don't know, I'm thinking about trying to sell it myself," lies Ed. "It'll be ready to go back on the market soon. I'm putting Mahodi on it full-time."

"What are you going to do about your house? Can you guys live with it all torn up in back?"

"It's only for a month. I'm going to start working on it myself. It'll go faster." Ed looks out at the field. "They've really improved this season. Dave is a good coach." He watches as Buddy's team comes in from the field for the last inning. The coach gives them the batting order and Buddy is almost always first.

Mickey is not listening. He's bored by baseball. Even when he was a kid, the only time he liked baseball was when he was up at bat, and that wasn't often enough to keep him in it once he hit twelve. He is also totally uninterested in the game and impatient that Ed's attention has slipped away. He prods Ed. "Listen," he says sotto voce, "I've got a little business opportunity you might be interested in."

Buddy is up at bat. "Drive it, Buddy!" shouts Ed. Buddy hits the ball solidly out into left field and runs like lightening for first, then second, and he's even going to make it to third. The parents in the bleachers cheer loudly. Ed hollers, "That a boy, Buddy!" What a great hit that was. He turns to share the moment with Mickey.

"It's a house I heard about," says Mickey. Good. He's got Ed's attention. "It's going on the market in the next couple of days. It's a steal. If you could get your hands on enough money for a month, all you'd have to do is sign on the X, slap on a coat of paint, and get it back on the market. The faster, the better."

Ed frowns at Mickey as his brain shifts gears. Mickey's proposal is distracting, but definitely interesting. A house with nothing to do but put it up for sale again? That could be some quick, easy cash. Ed's out of a job. Hey, maybe he could really give this real estate venture a whirl. Go for it all the way. Make a lot of money, and then get out and enjoy life, just like those people you hear about. That Ronald Whatever-his-name-is, that

Tatiana is always going on about. Maybe his moment has finally come.

Out of the corner of his eye, he sees Buddy steal home and he lets out a cheer along with all the other parents. The thing is, if he's clever, he could get this thing to play his way. The Arvee Street house is behind, he knows that. But if this one just needs a coat of paint to make thousands of dollars off it, why that could cover whatever payments he still owes on the Arvee house until he sells it. And, he hates to admit it, but he misses Tatiana. Yes, Tatiana. Not only that luscious mouth, those gorgeous legs and great breasts, but that wacky personality. Maybe he could get her back with this. It's real estate, after all.

"So, who's selling it, and where's it at?" asks Ed still looking at the field.

"It's a holding company I know of," says Mickey, keeping his voice low. "It's a property they had to foreclose on. Too bad, but it happens now and then. They're giving it away. You could probably net about hundred grand on this. Who knows? Depending on the market, maybe even more."

A hundred grand? thinks Ed. That would definitely address his cash problems, but he doesn't want to appear too eager. "I don't know, Mickey, I don't want to spread myself too thin. Cash-wise, I mean."

"Eddie!" says Mickey, playfully punching him. "Always the cautious one. You'll never make it like that. I can get you 110% financing again. Don't touch your other money. Keep 'em separate. Until you roll in your profits."

"Only needs a paint job, huh?" says Ed. He turns and looks at Mickey for a moment, then turns back to the baseball game.

Mickey leans closer to his prey. "It's in the South Wind development. Practically brand new house. All top of the line appliances. Great neighborhood." He pauses, waiting and watching.

"What kind of time frame are we looking at here?"

"Soon. It's gotta go soon. And if you're interested, you

should look before it goes on the market, that way you can skip the middle man and get an even better deal."

"Foreclosure, huh?" says Ed, thinking how it would feel to have truly substantial real estate in hand. And cash is always welcome. He's been puzzled lately at how his account balance has dropped.

"Come see for yourself," says Mickey, clapping him on the shoulder. "Nothing to lose."

"I'll give you a call," says Ed. He turns his attention back to the baseball game, but his fingers are itching to pick up his cell phone. Two more innings to go. Sometimes baseball games seem to go on forever.

That evening, tired from too many pedicures and too many manicures, Tatiana stands in front of her alter. She frowns at the photo of Lada. "I sure hope you know what you're doing," she says crossly.

At that moment, her cell phone rings. 'My Country 'Tis of Thee', it chimes. She picks it up and looks at the number. It's Ed. She doesn't answer. She sets it down on her bed and glares at it. Now what does he want? She glares at the phone until it stops ringing, and then she stares at it, waiting for the tone signal that he has left a voice message. There it is—the little electronic tone sprinkle. Now she considers the phone pensively. Should she listen to it? Should she ignore it? She looks at the photo of Lada in the flickering candlelight. What harm? She picks up the phone and hits the 'call mail box' button. The automatic voice announces one message. She waits, and then she hears his voice.

"Hi Tat." (He pauses) "I'm thinking about buying a house in South Wind Estates, a big one, to turn around and I thought you might like to come take a look at it with me tomorrow. Give me a call."

"Eddie?" says Tatiana, her voice rising into a question when Ed answers his cell phone two seconds later. "What time you going?"

"Huge is beautiful, small is worthless. If you want to be huge, you
have to think think huge, live huge and eat huge. I like huge."
Ronald Ace, The Art of Huge

11

"Here we are," says Ed as he takes a right onto Mario Drive and
enters between the low, curving stucco walls of the South Wind
Estates. Bright yellow marigolds and purple petunias planted
along a center divider invite them further. The sidewalks and
driveways are spotless. The ground cover still weed-free. And the
tallest trees barely top twenty feet. The large houses, featuring
small mazes of bedrooms and individual bathrooms look like
miniature castles, Italian villas, and Spanish haciendas, set off
on immaculate lawns. Wow, thinks Ed, payments must be so high
that the owners can't afford to not work full time and then some.
As they drive along the gradually circling street, Ed notices that
numerous homes have discreet "For Sale" signs next to a bush or
fence post.

"Oh! This is really nice neighborhood," exclaims Tatiana,
interrupting his observations. She is happy and charming again.
Plus, they have just had fabulous sex even if it was a quickie.
"Almost as nice as yours, Eddie," she adds. "And look at all the
'For Sale' signs! This is good sign. In my country, people only sell
when they know other people want to buy. If nobody want to
buy, why sell? "

Ed cannot argue with her logic. He breathes in the faint smell
of her body. More and more he agrees with her: Real estate is
great.

"Look! There it is!" She points to a house while she holds up the piece of paper with the address. "Yes. Is 165."

It's a corner house, in the Italian villa style, with small terraces and balconies erupting here and there, surrounded by a row of closely planted palm trees and a bright green lawn. The back of the house is screened off from view by a stucco wall. A stone pathway leads from the sidewalk to the front door.

"I bet they have pool," she says. "Why else not show neighbors what you have?"

Ed pulls up to the curb and Tatiana jumps out of the car.

"Hurry, Eddie!" she says. The red suit she chose makes her look stunning.

Ed locks the car and looks at the stone pathway. That's a nice touch, he thinks. "I wonder where Mickey is?" He says aloud. He looks up and down the street, but Mickey's car is nowhere to be seen. "Are you sure this is the right address," he asks. "I don't see a 'For Sale' sign." He gingerly itches his scalp and adjusts his tie. The tie was Tat's idea. She thought they should dress up for the occasion. Personally, he didn't think it was necessary, but now, looking at the neighborhood, he thinks she was right.

"Is right number," says Tatiana, glancing at the paper one more time. This is more beautiful than she imagined. This is like Xtreme Makeover. She is wondering if this house is her destiny. To live in this house, and to be rich, and to sell real estate. After all these years of desiring, maybe it is about to happen. The two of them stand on the corner waiting.

Mickey's black Escalade suddenly appears down the street and, in a second, he is parked and sprinting towards them, a coral tie flying behind him. Look at that guy trying to look sporty, thinks Ed.

"Hello! Hello!" says Mickey. He claps Ed on the shoulder, and then turns the full force of his gaze on Tatiana. He extends his hand towards her. "Mickey Schulz."

Ed puts his arm around Tatiana's shoulders. "We just got here," says Ed, ignoring him. "Nice neighborhood."

"I'm Mickey Schulz," says Mickey extending his hand even further towards Tatiana. Tatiana loosens her arm from Ed's grip and reaches out.

"Hello, Mickey."

"Tat, this is Mickey, the guy I've been telling you about. Mickey, Tatiana Talliin."

"Good to meet you." Mickey shakes hands with Tatiana while he mentally undresses her. What a babe. How did this schmuck score her, he wonders. "What a great neighborhood, huh? People are lining up to get in here. You'll understand why, when you see the house. Let's go on in and take a look." He casually brushes against Tatiana's shoulder as he leads the way. He types a code into the lock box, which is dangling from the front door handle, and extracts a key. With one click, the lock slips back and the door quietly swings open. Mickey steps back and motions for Tatiana and Ed to enter.

Ed puts his hand on the small of Tatiana's back and propels the two of them into the entry hall. He stops a moment and blinks as his eyes adjust to the change in light. Then he blinks again as he takes in the color scheme: The entire house is painted in tones of green and red. The two-story high entry hall is painted in dark green. To one side is a deep red colored living room. On the other, a formal dining room painted in apple green. Straight ahead is a great room hued in evergreen with bursts of ochre, while off to the side is a large brick-red kitchen. "Holy mother," says Ed, "who came up with this color scheme?"

Beside him, Tatiana sucks in her breath and gasps, "This is absolutely fab'lous!"

"What did I tell you?" says Mickey, pleased with himself. "Can you imagine the parties you could throw here? And for the price, in this market, it's like giving it away." He herds them inside and closes the door behind him.

Tatiana frees herself from Ed's hand and walks straight ahead, as if hypnotized. Mickey picks up her cue and follows close behind. Ed, however, seems to be in stuck in place. He's overwhelmed by...what? The immensity? The grandeur? He looks to the left and takes in the empty living room, then he looks to the right at the empty dining room, before wandering into the cavernous great room. A carpeted staircase leads off to the right. Ahead of him is a triple French door leading to a tiled patio.

"Oh, my God!" gasps Tatiana.

She has moved to the kitchen. Ed sees her walking past the cooking island until she stops before a giant stainless steel double refrigerator. "Look at size!" she says with awe.

"Sub-zero refrigerator," says Mickey, appearing from nowhere at her side. "Notice the brand new Wolf range, too," he says, gently taking her elbow and turning her back towards the island. "Top of the line, I'll have you know."

"Wolf?" she says, looking at Mickey with a questioning glance. "Is like GE?"

"You bet," he says. "Just like GE, only WAY more expensive."

"Mmmm," says Tatiana. She floats over to the cooking island and runs her fingers lightly over the stainless steel while she makes a mental note of the new brand name. Then the double French doors in the kitchen catch her attention. She walks over and looks out. "Oh, backyard very nice!" she exclaims. "Perfect for garden party." And indeed, the yard looks like a grossly foreshortened version of a Roman garden complete with aqua blue tiled pool and pillars.

Ed does not like the way Mickey is following Tatiana. "Isn't it great?" he says with forced enthusiasm, as he walks up behind Tatiana and slips his arm around her waist. "Great yard. I like the Italian thing."

"Check out the lighting," says Mickey, touching Tatiana's other arm to get her attention and pointing. "It was designed by Cordon Lighting and can be totally controlled." He takes a couple of manly strides to the control box on the wall between the kitchen and the great room, and demonstrates the concept to her.

"Ooo," she says appreciatively.

"Now, Ms. Talliin," he pauses for effect, "can I ask you to take a look at this?"

Mickey strides to the other side of the room and throws open a door to reveal a gigantic master bedroom suite with a private terrace.

"Oh!" gasps Tatiana, wiggling out of Ed's grasp and hurrying over to Mickey. "Ooo, Eddie!" she calls.

Ed smiles tightly and joins Tatiana and Mickey. "Nice," he says.

"But wait!" says Mickey. "How..." he pauses for dramatic effect, "do you like this?" He waltzes over to a double door in the room and, using both hands, pulls open both doors to reveal a twelve foot by twelve foot room complete with built-in his and hers drawers, shelves, clothes racks and mirrors. "Your dressing room!" he announces, grinning widely at Tatiana.

Tatiana stands in the middle of the room speechless with awe.

"But it's not all," says Mickey. He opens another molded door with an elegant handle. "Here is your bathroom."

She walks in and audibly sucks in her breath. There, straight ahead, with gold-plated fixtures and marble facing, is a large, oval, raised bathtub. "Oh. My. God." she says in a hushed voice. "Bath with double jets."

Mickey stays at the door, mesmerized by this ripe red apparition standing amidst the pale cool marble of the bathroom, as if in a church.

"Why the hell would anybody want something this big?" says Ed, brushing past Mickey.

Tatiana and Mickey simultaneously turn and stare at him in disbelief. Ed feels the air slowly being sucked out of the room. "What?"

No one answers. Then Mickey says, "Luxury, my friend. The feeling of pure luxury. Look around you! Every detail says that the person who owns this house has arrived."

"Eddie!" chides Tatiana. She steps closer to him and puts her hand lightly on his arm. "Eddie, this is American dream house." They are both staring at him.

Ed looks at Tatiana's clear blue eyes and that brilliant white smile. His eyes slide involuntarily down to her enticing cleavage framed in fire engine red, and he feels his groin start to wake up. This will not do. He's got to think of something else. "Ho!" he exclaims. He coughs and looks around the room. Licks his lips, smoothes down his comb-over. Finally, he blurts out, "Where's the laundry room?"

Mickey gives Ed a curious look. Why in the world does Ed want to know where the laundry room is? "It's off the garage," he answers. "We can stop by on the way out. It's a full feature laundry room with built in ironing and storage," he adds with no enthusiasm.

Mickey turns and gestures towards the bedroom. "This way, please. I'll show you the second floor bedrooms and baths. Nothing like this, of course, but nice." Ed and Tatiana, who takes a last lingering look at the various cupboards in the dressing room, follow Mickey obediently to the stairs.

"So," says Ed, edging a little closer to Mickey. "What did you say the price is on this?"

Mickey slides a glance at Ed and thinks, ah, I do have him interested. "How does seven hundred thousand sound? It's a terrible loss for the owners, but...oh well. It's a once-in-a-lifetime opportunity for the buyer." They stop at the foot of the stairs. "Make other people's misfortune your fortune, I always say. That's the way to play the game, eh?" He jovially punches Ed in the arm. "Right this way, Miss," he says, taking Tatiana's arm and leading her up the stairs. Ed follows so close he almost trips on her shoes when she stops on the fifth stair to look down at the view. "Oh Eddie," she says. "Is so nice to have stairways in your own house. Is like castle! We could sell house on golf course and live here!"

"Now wait a minute," says Ed contritely. "That's not the idea." He looks at Mickey.

"Well, in a way she's right," says Mickey. He throws a little smile at Tatiana as they continue up the stairs. "Because you would have to declare this your primary residence...just like we did for the other loan. So, theoretically, you could move in here. But I tell you, Miss, if you sell it, it's nothing but profit from OPM."

"OPM?" says Ed.

"Eddie! Don't tell me you haven't heard that one?" He winks at Tatiana. "Other. People's. Money. Just like the big dogs. Take the money, buy the house, change it and get it back on the market. When it sells, the profit is all yours."

Ed looks around at the generous hallway, the doors to the four bedrooms, the sunlight from the balconies. He surreptitiously rubs his scalp with his finger tips, trying not to mess up his hair. It would be nice to have a lot of money for a change. There's Meledy's college to think of. And he could pay back the loan he took out for the remodel. The prices of houses do just keep going up. It's gotta work. Maybe there's no such thing as a free lunch, but there are times when things are booming, and smart people take risks to be a part of it.

At that moment, Tatiana leans on his arm and reaches up to his ear to whisper. "This is amazing opportunity. Maybe only opportunity like this you get. This house is worth million at least. You gonna be like the Big Man." She nibbles his earlobe. "You gonna be...The Eddie."

The Eddie? Ed feels a tingle of sensation go down his spine. "So, how much time do I have to think it over?" he asks Mickey.

Mickey looks at him and shrugs. "Like I told you, it's going on the market tomorrow. You're the first to see it."

Ed looks around again at the green and red mirage that was somebody's fantasy of high living. He imagines it in white or pale yellow and immediately sees...Potential. Yes! This is loaded with potential. All it needs is a new coat of paint.

"What the hell," says Ed. "Let's do it! Three's a charm."

"That's good, Ed. That's very good." Mickey slaps Ed on the back. "You won't regret this."

The three amble gaily back towards the front entry, but then Ed remembers he wanted to see the laundry room. He walks back to the kitchen. "Where did you say the garage and laundry room were?" he hollers at Mickey.

But Mickey doesn't hear because he and Tatiana are now standing rather close to each other near the front door.

"You look so familiar!" says Tatiana. "Haven't I seen your picture somewhere?" She pauses a moment while she puts on her pouty, thinking look. "I know! You make seminars." she says.

Mickey is flattered. "Yes I do. As a matter of fact, I have one coming up on new opportunities in foreclosures and distressed assets next week, if you're interested. They are very much a thing of the future."

"Fork-loshers?" queries Tatiana.

"Yeah. It's a new approach to real estate. You could even bring Ed, although," at this he turns to look where Ed could be. He lowers his voice, "Although I doubt he'd be interested."

At that moment, Ed reappears. "I can't find it." He looks from Mickey to Tatiana. "What are you two talking about?" he asks with a puzzled smile on his face.

"Oh, nothing," says Tatiana sweetly. "The weather."

"So, sleep it over and give me a call first thing in the morning," says Mickey, clapping Ed on the shoulder for what feels like the hundredth time. "I can have my secretary draw up the papers by the end of next week. Nice meeting you, Ms. Talliin." he says. He reaches out to shake her hand, and surreptitiously presses a business card into her palm.

"Leaders, like myself, would like to say that we made ourselves, but the fact is, either you're born this way or you're not. So if you weren't born with a natural sucker-radar, buy my books. It's your best chance."
Ronald Ace, The Art of Being Me

12

About a week later, Ed finds himself again sitting in Mickey's airless conference room. No time for second thoughts with this guy, he thinks. He admires Mickey's heavy gold Rolex watch as Mickey deftly makes two stacks of papers out of one and shoves one towards Ed.

"You're really getting the hang of this," Mickey compliments Ed. "This is standard stuff again, so you'll recognize all of it. Here's the settlement statement, all the different fees are listed here, title search, escrow, pest and structural inspections, agent fee, et cetera. I've put them all into the loan for you so you don't have to pay anything up front. Wanted to make it easy for you. And here's your note. You need to sign...," Mickey hands Ed a gold Mont Blanc fountain pen while he points to a line near the bottom of the page. "Here, and...," Mickey flips the page, "here...and...here."

By the time he's signed his name five times, Ed feels like he's getting a fever, only he doesn't know why. Buddy had the sniffles a couple of days ago, but it didn't seem like anything serious. Maybe the house is too drafty. He has to put pressure on those guys to finish up the add-on so they can close it up. The hot summer weather hasn't kicked in yet, and it's been drafty at night.

Mickey pulls a last document from the bottom of the stack. "And sign here," he says, directing Ed's hand. Ed signs where

Mickey indicates, and then Mickey scoops the papers together, neatens them up into one stack, and shoves them back into the manila envelope he laid aside for the purpose. "I'll get these processed ASAP and express your copies so you have them for your record. And, by the way," Mickey reaches into his jacket pocket and pulls out a key. "Congratulations! Here's the key to your new home."

Ed feels like he's in a dream. He reaches out and takes the key in his hand and looks at it. It's all his now.

"So, guess what, kids?" says Ed, walking into the house. Meledy and Buddy tear their eyes away from the TV and look at him expectantly. He's grinning from ear to ear, almost as if he's high, thinks Meledy. Adults are so weird. First, her dad is gone more and more. Then, he's buying stuff like crazy, which is sort of okay, but also very random. Then he's moping around for weeks and they're living in a mess. Now, all of a sudden, he's happy and whistling and playing guessing games.

"What, Dad?" answers Buddy. He still loves his dad, even though he's been sadly disappointed lately.

"Daddy's got a new job. I'm a real estate investor now!"

"What's that?" asks Buddy.

Overhead, footsteps stomp heavily across the roof. Ed is so used to Mahodi and crew, that he doesn't even notice anymore if their truck is parked in front or not. They seem to be making some kind of progress on the house, but it sure is in fits and starts.

"It's someone who sells houses, stupid," answers Meledy, grabbing a handful of pretzels from the family size bag sitting on the new leather sofa between her and Buddy and turning her attention back to the TV. Ever since they got the huge new flat-screen, watching TV has been a lot more attractive, even with Buddy. Especially some of the stuff they show on MTV.

"You mean like Sammy's dad?" asks Buddy.

"Well, sort of," answers Ed. "Actually, no," he says on second thought looking at the TV. "How can you watch that stuff?" he asks. They both know well enough not to try to answer. Ed looks back at Buddy and sees Buddy is still looking at him expectantly, waiting for an answer. "Sammy's dad is a mortgage broker. He lends people money to buy houses. I'm going to sell the houses."

"I thought people are saying that real estate is slowing down," says Meledy.

"Where did you hear that?" says Ed with a chuckle.

"IDK. Internet? TV? Don't you listen to the news? You get a paper every morning." She says it with the scorn that only a fifteen-year old can muster.

"Listen, smart-aleck…"

"Dad!! Look out!!!" shouts Buddy as a tremendous cracking of lath and plaster is heard.

Ed looks up where Buddy is looking and, sure enough, at that second, the ceiling above Ed's head breaks into pieces while plaster rains down around him. A booted foot projects through the hole and rapidly morphs into a leg. One second later, an apologetic Liang Rong peers through the hole. Buddy and Meledy howl with laughter.

"You idiot!!!" shouts Ed, staring up at Liang Rong's disheveled, lopsided grin. He can't believe that this has happened. Nor can he believe that he just said the words he said: You Idiot. That was his dad's favorite name for him. It was never, 'Ed, that's not a crescent wrench,' or 'Son, you just burned the toast.' It was always, 'That's not a crescent wrench, you idiot!' or, 'Burned the toast again, huh, you idiot.' Ed hates the word idiot, but the old tapes are playing.

"You better have that closed up by tonight or you're fired! And tell Mahodi I want to see him tomorrow at nine a.m., got it?" he yells at Liang Rong who disappears into the attic. "This is getting to be a circus. Come on, kids. Shut off the TV and let's go out to dinner. Chinese? Pizza? What do you feel like?"

"Fresh Greens!" says Meledy.

"Burger Wow!" shouts Buddy.

"I get to choose. Buddy chose last time."

"You did not. We went to Chinese Buffet's last time. That was your choice."

"No, it wasn't. That was Dad's choice. Dad, that was your choice, right?"

"It doesn't matter," says Ed. "Let's live dangerously and go someplace we've never been before. Let's go to the Upper Scale Hotel and have dinner there. To celebrate."

"Do we have to dress up?" they moan in unison.

The Upper Scale Hotel is a mid-level luxury hotel, particularly known for its expansive view of the river and its conference room accommodations. Ed and the kids wander in past the frosted glass front doors and stand in the spacious lobby.

"Wow, look at that!" exclaims Buddy. He points to a gigantic wooden figurehead mounted on the wall. "What is it?"

"It's a flying buttress, dummy," answers Meledy.

Buddy looks suitably impressed. "Well, it sure looks like she's ready to fly alright."

Ed casually glances around. He notices that there's a real estate seminar in one of the conference rooms down the hall, and a handful of people mingle at the bar. The entrance to the restaurant is straight ahead.

"Good evening, Sir," smiles the hostess as they approach. "Hi, kids. One child's menu?"

Meledy pulls herself up a little taller and smiles endearingly at Buddy. "Yes, thank you," she says, before Buddy can protest.

"By the window?" asks the hostess.

"That would be great," says Ed, following her into the dining room. "Pretty quiet here tonight," he remarks as a group of people pass by the entrance of the restaurant.

"I think there's some dinner seminar down the hall," she answers. She stops and places two menus, a paper placemat and cup of crayons on a table next to the window. "Your waiter will be with you in a moment. Enjoy your dinner."

Down the hall, in the Paddle Wheel Room, seven round tables have been set up for dinner with white cloths in a semi-circle around the podium. The room has a cavernous feel to it in spite of some skirted tables off to the side displaying books and DVD's for sale. The overhead recessed lights shine weakly down on the titles. There's "Mickey's Guide to Real Estate Scams," "Mickey's 50 Best Tips to Sell Real Estate," "Mickey Schulz's Way to Make Big Bucks," and "Mickey Does Debt," as well as his inspirational tape "Mickey's Guide to Preying" along with brochures and business cards. Two pretty, young women stand behind the tables looking bored, ready to take anyone's money should they decide to buy.

Tatiana arrives early and spends a long time perusing the goods. She finally settles on Mickey's 50 Best Tips. That sounds straight-forward enough and should be a good companion to the Ronald Ace book she just purchased, "How to Do Real Estate Like a Pro."

She takes her book and chooses the center-front table, so she is looking straight at the podium. The spotlights gleam on the gold and red banner hanging on the wall behind the podium. "Welcome to **Your** Real Estate Future" it reads. Yes, she thinks, MY real estate future is about to begin!

The rest of the seminar participants begin arriving in small groups, and soon her table is filled—with women. She glances casually at them. Then she looks around at the other tables and notices that, a) there are many more women than men; b) the men are frumpy and old; and c) she is by far the most attractive woman. She smiles to herself in satisfaction. At that moment, the server plops down a plate of airline-style food in front of her. Tatiana looks skeptically at the plate.

"Is beef?" she asks, turning to the woman sitting next to her.

The woman pokes at the dark brown food on her plate. "I think so. I'm Beth, by the way."

"Humph," says Tatiana. "How much you pay for this?"

"I thought it was fifty dollars for everyone." answers the woman. "How much did you pay?"

"Oh, I know speaker," says Tatiana airily.

"You're so lucky!" says Beth. "I just love his book. I increased my income per sale by almost 10% using the tips in his book! Where did you meet him?"

Just at that moment, the lights dim and the servers disappear. Apparently they are to eat while they listen to Mickey's presentation. Tatiana reaches down into her purse and digs out a little notepad and pen, and puts them ready by her plate. Then she takes a few more bites of the beef. The lights grow even dimmer, and then, there he is! Mickey Schulz, real estate magnate! Tatiana can hardly swallow, she's so excited.

"Hi, folks, and welcome!" he shouts. "I'm Mickey Schulz and if you have a pulse, I can get you a loan! Welcome to my seminar on how to make money—tons of money—in today's real estate market." He stops to take a breath of air and, in spite of the air conditioning, Tatiana can see that he's already sweating. He exudes pure energy and drive. He IS real estate.

"Everybody wants to be rich, right? But you," he jabs at the air in front of him, "you are not everybody, because you're here at this seminar to actually learn HOW those big bucks are made. How do you get prospective home owners to let you deliver the loans that will make you the money you deserve no matter what their assets? I am here to tell you all about non-traditional financing and how you can make it happen."

Mickey stares directly at Tatiana to let her know he's zeroed in on her and he'll be waiting. She said she'd come, when he gave her the invitation, but you never know when a woman might stand you up, fifty-dollar dinner or no. She smiles alluringly and winks. Reassured, he breaks his gaze and moves on to other faces. He likes to give each attendee a least one second of personal eye contact. It connects him to them. And most of them aren't here to do what he does anyway. They're simply potential clients. They only think they want to find out how to do it. In the end, they will realize how much better he is at it than they, and this will make them feel confident entrusting him with their desires.

"When I first got into the business," he says, smiling genially at everyone as if he knows them personally (the women all shift in their seats), "it was hard to qualify someone for a loan. They had to have twenty percent down to buy a house. Cash! There were a few tricks we could do if someone was a bit short, but not many. And the banks would only lend to people if their payments were no higher than a quarter of their income." He grins widely. "But now..." he pauses for dramatic effect, "...now, we can massage things however we need to make it work. With all the packages and plans, quick qualifiers, reverse equity, adjustable interest, and things like stated income, you create the real estate opportunities your clients think they deserve.

"You find a way to fund the loan. And then, it's a wonderful world of commissions and fees. If something doesn't work out down the line...who knows? They may even come back to you for refinancing.

"Deregulation has been the greatest development in the real estate mortgage business since women were allowed to own property." He pauses for the audience's chuckle, and then continues. "It's a win-win situation: We create value for our customers and capture the financial opportunities that result. People who couldn't afford houses get houses, people looking for streams of high-interest income find it in the repackaged loans, and lots of commissions are made by everyone all around. Genius, pure genius."

Tatiana sits breathless. This is even better than she thought. She can't wait to tell Cyndee about it.

"And now, friends," continues Mickey, "it's getting even better because, not only can you sell a mortgage with only 5 or even 3.5% down, you can let people take out cash and the government will guarantee the loans. It's an ownership society, and that's why you're here. Because you want to learn the ins and outs of how you can make it happen for your clients."

When the short seminar is over (the majority of the room rental is for allowing people to browse his wares and to chat), Mickey approaches Tatiana.

"Ms. Talliin!" he says. "I am glad you made it. Did you find anything interesting in my presentation?"

"Oh, yes," she says enthusiastically. "I learn something very important. It don't matter what house you sell to what person. What matters is, you get signature. Then you get commission. Rest is not your problem. But I'm not sure I'm understanding fork-loshers. Maybe you have time to explain after here?" She looks at him flirtatiously.

"Of course! I was hoping I could do that," says Mickey. "Let me finish up here and then we can have a drink in the hotel lounge."

"Wonderful!" says Tatiana "I wait for you in hotel lobby." Tatiana walks down the hall from the Paddle Wheel Room, past the restaurant with the beautiful view, to the lobby where she glances briefly out the glass doors before turning right into the bar area. Strange. It almost looked like Ed's car pulling out of the parking lot. But that would be impossible. He's with the kids tonight.

By the time Mickey finally joins her at the bar, Ed, Melody and Buddy are indeed sitting cozily back at home. They have just cued up "Indiana Jones and the Last Crusades," one of Ed's favorites and are all set to watch.

"Tatiana?" says Mickey, coming up behind her.

She is a bit cross, since she's been waiting a long time and doesn't really like to drink, or wait. But when she turns to him, he doesn't give her a chance to say anything. He leans towards her and kisses her slowly and firmly on the side of her neck, just where her hair begins to cascade down her back, and then makes a little wet circle with his tongue.

"Mickey!" she chides and playfully slaps him on the shoulder.

He holds up a wallet sized envelope with a hotel room card sticking out. "Are you ready to begin your lessons?" he says.

She looks at the envelope with the Upper Scale Hotel monogram on it and sees, written by hand, Room #2018. "Mmm, you think you can explain better if we have more privacy?"

"Absolutely. I'll not only explain foreclosures, by the time I'm finished, you'll know the difference between short sales and long full loads too."

She giggles. "You are man who knows what he wants!" She stands up, he proffers his arm, and together they amble toward the elevator.

"Send up a magnum of champagne," he tells the desk clerk as they pass by.

Much later that night, Tatiana solemnly stands in front of her alter to Lada wearing the new red camisole and panties she bought along with her suit. The candles are lit, fresh flowers are in the vase.

"Oh, beautiful one," she says, her voice husky with emotion. "Now I understand! You send me wrong one to prepare me for right one. You are so wise. One day, God willing, I be like you. 'The Mickey.' It sound so much better." She reaches out her hands and gently picks up the golden framed photograph of Lada and brings it to her lips for a reverent kiss. "Thank you."

She stretches out on her satin sheets and goes over the fabulous evening she has just had. Everything is so simple, once you grasp the principle, she thinks. Maybe she can find special upp for her smart phone to figure this out. Happy, she falls into a deep sleep.

"Don't listen to negative voices, don't believe them! Buy my
books and I'll tell you how to be huge like me."
Ronald Ace, Don't Be A Loser

13

The next morning, Ed wakes up feeling in fine form. The sun is shining and he's the proud owner of three houses. Plus, he's got two great kids, he's hooked up with a beautiful girlfriend (again), and he doesn't work at the 'shitter plant' anymore! He'll miss the guys, but he sure won't miss the job. The first thing, he thinks, is to get the kids off to school and get started on his physical fitness program. He's gotten a little flabby over the past year or two, ever since he hit forty, but he always had his schedule to blame. Now he's a free man.

"Up and at 'em, kids!" he calls down the hallway. "Seven o'clock!" He pulls on a pair of grey sweat pants and a baseball tee-shirt Meledy gave him for Christmas last year. Brushes his teeth, throws water on his face, carefully combs his hair across the top of his head and then takes a moment to look at himself in the mirror. Gives himself a rakish smile. "Hi, I'm Ed Fasouli, real estate agent. Here's my card," he says to the mirror. He holds out his hand as if proffering a card. Yeah, baby. Upwards and onwards. He grabs his old running shoes before going into the kitchen.

Now there's one thing about Ed that most people wouldn't expect: He is passionate about his morning coffee. He knows that everybody has their ideas about what's best, and he doesn't care, all he knows is he wants his coffee to taste exactly like he likes it, not somebody else. So he sticks to his Braun automatic, six-cup coffee maker, unbleached paper filters, filtered water, and only the best coffee. He's currently working on a half-pound of an organic coffee blend from the local Petter Coffee Roasting Company. It's got a rich, aromatic—not burned—flavor. He hits the 'brew' button on the coffee maker, and sets out the bags of cereal and three bowls and spoons on the table.

"Can't we get something better than this bagged stuff?" complains Meledy, as she walks into the kitchen and dumps her backpack on the floor beside her chair. "This tastes like sugared dust. We have money now. Can't we buy stop buying all this generic stuff? Brand names really are better."

"Ah come on, Mel," he says, "it's the same stuff. The advertising just tastes better. But tell you what, I'll get some the next time I go grocery shopping, okay?"

"I have dibs on the Froot'n'Toot's!" calls Buddy rushing into the room.

Ed wanders out the front door to get the morning paper, checks for golf balls on the front lawn, curses once more at the refrigerator box still standing on the driveway, and heads back in. Maybe he'll be using those golf balls himself one day soon. Ah, coffee's ready. He pours himself a cup, adds a little milk, and sits down to eat, read, and sip. Life is good.

A half an hour later, Ed heads out to start up the car. The Mercedes is still parked on the street. Buddy comes tearing out the front door. "Shot-gun!" he yells and runs for the front passenger door, almost tripping on the buckled sidewalk next to the elm tree.

"It's my turn!" shouts Meledy in hot pursuit behind him. She's holding her shoes and hair brush in one hand, her backpack slung over her shoulder. "It's my turn! You got to ride shot-gun yesterday."

But she's one second too late. Buddy beats her into the seat and pulls the door closed in front of her nose.

"Butt-head," says Meledy. She kicks the door and gets into the back.

"Mel, I promise you get front seat tomorrow. And the next day," says Ed, driving off down the street. He drops Buddy off at Middle School, reminds him about picking him up to go to the batting cages after school, and then drives on to the high school where he stops one block down, near the corner.

"Mel?" says Ed, as she gets out. He sees her focus has already shifted to the friends and challenges awaiting her at High School, but he wants to savor her presence for one more second.

"Yeah, Dad?"

"Love you."

She smiles at him and shakes her head. "See you tonight." And off she disappears into the trail of kids herding towards the school.

When Ed gets back to the house, Mahodi's truck is parked halfway off the driveway, next to the dumpster. The eternal dumpster. The dumpster that seems like it is now a permanent part of his driveway. He parks the station wagon in its new spot along the sidewalk and gets out. As he does, he notices Michelle, in a sleeveless white tank top and cotton skirt, across the street, pruning back some pyracanthas.

"Hey there, stranger!" he calls out affably, hoping that whatever was wrong last time has blown over. He ambles across the street and stands next to her. "Did Mickey take Sammy to school this morning?"

"Yeah, he said he had an early meeting somewhere," she answers, without turning around.

Okay, so that's the way it is. Ed sighs, watches for a few seconds, then says, "Those are pretty prickly plants to be trimming without gloves, aren't they?"

"They're not bad," she says, as she bends down to get a branch near the back.

Ed stands there a little longer. "I guess you're giving me the brush-off," he says finally.

She clips her branch, pulls it out from the bush and adds it to the pile beside her. Then she turns and looks at him evenly. "So, how's the big real estate baron?"

"Is that possibly sarcasm I hear in your voice? I thought maybe we could move on since our last encounter."

"I don't know why you'd think that. I haven't seen or spoken to you since."

"Well, I've been kind of busy. But I've missed seeing you around."

"Why would you miss me when you have so much other excitement in your life? I probably don't even know the half of it. All I know is that your kids miss you. And from my point of view, it looks like you're putting that sleazy girlfriend ahead of them."

"I am not. What makes you say that? I even took them out to dinner."

"Anybody who gets mixed up in business with Mickey, as far as I'm concerned, is as underhanded as he is."

"Underhanded? What are you saying here? I think you just feel bad because I have a girlfriend. Well, excuse me, but which one of us here is married?"

"It has nothing to do with the fact that I'm married...or that you have a girlfriend." She glares at him. "I am not having this conversation. I have to go." And with that she leaves her pile of clippings and turns and walks into the house.

"Michelle!" calls Ed. But she ignores him and the door slams behind her. That went well, thinks Ed. Why does she think Mickey is underhanded? He and Michelle have always been straight with each other. She was even honest enough to explain to him that, after giving birth to Buddy, Jayne couldn't stand the idea of having a vagina anymore. Women, he thinks, are too deep for their own good, and he takes off jogging down the street.

When Ed gets back to his house, Mahodi's truck is gone and so is the refrigerator box. Progress! But when he walks into his kitchen to get a drink of water, he is not so sure. The original idea for the house had been to put a second story on, but—since that would have required proper permitting, and Ed is in a hurry—the house is simply being extended into the back. That way, you can't see anything from the street, just in case the permits aren't quite on the up and up. Although, when he stops to think about it, any idiot knows what's going on.

Ed stands at the kitchen sink (the kitchen is supposed to be remodeled too, if Mahodi and company ever get the extension done) drinking a glass of water and looks out at the backyard. It is now mostly dirt all the way back to the cyclone fence where the golf course begins, and there is a large irregular hole dug into the ground, supposedly for the pool. The backhoe is still sitting precariously at the edge of the hole, and most of the shrubbery around it has been mashed beyond recognition. Not very nice.

To his left, the trees and bushes have been completely torn up and the dirt unevenly flattened. This is the area where the back is being rearranged for the master bedroom extension, the idea being that it will extend perpendicularly from the kitchen, making an L-shape. A rudimentary foundation has been poured for the extension, and holes have been dug for concrete footings which will support a deck. The deck, which comes off the bedroom, is for the hot tub (*hot tube*, he thinks affectionately), although when this is supposed to happen, he has no idea. The garage wall has already been torn up in places (as if with a sledge hammer) to connect the extension. The wall beyond the back door is also gone now (as are the washer and dryer), and a sheet of blue plastic hangs in its place. The garage will eventually be transformed into a family room, while the current cement driveway is slated to morph into a carport.

To Ed's right, as he stands at the sink, drinking his second glass of water, the current family/dining room is supposed to open out onto a deck and pool area with large French doors. But right now, the hole cut into the wall is much too small for either the doors or the proportion of the room. And for some reason, there is a second, larger hole in the wall between it and the kitchen. It all feels very confusing, even though it looked absolutely logical on paper.

He puts his glass down on the counter and decides, in the time-honored tradition of landowners everywhere, to visit his properties. And then he can take Tatiana to lunch. Which means he needs to clean himself up. He grabs one of the kid's cereal bars for a snack and, in passing by the counter on his way to the bedroom, notices that a large, unfamiliar envelope has appeared. Where did this come from, he wonders. He pauses to picks it up and sees that it's a express envelope from Mickey. It must have arrived while he was out jogging, and Mahodi put it on the counter. He slides a knife under the flap and peeps in. Just what he thought: the house documents.

Ed puts it into the over-filled in-basket. There is way too much in there. He frowns at the basket and makes a mental note: Must look through tonight.

He changes clothes (slacks and a button-up shirt; hopefully Tatiana is available, although she hasn't been answering her phone again lately), grabs the keys for the BMW and heads off to Arvee Street. While the car doesn't feel nearly as sexy without Tatiana, still, it is great to drive. There's something about a sports car that just make you yearn to step hard on the accelerator. He pulls up to the sidewalk and slams on the brakes, leaving neat black skid marks. How he loves this car. He hops out, expecting to see Mahodi, and instead sees that the dumpster parked in the middle of the driveway is now totally overflowing with odd, unlikely objects while crumpled newspaper, wads of blue wall tape, and pieces of plastic wrap cover the ground around it. A fifties-style, stand-up lamp, portable TV with rabbits ears (good grief, who has those anymore?), and kid bike flop on top of cardboard, broken sheet rock, and empty paint cans. It looks like a recycling center.

He gingerly makes his way to the front door. He presses down on the handle, but the door is locked. He sidesteps into the dirt beside the front walkway and tries to look in the front window, but the window is so occluded with dust and paint, it's impossible to see anything.

Ed was sure that Mahodi had said they were going to be working here today, but obviously they must be dealing with the refrigerator. He goes to the side of the house, stumbles through the overgrowth in his casual leather loafers, almost trips over an exposed root from the neighbor's pepper tree, and picks his way through the mess to the back door. He looks in the filthy back window. Something looks changed. He tries the back door. It's locked, and Mahodi has the only key. He looks around. A rusting butter knife in the dirt beside him catches his eye. He picks it up and jams it between the doorframe and the door. He wiggles it up and down and then presses in where the door handle and locking mechanism are. The paint cracks under the pressure and the soft, rotten wood underneath gives way like cake, exposing the lock hardware. He uses his fingers to press the lock open. They should have replaced this door, he frowns. He shouldn't have to tell them everything.

Ed pulls the door open and steps inside the newly painted kitchen. The new, bottom-of-the-line, basic white appliances look—new. It's an improvement. The stainless steel sink looks good too. Ed taps it with his hand. It echoes hollowly back. He brushes the cabinets to feel the finish. It's not great, but it's okay, and the white looks clean at least. One cabinet is slightly ajar and he gives it a tap close. It springs back, almost knocking him in the head.

"For Pete's sake," mutters Ed. You'd think they would've fixed it when they painted. They must have noticed it. He definitely needs to start supervising Mahodi more closely. Good thing he has time now. The way he figures it, he wants to make at least a hundred grand when he sells the place. You gotta be optimistic. And now that he's not working, he's got the time to push this baby on the market. He makes another mental note: Exterior. Back door. Kitchen cupboard.

He crosses the kitchen threshold and stops at the entrance

to the living room area, blinking. The amount of ambient light is astonishing! It seems so different from the last time he was here! They must have painted. He waits for his eyes to adjust. Then he gasps and his stomach clenches like in a free-fall. All of the interior walls in the house are gone. The house is one huge room with only the three walls surrounding the bathroom off to the side. How could this have happened? What kind of horrible miscommunication could have led to this...this...nightmare!

Before he can say 'idiot', he has his cell phone out of his pocket and speed dials Mahodi.

Mahodi answers his phone, politely as always. "International Networking Production Technology Construction Company. Have a good day. May I be helping you?"

"Mahodi!" Ed shouts into his phone. "What have you done to this house? There are no walls!"

"Ah yes, sir, Mr. Fasoline, sir," answers Mahodi nervously. "We are wondering if you are saying, 'make a room' meaning to add more walls to make room, or if you are saying, 'make a room' meaning to remove walls to make a room, and we are coming to the conclusion that it is the second you are meaning because to be meaning the first would be meaning that one room would be not even large enough for a small bed. And so we are making a great room. Are you not pleased, sir?"

Ed feels the biggest headache he has ever had in his life coming on. He wants to run, scream, tear his stupid combed-over hair out, but instead, all he does is stand there with his mouth open.

"Mr. Vasoline, sir?" says Mahodi at the other end of the line. Still there is silence.

"Mr....Fasouline?" whispers Mahodi, trying another pronunciation. "Are you there?"

"Yes, Mahodi," answers Ed's tired voice. "Yes, I'm here. I was meaning the first, not the second. Why didn't you call me?"

"We did. But you are not answering and we are needing to exploit window of opportunity for work on the house."

"I need to get this dump on the market in three weeks. I can't sell the house like this."

"Oh," answers Mahodi with uncertainty. "This is perhaps a regretfully situation." He pauses waiting for Ed, but Ed is still too stunned to get his thoughts together.

"Mr. Foosoline?" says Mahodi, hopefully.

Ed nervously itches his scalp and smoothes his comb-over. "Yes, Mahodi?"

"Well, at least you are having new people to live in the big house already."

"What?" croaks Ed.

"New people. At least you are already having new people for your big house."

"New people at the big house?" Ed's mind backtracks. When did he tell Mahodi about the house in South Wind? He vaguely remembers leaving a message, the day after he toured the house. No, he was with Tatiana that evening. So it must have been the day after. Sort of a pre-organizer kind of message. About painting. Yes, it was about painting the big house. That Mahodi should put it into his longer range planning. Ed pauses. And now Mahodi is telling him there are people in the house?

"What do you mean, Mahodi?"

"I am just over at the big house to look for painting since you are telling me that this will also need to be done. And while I am waiting for Arvee Street to dry and pool kit to arrive…and credit from Home Warehouse to buy wood for your house, not to forget that…I am thinking, Why not start priming new big house to get a hole of the game. If you take my meaning.

"Only, when we arrive, I am seeing a very large moving truck parked in the drive, and there is furniture being moved into the house. Are you not knowing about this, sir?"

Ed slams his phone closed and runs out the back door, trips on the pepper tree root again, skirts the dumpster, and jumps into his red BMW. He hits the accelerator pedal and screeches off in the direction of the South Wind Estates.

Traffic is heavily congested as he makes his way across town because it is the end of lunch hour. He drives past low-end malls with their mega-superstores and greasy eateries. Over the freeway with the trucks trying to go north or south amidst the hurrying cars. Then downtown with its lunch crowd at boutique sushi and pasta places, not to mention the Planetbucks and Hornbucks and whatever-bucks coffee. Then it's through the old neighborhood, which is now nothing but attorney and insurance offices, and finally to the belt of new developments along the eastern foothills. South Wind Estates is up in the foothills, and almost outside the city limits. In fact, it was once outside city limits, but was quickly rezoned when city fathers realized the potential increase in tax base.

Ed finally sees the curved stucco walls of the South Wind Estates up ahead and turns onto Maria Street. It took him almost an hour to drive twenty miles. He quickly passes the 'For Sale' signs and pulls up to the big, Italian villa-style house on the corner. His house.

And what does he see? Indeed, there is a large moving van parked in the driveway and two beefy men carrying a wall-sized plasma screen television out of the van and through the front door. Ed sits in his car staring at the scene. What weird twist could have possibly occurred for him to have just signed the purchase papers to a house that is now about to be occupied by someone he has never met without his knowledge? Mickey sold him the house. Mickey said that the house had not even been put on the market. That's why Ed paid a little more, exactly for that reason. Mickey gave him the papers, and he signed. The papers are sitting in an express mail envelope on his kitchen counter. At least, he thinks that's what they are. So, who are these people?

He gets out of his car and walks up to the house. On the other side of the van, is Mahodi's truck, and Mahodi, Liang Rong and Carlos are squatting next to it, dressed in their painters overalls, watching the movers as if watching a performance event. They haven't even touched the cans of paint and ladders in the truck.

"When did you get here?" asks Ed.

"Oh, it is being at midday minus a quarter," answers Mahodi.

"Noon?" Ed looks questioningly at Mahodi, then Carlos, then Liang Rong who stares back at him with a very amused look on his face. Ed glares at him. "So when did the movers get here?"

Mahodi shrugs his shoulders. "This I am not knowing. Truck was here when we arrived." He wobbles his head to the side. "This is what I am saying to you on the telephone, I am thinking that you have been selling the house already and you are knowing this."

Ed strides over to the moving van and peers into it. There's nothing left but a lone rocking chair pushed against the back. He marches up to the door. The lock box is still hanging from the door handle. How in the world did these people get a key for the house? Did Mickey forget to take it off the multiple listing?

He storms into the house, through the dark green entry hall and straight towards the red living room. But then he hears voices coming from the dining room. He whirls around and strides across the doorway, ready to shout and prevail over these interlopers.

A man the size of a linebacker, inked on both arms, wearing a sleeveless tee-shirt, a gold chain around his neck, stands in the middle of the room. Whatever it was Ed had on his tongue to say slips immediately into oblivion.

"Over there!" barks the guy to two movers, who stand there holding the gigantic plasma screen TV. The guy points to the far wall and Ed can see the musculature on his arm through the sleeve of tattooing. Opposite the TV wall, is a huge, home work-out set-up and treadmill.

"Attack!" screams a pudgy kid popping out from behind an overstuffed armchair in the corner of the room. He runs towards the movers and kicks one of them in the shins. "Ha! ha! Gotcha!" he laughs.

"You little shit," yelps the mover.

"Lightening!" shouts a woman, entering the room and brushing past Ed as if he was just another piece of furniture. "I told you to play outside." She turns to the man—her husband?— and Ed sees a tattoo peeking out from above her low-waisted sweatpants and well-sculpted buttocks. "I really think it should be on this wall," she says. "There'll be way too much reflection. That was the problem we had before, don't you remember?"

"Excuse me," says Ed, trying to maintain his composure. "You must have the wrong house. This is my house."

The man and the woman both turn simultaneously toward him in surprise.

"Who the fuck are you?" says the man to Ed.

"I own this house," says Ed. He holds up a key. "I just bought it."

"Like, not," says the woman. Her lip curls.

"Excuse me," says Ed, incredulously. "Who are you?

"Who are we?" asks the man and woman in unison.

"We are the renters," growls the man. "R-a-n-t-r-s, or however the fuck you spell it. We rented this place off Lifter's List. So if you applied for it, and somebody told you, you could have it, well…" he laughs wickedly. "Oops! Now get the hell out."

"I don't want to rent it," sputters Ed. "I bought it!"

"Uh," interrupts one of the movers who has been standing there watching the exchange while he and his partner hold the TV, "should we go ahead and put it down here and you can, uh, decide later?"

"Who did you rent this from?" Ed's voice is rising. "What's his name?"

"Her name," says the woman.

"What's her name? Tell me her name and phone number. This is my house!"

"Whoa, asshole. I don't know what you're talking about. And who we rented this from is none of your business. Get out of here," shouts the man.

"Yeah, asshole," giggles the boy, who has not gone outside. He jumps back onto the overstuffed chair and bounces up and down.

"You know what," interjects the woman, taking a threatening step towards Ed. She's wearing a tank top, and now Ed can see that she's got another tattoo above her left breast and muscles in her upper arms too. "You are trespassing, so I think you better get out of here, or I'm going to call the police. If you have a problem, go spend some money on a lawyer!"

"Trespasser, trespasser!!" shouts the boy like an ornery parrot.

"Trespasser?" says Ed. He feels dizzy, like he's not getting enough air.

The man pushes the woman aside, grabs Ed by his button-down Oxford cloth shirt and pulls him close. Ed can feel his breath on his face. "Listen, buddy, we want to finish our moving here. Now get out!" He yanks Ed through the hallway to the front door and physically throws him out the door. Ed stumbles to the porch as he hears the jingle of the guy's gold watch and sees a fleeting flash of reflected sunlight before the door slams shut.

Stunned, Ed stands at the entrance of the huge, luxurious house he has just paid over $750,000 for and stares vacuously at the empty moving van.

"Shall we be not painting, sir...?" Mahodi's voice breaks through Ed's empty head.

Ed turns slowly on him, sees Mahodi standing before him. Notices the other two idiots still squatting in the shade of the truck. And the bile in his stomach rises.

"You idiots! Get the hell out of here," he screams. "Go put the walls back in where you tore them out!" He jumps into his car. Where's that asshole, Mickey Schulz? Ed angrily grabs his phone and dials Mickey's cell number for the umpteenth time.

"Mickey Schulz here," says the automatic voice recording. "I'm doing business right now. Leave your name and number, and I'll get back to you. Don't page me because I won't answer."

"Mickey!" hisses Ed tensely into the phone. "Where the hell are you? And who the hell has moved into my house?" He doesn't even close the phone. He just throws it onto the floor of the car, and tears off down the street, heedless of the stop sign.

James MacUffy, town patrol officer, has been sitting in his patrol car in the shade of a Japanese maple tree pretending to do a little paperwork. Actually, his wife has been nagging him about taking out a loan—while money is so cheap right now—to remodel their kitchen. He really doesn't want to do it, but then again, he did just put that chunk of money into buying a fishing boat with his buddy, and ever since she found out about it, she's not given him a moment's rest. So he doesn't see many options for himself.

He scribbles a few numbers on his notebook pad, and glances up. Just in time to see a brand new, red BMW Z4 tear through the intersection without so much as a nod to the stop sign. "Oh, man!" he chortles to himself. "Let's go get 'em." He cranks up the siren extra loud as he tears off after Ed.

14

Michelle is actually a fun, down-to-earth person. She also has a streak of pragmatism a mile wide. For instance, when she got pregnant from Mickey, she made a decision to pursue a life not dependent on the kind of happy pairing that every woman thinks she yearns for and needs. Mickey has his faults. He is—even she knows this—basically an arrogant prick. But a rich one. So she chose a life in the Country Club Estates, across the street from Ed (that was really quite a coup on Mickey's part), free of financial worries. She has a good time being a mom and likes having Buddy and Meledy around. And now that the kids are older, she has fun with her evening 'Tupperware' parties every month. She likes doing the research and bringing her friends and acquaintances the latest and most fun sex toys and gadgets on the market. Her Passion Parties were a big success. Then she started her Naughty Nancy series, which is going even better. Now she's working on an idea to get men involved too. 'Fun with Big and Bigger,' she's dubbing the events. With Mickey gone so many nights a week, it's a cinch finding time to host them. And it's kind of fun that Mickey really does think she's selling Tupperware.

The only part of her life that is off-kilter lately is Ed. She liked it the way it was, without that bimbo girlfriend. After Jayne left—God bless her heart—she got to see Ed almost on a daily basis. She refused to get involved with him sexually, because that would have opened a can of worms. But the way she sees it, she's almost got the best of both worlds.

When Michelle walks into the Golden Toenail Spa, it looks almost empty. "Pedicure and manicure," she tells the petite Asian woman, Amy, behind the desk.

Amy leads her to the nearest padded, plastic covered, reclining chair and efficiently fills the foot bath with warm water. "Feet here," she says, indicating the bath. Then she puts a small plastic container with warm water on the arm rest and has Michelle dip her fingers in to soak.

Michelle feels a mixture of impatience and relaxation as she sits in the chair. Amy doesn't sound like she knows much English, nor does she seem the talkative type. Michelle amuses herself by thinking about how she'd like to rearrange the living room. She's sick to death of neutrals. It's time for bright colors. She saw a room in a magazine done in fuchsia and brown and a tad of green apple she liked. That would go with the sofa which is still rather new and in good shape. Michelle's thoughts pause for a moment as she notices a familiar voice in the background.

"Is very informationative," says the female voice with the accent.

"Did he say it was legal?" asks a second female voice.

Where does she know that voice from, wonders Michelle. She turns her head towards the sound, but a gilded wooden Chinese screen cuts off her view. The voices are coming from behind. She thinks a moment. Then she remembers the accent. It's Ed's bimbo. Michelle turns her full attention to the conversation.

Two stations down, Cyndee interrupts their conversation to text a friend back [am@goldenT-nails. fab2take break], and then turns her attention back to Tatiana who is giving Cyndee a pedicure. "So what'd he say?" she asks.

"Well, he did not say was legal," answers Tatiana. "He says is good tool. What color today?"

"That Mickey Schulz," says Cyndee. "He's such a shark! I'll take coral. I think he's got his finger in a lot of things. You know, like mortgage company, title insurer, holding company and, and, and. Did you talk to him afterwards?"

"You bet!" giggles Tatiana. "We doing more than talk. But I don't know why they call him BIG Mickey." She and Cyndee both laugh out loud.

Michelle feels her face suddenly burn like a spotlight. She yanks her hand away from the poor manicurist who doesn't know what she has done wrong.

"I have to go. I just realized, I forgot something," she stutters to Amy. She slips her wet feet into her shoes, grabs a twenty dollar bill out of her wallet, throws it down, and bolts out of the spa.

Amy stares after her in complete astonishment. She'd only finished three nails on one hand. She shrugs her shoulders and ambles back towards the cubbyholes.

"What was that," asks Tatiana as she passes by.

"How I know?" answers Amy, holding out the money. "But I got pay."

Tatiana paints a coat of coral nail polish on Cyndee's toes and sits back to wait for it to dry.

"How did you get a visa to enter the country?" asks Cyndee.

Tatiana looks at her for a moment. It's been a slow day and she's glad for a little diversion. "Come, I show you," she answers. "Then we do finger nails." She stands up and motions to Cyndee to follow her. They walk back to the cubbyholes behind the brocade curtain.

"Whoa," says Cyndee looking around. "This is pretty rustic."

Tatiana shrugs. "Is okay." She goes to her cubbyhole and lifts the cotton cloth. Cyndee peers in curiously. There, in that tiny space, is a mini-shrine to Lada and Ronald Ace. Cyndee laughs. "What's this?"

Tatiana smiles at Cyndee like the Cheshire Cat. "I have religious visa. I'm Aceist."

Cyndee looks again at the photos of the Aces and then at

Trumped

Tatiana. "They let you enter because of your religion? That's a good one."

"No, no," says Tatiana with a twinkle in her eye. "Religion was visa." She adjusts her posture and pulls back her shoulders. "D cups were entry."

"Okay, let me get this straight," says Cyndee mirthfully. "You told them you were coming for religious purposes, and then what?"

"No, Cyndee. First I go to embassy and apply for visa. So, I get visa in Astonia. Then, I come here. But you need entry stamp on visa to get out of airport. If Homeland Security don't like you, they don't have to let you in. Then you go back home and argue with embassy. But I can't afford to do that. So I make sure I get my visa."

"You are a very resourceful woman," says Cyndee with new interest. She is standing a fingernail's length away from Tatiana now. She reaches out and sensually runs her hand over Tatiana's fabulous D cups. Tatiana smiles her brilliant flirtatious smile. She's pleased that Cyndee has noticed. "Maybe you'd like to work for me," says Cyndee. "I could start you as my escrow coordinator."

Tatiana looks at her. Cyndee is not an unattractive woman, and she knows a lot about the business. Tatiana leans over and plants a luxurious kiss on Cyndee's well-shaped lips.

Out on the sidewalk, Michelle storms blindly down the street, walking as fast as she can. She walks three city blocks until she finally slows down to a normal pace. Oh, this is it. This is the last straw. How low can people go for their own gain? And the irony of it! Mickey is screwing the woman who was screwing Ed, which is sort of a new way for Mickey to screw Ed. She laughs a bitter laugh. Ed is such an idiot. He deserves to get screwed.

Deserves to get screwed? Michelle is caught up short when she hears herself thinking that. Is she actually that jealous? She marches to her car and drives straight home.

When she arrives, she goes up to her bedroom and sits on the bed staring out the window at the leaves of Ed's magnificent elm trees across the street. Of course she still loves Ed. Who is she kidding? She can try to hide it from herself as much as she wants. In fact, she's tried to hide it from herself ever since Mickey told her Ed 'needed a challenge in his life.' But frankly, the longer she lives with Mickey, the more she doubts the honesty of his version of what happened. The way he sauntered out of the recruiting office, after telling her to come downtown for a surprise birthday celebration.

"Hey, Michelle," he'd said thickly. "Guess what? You're not going to believe this, but Ed just enlisted in the Navy!" He broke up laughing and rolled his eyes. "He did it! It's all finished!" Then his expression took on a look of sympathy. "He wanted me to let you know."

Michelle was stunned. She couldn't believe her ears. She and Ed had plans! She was going to study landscape architecture, and he was going to be an architect—when he got enough money for school. She stood there staring at Mickey like he was some strange worm that had crawled out from under a tomato leaf.

"Don't take it so hard, Michelle," said Mickey, patting her on the back gently. "He's just bored. He needs a challenge. A little adrenalin. It's nothing against you." He watched her with a barely concealed look of satisfaction.

Michelle stood frozen in place.

"Come on, Michelle," said Mickey. "It's okay. Life goes on. Let's go get something to drink." He put his arm protectively around her shoulders. "Come on. Let's go do something fun." And he led her away down the sidewalk.

And the strange thing is, after that, Ed never wrote to her, barely even talked to her when he was home on furlough. While Mickey called her almost every day to see how she was 'holding up.' And then came the big mistake, the total cliché. TGIF, alcohol, and his place.

Mickey is a horrible father. Maybe it's time to make a change.

Too bad her dad isn't still around. He could help her really nail him. But she isn't the daughter of an attorney for nothing. She's been keeping notes on his deals and tracking down his accounts. She should be able to get a very good settlement from him. Especially when he finds out how much she really knows about his business dealings. Yes, maybe it's time to get out.

Michelle checks the time on her phone. School's almost out. She goes to the bathroom and splashes cold water on her face. Takes her hair out of the pony tail and brushes it until it's smooth and silky. Then she looks at herself in the mirror. She should get in touch with Adam Sandier, the guy who took over her dad's practice. She doesn't really like him because he seems aggressive. He operates on a different level of ethics than her dad did. But he wins his cases and gets the best settlements for his clients, and that is what she needs: A cut-throat for a cut-throat. A predator for a predator. She loves the idea of Adam and Mickey hissing and spitting at each other from across the table, both of them puffed up like roosters.

Michelle jots down Adam's phone number from the directory, and then remembers that she ran the dildo collection through the dishwasher for next week's event. She deftly unloads it, packs the clean items in the presentation box, and then glances at the clock. Uh-oh. She's late. She'll have to call Adam after she picks up Sammy. She quickly shoves the box in the guest bedroom closet, grabs her purse and leaves the house. As she drives to Sammy's school, she thinks, why not pick up Sammy and just drive over to Adam's office? See him in person, and find out what his timeframe is.

Traffic is abominable. The whole area is a mess because the street has been torn up and all lanes flow into one. There's an underground problem. As she crawls past the spot where the street is opened up, she counts the number of workmen surrounding the hole. Thirteen. Good God. My tax dollars at work, she thinks. Well, at least they have jobs. By the time she pulls up in front of

Sammy's school, only a small handful of children remain. One of them is Buddy.

"Hey Buddy!" exclaims Michelle. "What are you still doing here?"

"My dad said he was going to pick me up to go to the batting cages," answers Buddy dolefully. "So I didn't take the bus."

"Humph!" says Michelle. "Looks like he forgot, huh?"

"Can he come with us, Mom? Please?" begs Sammy.

"Of course, he can!" says Michelle. The kids throw their backpacks into the car and pile onto the back seat. "Tell you what. I have to go into town to see an old acquaintance. Let's stop at Burger Wow and get some fries so you guys don't starve."

"Yeah!" they chorus in unison. Little boys are so wonderful, thinks Michelle. What the heck happens?

"Put yourself into a challenging situation and feel the adrenaline.
That adrenaline? That's what you want to feel every day. And if you
don't have a challenge, buy extra caffeine."
Ronald Ace, The Art of Being Me

15

When Ed pulls up to his house, he is fuming. He gets out of the car and slams the door. As if on cue, a large delivery truck pulls around the corner and stops in front of his driveway. It's the Sanity Pool Wholesalers delivery of the in-ground pool kit.

"How ya doin'?" says the driver as he opens the back doors to the van. There, inside a space as big as a warehouse, are boxes and boxes of...pool parts? The driver has a digital sign box in his hand. "Sign here," he says.

"What's this?"

"It's the receipt for your pool."

"How do I know everything is here? You haven't even unloaded it."

"Look, I'm on a schedule. Do you want your pool or not?"

"What if I said, no," says Ed. He doesn't like the guy's tone at all.

"I'm here, and I'm here now. If you don't take delivery of this pool, and sign for the rest of the money, mister, you lose your deposit. Read the fine print on your contract. Now, do you want to sign here, or not?"

Where the hell is Mahodi, thinks Ed. He glares at the man, and then snatches the invoice from his hand. It's a list of about twenty-five items, and it shows that a deposit of $3,000 was paid.

"Oh, all right. But I want my copy now. I want to check the stuff off as you unload it."

"Whatever," says the guy. He hands the digital sign box to Ed. "Sign here."

"How are you going to unload this stuff?" asks Ed.

"With the hydraulic lift, what else?"

"But, how are you going to get it to the backyard? The pool goes in the back."

The guy looks at Ed as if he's just stepped off the moon.

"That's your problem, not mine." He snatches the box from Ed, hits a button, prints out an automatic receipt and disappears into the truck. Two minutes later he's already lowering the first palette of boxes and steel plates.

Ed reads down the list: Dig sheets, video, walls and bracing, coping, liner, hardware kit, deep end ladders, skimmer, pump and filter, rebar stakes, wall foam and adhesive. "How the hell am I supposed to know what is what?" he calls to the driver.

The driver pauses, looks at Ed and then says, "Do you see the bar code numbers in front of each item?" Ed looks at the invoice and sure enough, each item has a string of about twelve numbers in front of it. "Well, each one of those numbers correlates with a number on a box," says the driver as if he is talking to a second grader. "Now, if you don't mind, I've got about a thousand more deliveries to make today."

"Oh, man," says Ed. He shakes his head at the rapidly growing stack of boxes on his driveway, and then goes to the car to look for his cell phone. He searches the floor and under the seats with his hand, and, finally, about as far back as he can reach, he feels it lodged under the metal frame of the seat. He drags it out, opens it, and automatically hits Mahodi's speed dial number. He hears the whine of the truck's hydraulic lift, but nothing from the phone. He stares at the screen. What else? The cell phone is dead. He shakes his head and sinks down on the hood of the car to watch the rest of the show.

Twenty minutes later, the Sanity Pool Wholesaler driver revs the motor of his truck, and without even saying goodbye, drives off down the street. Ed goes into the house to get a beer and try to reach somebody, but all he does is leave messages. Messages. The new purgatory of his life. Then he sinks down on the sofa and waits.

An hour and two beers later, Mahodi arrives at the house with Liang Rong and Carlos. Within thirty minutes, they've moved all thirty boxes from the pool kit into the back yard and spread them out on the ground next to the precarious backhoe. As they begin unpacking, Mahodi drags the outdoor table over and sets up his laptop.

"Carlos?" he calls. "You see installation video?"

Carlos rummages around among boxes and holds up a small one. Mahodi pops in the installation DVD.

"Haven't you guys ever done this before?" asks Ed, a slow feeling of panic rising in his gut.

"Oh, sure," says Mahodi. "But that was other company. Every company different. Now, if you are pleased to be quiet." He hits the play button.

"Congratulations on your purchase of a Sanity Wholesale Pool," says a God-like voice as the camera zooms out from a close-up of a pool. "This will be a purchase that you will cherish and enjoy for many years to come with only a minimum of maintenance. And now, let us show you how you are going to make your dream of your own home swimming pool a reality." A digital, beat-intense music track fades up, and the picture switches to a smiling, buxom blond in a pool-blue bikini wearing high heels. She stands in a large warehouse surrounded by packages.

Liang Rong and Carlos, hearing the music pulsating from the laptop, stop unpacking the pool and come over to watch the video.

"Where I know music?" asks Liang Rong, a puzzled look on his face.

"Yo se!" exclaims Carlos, punching Liang Rong. "Eez porn musica." He and Liang Rong burst out laughing.

The music fades down, and the woman begins to speak.

"Welcome," she says, "to the Sanity Pools installation guide. This guide will help you step-by-step as you install your pool."

Mahodi, who is intently watching the video, calls out. "Hey, Mr. Vasoline! Are you wanting to be interested to see the installation explanation?"

Ed joins the three of them. He never knew a pool installation video could be so…mesmerizing.

"Before we begin," continues the woman, "let's make sure that you have all the parts. First, you will need your dig sheets. They look like this," she holds up a large drawing in front of her chest and smiles. "This is to ensure that you dig your hole in the appropriate dimensions. Next, you will need to check your permitting specifications. This is a small sheet, like this."

Mahodi unfolds the dig sheet and takes a cursory look. He frowns and looks at the hole they've dug, then he looks back at the dig sheet. He pauses the video.

"What's wrong?" says Ed.

Mahodi says nothing, just keeps studying the plan and looking back at the actual hole. Finally he says, "Mr. Vasoline, I am thinking that perhaps we must be doing some adaptation. It seems, you are selecting the pool 'Tulsa,' and when I am going to website, I am seeing the pool style 'Kansas,' but not 'Tulsa.' And so I am thinking, Tulsa is in Kansas and so you must be meaning 'Kansas'-style pool. But now I am realizing Tulsa is not in Kansas. Toto was in Kansas. Tulsa is in Oklahoma. So we are having slight credibility gap between pool shape and pool hole, but never to mind. This is small apples."

Mahodi turns his attention back to the video, while Ed stands there, sputtering in the waning afternoon. He surveys all of the unpacked sections of polymer wall, the plumbing kit and step jets, flex hose and timers, spread across the ground along with the rebar stakes and wall bracing. For the first time, he begins to wonder if all this richness is making him go slowly, but surely, crazy.

By the time Mahodi and his crew have made order among all the various elements of the pool, and have marked the ground with spray paint for the additional excavating, the sun is about to melt on the horizon. The moment they are gone, Ed remembers his children. He hasn't seen or heard from either of them all day. They should have been home from school hours ago. Why didn't they look for him? Oh no. He forgot Buddy at school.

He runs into the house to grab his keys and wallet, when the blinking eye of the answering machine catches his attention.

"You have two messages," says the digital voice. Beep. "Dad, I'm with Sammy, and I'm going to sleep at his house tonight," says Buddy in a toneless, digital voice. Beep. "I'm spending the weekend at Kassi's. You never answer your phone anymore," says an angry digital teenage voice. Beep. Melody. "To erase messages…" Ed slams his hand down on the answer machine to shut it off. Great. Now he's let his kids down, in addition to everything else. And there's no other parent to blame. He hates that part of single parenting.

He glares at the dirty dishes in the sink, the drying food on the kitchen table, and the filth on the linoleum floor. On the counter, the overflowing in-basket of unopened mail. Ed's throat constricts. His head feels light. He grabs the last beer out of the refrigerator and staggers to the living room. He collapses onto the couch and barely manages to grab the remote and turn on the TV. A newscaster appears, droning, "Meanwhile, in real estate today, prices dropped another 8%. This is the second consecutive quarter of dismal news…" Ed changes the channel. There has to be at least three dozen pieces of mail in that stack! And not a single one of them opened. Xtreme Makeover returns from commercial break. He doesn't want hear this either. He finds a rerun of Crime Scene and stares vacuously at the TV, sipping his beer.

He feels like he's been in a car wreck. He's certainly been in some kind of wreck. He puts his head back and closes his eyes. Everything was going so well. Unbidden, the moment that he wants to forget for the rest of his life comes back to him in living color memory.

It's his twenty-first birthday. And Mickey is insisting that they have to get drunk. Ed was a sophomore at the junior college, and he skipped classes to get drunk with Mickey. First thing in the morning, a brewski, then some more brewskis. By noon, they were working on the wine. By mid-afternoon, they were raiding Mickey's parent's bar. And by the time late afternoon pulled around, there they were, reeking of alcohol, standing in front of the large plate glass windows of the Navy recruitment office.

He could've finished college, like his mother would have wanted. Even his old man, who criticized him for not contributing anything useful to society, wanted him to finish the JC. But no, instead he went and got drunk with Mickey.

"Let's go see the world, man," said Mickey, punching Ed in the arm, but Ed was so drunk he didn't feel a thing. "Come on, man. Effin hell, let's do something," said Mickey. He laughed, and drool spattered in the air. "Let's go be men!"

The sight of Mickey careening into the wall made Ed laugh so hard, he felt like he was about to pee. Life was hilarious! It was his birthday! And he was twenty-one! Who cared about anything except having fun! Forget about his girlfriend! His mother was long dead. His dad old. None of that mattered. There was just him and Mickey, and they were about to do something crazy and join the Navy because they were buddies.

Together they staggered into the linoleum-covered recruitment office where metal folding chairs waited in tight short rows. A young enlisted man, neatly buttoned, face blank of any judgment on the boys' behavior, greeted them. Several young men were ahead of them. The enlisted man guided them to the folding chairs, made sure they didn't collapse into the chairs, and handed them each a clipboard with an application. Mickey and Ed started filling out the paperwork.

Ed, always the more serious one, actually filled out the form in loose handwriting. Driver's license. Schools attended. Social security number. Medical conditions.

Mickey joked with the young enlisted man, "Do you need to know how long my dick is?"

"No, Sir," answered the enlisted man with a complete poker face, "that'll be unnecessary."

"Why don't you ask how much I pee every day?"

"We only need essential information, Sir."

The man reached for Mickey's clipboard.

"You first, buddy! It's your birthday!" said Mickey, pushing Ed's clipboard forward.

Ed looked sheepishly around, and handed over his clipboard to the enlisted man.

"Right this way," said the man stiffly.

Ed turned, grinning foolishly. "See you up there," he said to Mickey, just as Mickey glanced at his watch, turned and stared out the plate glass window of the building. "Mickey!" But Mickey didn't hear him. Ed felt the alcohol beginning to wear off.

"Sir? Have a seat," he remembers the recruiting officer saying. Ed felt himself gently pushed into a chair. This chair was solid wood with a padded seat. In front of him was a very imposing wooden desk. And next to it, an American flag dangled on a thick gold pole. The subordinate officer handed the clipboard to the recruiting officer. The RO glanced briefly at the application, flipped the page, scanned the second page, then the next until he reached the last page. "It looks like everything is in order here," he said to Ed. "Just sign here, please." It was a command, not a request. He pushed the form in front of Ed and handed him a new, black pen.

The moment he dotted the last 'i', Ed remembers turning to look for Mickey, his co-conspirator in this adventure and next in line. But all he saw was Mickey's back disappearing out the front door.

"Wait a minute," he said to the RO. But Ed's application form had already been whisked away for processing, and the RO stood with his hand outstretched.

"Welcome to the Navy, seaman recruit Fasoli." Ed didn't

dare correct him. He remembers hearing the heels of the officer click as he saluted Ed crisply. "You will report for your physical tomorrow morning at 0800 hours. We have to inform you that it is a federal offense to not appear for duty..." his voice trailed off.

In a daze, Ed turned again to look for Mickey, and he saw him all right. There, on the sidewalk, outside the recruiting office, and he was not alone. Ed's girlfriend, Michelle was standing in front of him with a strange look on her face. Then he saw Mickey take her arm and lead her away, changing his life forever.

"You can be qualified now by just calling 1-800-1231!" shouts a man on the TV, waking Ed out of his reverie. "Make your dream come true! You deserve to be rich. Just call us! That number again is 1-800-1231. We're waiting!"

Waiting. Ed stares at the TV for a moment longer, then he gets up and brings the overflowing in-basket from the kitchen. Sets it down next to him on the new leather sofa, and begins to go through the pile.

One by one, he takes each envelope into his hand. Credit card application, school announcement, electric bill, mortgage payment. He separates them into piles. One by one, he opens the envelopes, pulls out the contents, scans it, and then puts it in a pile. Utilities and telephone in one pile, various payments in another, bank statements in a third. How can he have so many bills? He doesn't carry credit cards. Okay, so he missed a phone bill two months ago, but he did pay last month. That's not so tragic. But somehow he missed his utilities bill. What a minute. That's for the Arvee house. He forgot he needed to pay the utilities there.

Ed finds his most recent bank statements and is astonished to see how low the balance has fallen in both his checking and saving accounts. Where is all his money? He puts it aside. Opens another envelope. It's a relatively new payment due to Mickey, and it's over three thousand dollars. Ed's eyes nearly drop out of their sockets. How can he owe over three thousand dollars

to Mickey? Mickey must have combined some of the payments.
But how could he have done that? And here's a bill for the Arvee
Street house for $2,199, and he still owes $286,000 on it in spite
of the two payments he made. How can that be? Ed swallows and
feels his tongue stick against the roof of his mouth. He lays out,
on the table in front of him, all of the envelopes and invoices he
finds that have Country Club Mortgage Co. or MD LLC written
on them, paid or not. He gets his check book and starts trying to
figure things out.

He finds two payments made to CCM for $1,766. That's for
the loan for remodeling. Then he finds a similar one that he seems
to have missed paying, because there's another one that charges a
late fee. Shit. Okay, those all have the same address and are from
CCM. What is this $3,000 one? He reads it carefully. It is indeed
for his house, but it shows a three-month adjustment. Ed's heart
beats faster. He grabs the other mortgage payments. They are for
MD LLC. The Arvee Street house was $1,014 a month. Of course,
that was Mickey's intro rate. Ed had two months before it went
up. Back then that seemed like plenty of time to turn the house
around. But now, he has a bill with yesterday's date for that
house for $2,199. Are the two months over already and $2,199 is
the new payment? Two thousand one hundred and ninety-nine
dollars for a house that is now a total cluster-fuck?

The anxiety that has been pulling around his neck like an
uncomfortable necktie is feeling more like a noose by the minute.
He searches for the payment slips for the South Wind house. He
agreed to $2,821 a month, which seemed kind of high, but he
thought it would be exactly that: just a month. And then he'd
have it sold. Next month, he's going to owe…he reads down the
statement…$6,686? There's no way he can pay that. And he's got
the renters to contend with. That means in about…two weeks
he is going to have to come up with $11,500 a month to meet his
obligations.

The papers drop from his hand and Ed collapses back into
the sofa, eyes glazed, staring at the empty basket. And of all

things, as if uncovered by an excavation, an old photo of his dad standing next a '58 convertible Thunderbird comes into focus. The car Ed's dad gave him for his eighteenth birthday. The car he later sold to Mickey for next to nothing because it needed a new carburetor, and he had joined the Navy.

'You idiot!' His dad's words fill his head like the sound of a dentist's drill. Ed hears a hoarse, hollow cry of pain fill the room—his own voice. He feels like the world's biggest idiot. And he thought he was going to be rich.

"When I, like, have an ueber-bad day, I go get really wasted, cause I
know when I wake up things will most definitely be different."
DJ Ace (Ronald Ace's illegitimate son), REmixRag, 2006

16

Ed sits on the sofa and he can't stop crying. He's losing his sanity!
He has never been in debt in his life, and, now, not only is he in
debt, he's about to go bankrupt and lose everything. What will
happen with Meledy and Buddy? He's dedicated his life to keeping
them safe. And now it's their lives, their home, their future he's
put in jeopardy. How can he possibly pay back all that he owes?
He feels darkness closing in around him as he sits there sobbing
with only the TV muttering in the background.

Then all at once, in the distance, Ed picks up the low rumble
of a deep-throated engine. It grows louder and more distinct as
it approaches. Suddenly, the living room is flooded with bright,
harsh light. Vibrations go up through Ed's feet and terror clenches
his gut. He turns towards the window and hastily wipes his eyes
on his sleeve, runs his fingers through his comb-over. Holds his
breath. Could it possibly be....

Out on his front lawn, the looming frame of a huge Ford truck
with double headlights and a row of four driving lights across
the top comes to a stop ten feet from the door. The engine cuts
out and the lights go black. The driver's door opens, then slams
briskly. Ed hears sharp, heavy boot heels on the cement pathway
walking straight to the front door. The doorbell rings.

Ed breaks into a cold sweat. It can't be. The date is wrong.
He tries to compress himself against the back of the sofa, to

S. Pareto Rose

make himself invisible. He's shaking in the center of his very manhood.

The bell rings forcefully again. "I know you're in there, Ed," says an impatient voice.

Ed stands up and slowly creeps towards the front. Why, oh why, of all times, does she have to arrive now?

The doorbell bleats angrily now.

Ed has no choice. She'll break the door down. He opens. A tall, handsome cowboy dressed in a plaid shirt and jeans, with Elvis-styled hair, stands in front of the door.

"Ed!" he says, smiling. "I thought I was going to have to break the door down!"

Ed swallows hard. "Jayne," he says unenthusiastically. "What are you doing here?"

"Dick, Ed, it's Dick," says Jayne, and gives Ed a big bear hug before turning back towards the truck. "Montana! Come on in! He is here. I figured as much." Dick takes a step back and scrutinizes Ed. "What the hell is wrong with you? You look like cow dung. Doesn't he, Montana?"

Montana stands next to Dick and peers curiously at Ed. Montana has a much slighter build than Dick, but he's wearing the same jeans and cowboy shirt and tooled leather belt. "The teeth look good," he shrugs.

Dazed, Ed steps aside. "All right. Come on in," he says.

Dick and Montana step into the living room and pause. An amused smile passes over Dick's face and he chuckles. "Well, looks like you've finally decided to update the look a little. What are you doing to the house?" He wanders back towards the kitchen, throwing a glance down the hall, as if he still has some kind of ownership. "What's this style called? Home improvement gone solo?"

"Very funny," says Ed. He hears a sound at the front door and whips around, only to see Buddy trying to sneak in the front door.

"Buddy!" says Ed, "What are you doing up at this hour?"

"Buddy!" cries Dick, spinning around and holding out his arms.

"Mommy!" shouts Buddy, running into the open arms. They give each other a huge bear hug, and then Dick pushes him away. "Look how you've grown! My god, when did we have our last camping trip? Has it been that long?"

"It's only been a year," says Buddy downplaying his feeling of pride.

"How did you know I was here?"

"I saw your truck lights. Nobody has truck lights like you! And Sammy sleeps in the front bedroom. The lights woke me up, and I climbed out the window."

"You rascal," Dick tousles his hair. "So what's been going on? Fill me in."

In the brief awkward silence that follows, Ed looks down at the floor in embarrassment.

Buddy saves the moment. "Daddy's a real estate investor now," he pipes up. "And he's always busy."

Dick looks incredulously at Ed. "You've gone into real estate? Are you nuts? Haven't you heard the market is about to crash?"

Ed slumps back down on the sofa and holds his head in his hands. "I know, I know," he says miserably. Dick looks at him in puzzlement.

"What did you do?"

"I bought a couple of houses."

"You bought a couple of houses? When did you learn about real estate?"

Now Ed looks even more miserable, if that's possible. It sounds so stupid here in front of Jayne. He never bothered. He can't believe it himself, that he took such a stupid risk.

"Daddy has a girlfriend and she likes real estate," says Buddy, trying to be helpful.

Dick bursts out laughing. "You went and bought two houses in order to impress a pair of tits?" He says this as if he's just heard a great joke. "And now what? You can't make your payments? Is that the problem?"

"It's worse," moans Ed.

"Are you kidding?"

"I actually took money out of the house."

"You mean, you took money out of the house to make the down payments on the two houses?"

Ed squirms uncomfortably. "The money from my house is almost gone. I bought stuff, and I'm remodeling. I didn't put anything down on the other two houses. They're just flipper houses. You know, fast cash."

"You didn't have to put anything down?" asks Dick incredulously. "How does that work?" He says this as if he's trying to understand why the Feds raise and lower interest rates.

"I don't know. You borrow 110% of the price of the house and then, when you sell it, you get more than 10% profit, so you just pay the whole thing back and keep the extra."

"So, what's the problem?"

"They're adjustable loans. I could afford the payments the first two months, but now, they're going up and the houses are nowhere near ready to sell. And I don't have an income anymore."

Dick lets out a low whistle. "You got fired?"

Ed shakes his head.

"You quit your job? Impressive. So how much are you in debt for?"

Ed mumbles.

"What?" Dick leans closer to Ed. "What did you say?"

"I said, aboutamillionandahalfdollars."

"A million and a half dollars???!!" sputters Dick.

Ed starts weeping again. "He's going to take my house. What am I going to do? I'm broke."

"For hella sake!" yells Dick. In one lightening quick movement, he juts out his chin and delivers a solid hand-slap on Ed's cheek.

"You can ACT LIKE A MAN!" he fumes. Ed reels backward into the sofa.

"Dick!" says Montana sharply. "Stop! I am going to get us all some drinks. Stiff drinks. Come on, Buddy, help me out so I don't get lost in that mess."

Buddy, standing next to him with wide eyes, is clueless about what is going on. He's never seen his dad like this before. Nor his mom, actually, because he mostly sees her in the summer up in Oregon. He eagerly follows Montana.

Dick checks himself, pulls back from Ed. "Sorry," he says in a lowered tone. "Sorry, Ed. It's the testosterone shots. They...uh... make me a little crazy sometimes. But...what's with the hair?"

Ed cringes. "Drop it. So, where'd you get the money?"

"Mickey," mumbles Ed.

Dick has to laugh again. This is unbelievable. "Mickey? Mickey Schulz? You let fat boy con you? I bet he's already screwing your girlfriend!"

Screwing my girlfriend? Ed feels a jolt of electricity hit him. Of course! Mickey is screwing Tatiana! It's so obvious!

"You...asshole!" shouts Ed, and lunges at Dick. "You have made my life nothing but misery! You chose your 'alternate' lifestyle and left me here to field all the local gossip and jokes." He reaches for Dick's neck. He wants to throttle him. "You...!"

"Whoa!" says Dick, jumping over the arm of the sofa. "Calm down! I'm not screwing your girlfriend! I'm friend, not foe."

Montana walks in with a tray of mugs and a bottle of bourbon at that moment. He drops the tray on the coffee table and grabs Ed's arm.

"Take it easy, Ed! Look. Buddy brought you some cocoa."

Ed, as if coming out of a trance, looks at Montana, then at Buddy.

"Here, Dad," says Buddy, holding out the mug. "Montana taught me how to spike it real good."

Ed takes the mug and sits back down. Dick sits at the other end of the new leather sofa, while Buddy perches on the arm of the over-stuffed chair Montana sits in. The in-basket, that was on the coffee table, was knocked off in the shuffle and envelopes and papers are scattered about. Dick looks at Ed, and Ed stares hostilely back.

"I'm sorry I set you off," says Dick finally. "Let's give the whole thing a think. Okay, so you have two loans or three?"

"Actually, three," answers Ed miserably, after a moment's hesitation.

"Three?" says Dick, trying to keep the sarcasm out of his voice. "So the first one is where you 'took' money out of the house. I love that euphemism. What are the other two?"

"For speculation, like I said. Easy money. One is a little house on Arvee Street, and the other is that new development of super-size houses over in the northwest. I was supposed to use the extra ten percent loan to fix them up and sell them before the loans adjusted and make a pile of money. Then I was going to pay back the home equity loan."

"How in the world did you get talked into that?"

"I don't know," says Ed impatiently. "My brain hasn't been functioning since I met this woman. I just wanted to impress her. The flipping houses thing was her idea. I talked it over with Mickey, and he figured out how to make it work."

"So, you didn't go to a bank? You borrowed everything from Mickey? And you didn't put anything down."

Ed lowers his eyes.

Dick gives a whistle. "If Mickey is using this house for collateral—it is totally paid for after all—that means you're probably fucked. He is some operator." Dick wags his head in appreciation of what Mickey's done.

"The worst is," says Ed, "one house is totally torn apart, and the other has some strange people living in it who claim they're renters."

"Hey, did your dad ever homestead?" interrupts Montana.

"What's homesteading?" asks Ed.

"Wait a minute!" exclaims Dick, setting his hot chocolate

down. "That's an idea. Your dad thought you were an idiot, remember? This place was in a trust before we even got married."

Ed frowns. "I'd sort of forgotten that whole thing, but I think you're right. But, so what if he did?"

"Man, you didn't do your homework, did you? You can't sell a house that's in a trust. I found that out when we bought our place in Oregon. The owner had to take it out of the trust to sell it to us. It took days to get the paperwork settled."

"But I'm not selling my house, I just took money out of it."

"Taking money out is just borrowing, Ed. And when it comes to property, it doesn't matter whether you sell or borrow against it. The bottom line is that you've done what they call 'encumber the property.' You've used it as a guarantee that you'll pay back the money Mickey loaned to you. Unless you can prove that those loans were made in bad faith or whatever, you're in bad shape. Ed," says Dick with a scornful tone, "didn't you try to find out what you were doing first?"

Ed studies his fancy loafers. Looks at the stitching on them. What a waste of money, just for a pair of shoes. He shrugs. "I was in a hurry. Mickey did it all overnight."

Dick rolls his eyes. "Overnight? Well, Mickey would've known whether or not the deed to the house is held in a trust, if he did a title search. Hmm," Dick stops to think a moment. "Maybe, just maybe, Mickey didn't do a title search. Michelle always said he had a finger in everything, meaning of course different businesses. You would've had to contact your lawyer to get the house out of trust, if he did it right. Maybe he did it for you. Go look at your documents. See if one is listed."

Ed gets up and walks over to the computer where a cardboard filing box is sitting. He brings it over to the sofa and riffles through it. There it is. He pulls out the envelope with the first batch of loan documents from Mickey. The ones for his equity loan. He puts the pages on the sofa between him and Dick. "Is this it?" he asks. He holds up the borrower statement. "This has statement of fees, loan processing, escrow and here's a title search. For $2,600." He shows Dick the document.

"So, he did do one. Well then, maybe you took your house out of the trust?" says Dick.

Ed thinks back. He remembers his old man threatening to 'lock up' his estate. And he knows his dad used to talk to Michelle's dad. And he remembers that when his dad died, Ed went to the law office and sat there while they told him a bunch of stuff, and that was it. There wasn't much to do.

"No. Nothing's changed since Dad died." answers Ed finally. "All I get is a letter telling me how much property tax to pay. So that's what I do."

"Well then, it is still in trust."

"You mean, Mickey can't use it as a guarantee?" For the first time Ed sees a sliver of hope. It's about the size of a cactus needle, but hope nevertheless.

"Well, theoretically. But I'm no expert."

Ed muses over that, and then a new thought comes to him. Where did all that cash come from? "You know, he gave me about $50,000 worth of cash. Do you think that's in the first loan?"

"I don't know but if I were you, I'd go over all three of your loan docs with a fine-toothed comb. If you know what you're looking for, I bet you'll find something. Mickey doesn't know how to do anything honestly. It's in his genes. Not even marriage." Dick smiles warmly at Montana. "But he knows business."

"Are we going to be all right?" asks Buddy in a small voice. He's been quietly sitting there playing with the melting marshmallows in his cocoa.

Ed smiles ruefully at Buddy who looks back at him in consternation. "Don't worry Buddy, we'll get to the bottom of this. I've learned a few things about trouble-shooting at the sewer plant. The most important being: you always start where it stinks the worst, and work your way forward."

"You've got to build a case against him," says Dick. "That's your only hope. Otherwise you're liable no matter what kind of shit he sold you."

"Is Sammy's dad in trouble?" asks Buddy.

Ed tries hard not to swear. "Let's put it this way," he says, "maybe both of us agreed to things we shouldn't have agreed to. But it doesn't make any difference for your friendship with Sammy, okay? Or Michelle," he adds.

"Good," says Buddy, reassured. "Because I don't want to ever move. This is the best house in the world."

"Don't you worry," says Ed, doing his best to sound convincing. "We're going to make an invincible game plan. We're going to be all right. But can I have, like, five more spikes in my cocoa?"

"Sure!" says Buddy grabbing the bottle of bourbon.

Dick stands up, and Montana picks up the cue and does likewise. "Well, I guess we'll head off for tonight and leave you two. We certainly don't want to stay here. Mel said she's coming back tomorrow, by the way. She just wanted some time to cool off."

"You talked to her?" asks Ed in surprise.

Dick winks at Buddy. "See you tomorrow, Buddy," he says, giving Buddy a quick hug. Ed stands up and shuffles towards the door with them. Dick pauses for a second and looks at Ed. "Why don't you finally give that asshole what he deserves? Do it for all of us." And he gives Ed a punch on the shoulder as he follows Montana out the door.

"Even if you're a loser, don't act like one. Act like you're me and you will be surprised how people will flock around you like flies at a picnic."
Ronald Ace, Don't Be A Loser

17

The county library is an impressive, modern building with tall ceilings, books, chairs and tables, drinking fountains and a whole wall of computers that are hooked up to the internet. When Ed arrives, dressed in jeans and tee-shirt shirt, his hair tousled and normal, carrying a bag with all his loan documents and a notebook, a small handful of other people, mostly itinerants or job-seekers sucking at empty coffee cups, are already waiting at the front door. At nine a.m. sharp, a library employee approaches from inside, turns the lock, and pushes open the glass door.

"Morning," mumbles the library employee, as people file past him.

"Hi, there," says Ed, pausing. He wants to ask the man if he knows where the real estate section is. But then he notices that the man, whose badge says 'Gus Ledbetter, Volunteer,' looks like he should have retired twenty years ago. "Hi," he repeats and moves on into the building.

Ed walks to the main hall and stops. He breathes in the musty smell of books and looks around with a pleasant smile pasted on his face. It's been so long since he's used a library that he can barely remember what to do. An island in the center holds a bright display of new history and political books. Over on the right is an old wooden catalog with its small rectangular drawers.

Adjacent to that, along the wall, is a row of computer desks. The reference desk is at the back, next to the periodical section.

Ed decides that his first goal should be to get an idea of what 'real estate' actually involves, and secondly, to find out what exactly is required when someone purchases a house. He's got a sheaf of papers for each one of his loans, but honestly, he has no serious understanding of what anything is, and he needs to know. He sits down in front of the online catalog and stares at the screen. Finally he types in 'real estate.' Up comes a long list of titles and call numbers. As he goes down the list, reading the titles and authors and publishing dates of each entry, most of them sound useless. "How to Probate an Estate in California," "How to Sell a House Fast in a Slow Real Estate Market: A 30-day Plan for Motivated Sellers," "Panic: The Story of Modern Financial Insanity," "Liz Earman's 2005 Action Plan," "Death Revokes the Offer," "Trump University Wealth Building 101." None of it sounds like what he's looking for. He scrolls down faster, and finally comes to an eligible title: "Barron's Real Estate Handbook" by Jack P. Freidman. He jots down the call number. 333.33 Friedman. The next one he jots down is "Home Buying for Dummies" by Eric Tyson and Ray Brown. Now we're talking.

By the time he's scrolled through all seven hundred eighty-three entries, his brain is completely dull. He wanders around the carpeted library floor until he stumbles across the aisle labeled 'Economics and Investing/300-400.' He turns into the aisle and scans up and down the mostly empty shelves, searching for the call numbers he jotted down. But most of them seem to be checked-out. Of the handful of books there, most of them are like Mickey's—stuff about motivating people to buy real estate. He decides on "California Real Estate Practice" and "The Better Business Bureau Guide to Buying a Home," then finds himself a quiet table by the window. He puts his bag down, gets out his notebook, and prepares to learn. He opens the book. It's old—1987. You'd think a county library would have a newer version. It's probably checked-out. He reads the table of contents anyways:

Sources of Law and the Judicial System; Law of Agency; Duties and Responsibilities of Licensees; Regulation of Licensees; Law of Contracts; Real Estate Contracts; Property, Estates and Recordings; Ownership of Real Property; Acquisitions and Conveyances; Real Property; Security Devices; Involuntary Liens and Homesteads; The Language of Real Estate… His eyes glaze over. He needs something simpler. He closes the book and opens the Better Business Guide. Does the same thing here. Find Your Dream Home…no. Location, Location, Location, Your Perfect Neighborhood…definitely not. Choose the Right Agent…too late. Secure Financing Types of Mortgages…too late. Investigate the Market, What's Available…too late. View Properties…forget it. Buying a New Home…no. Make an Offer…too late. Disgusted and impatient, Ed slams the book closed, takes the bagel sandwich he bought out of his bag, and eats.

From where he is sitting, Ed has two views. He can look out the window or, at the end of the aisle, as if framed, he can observe the reference desk. Behind the tall counter of the reference section, he notices three people. They apparently are librarians, and they all look way too knowledgeable. They look intimidatingly knowledgeable. One of them, a pudgy, unfriendly looking woman with steel-grey hair, spends a lot of time sitting at a desk. The bald, pasty looking guy, with an air of arrogance, seems to stand at the counter a lot. And appearing and disappearing constantly is a young, pretty woman with black-hair.

Ed considers his options while he discretely finishes his bagel, and washes it down with a bottle of double espresso with cream, purchased just for the occasion. He needs help. He has no idea where to begin, nor what is really the serious reference book for the field. This book—he looks at the Pivar—needs a class and a teacher. The other book is not for someone in serious trouble. Ed hates to ask the guy who looks like an asshole, but the day is ticking away, and he's not seeing a lot of alternatives.

"Excuse me," he says politely, going up to the reference counter addressing the only person there. "Could you tell me what the definitive book about real estate and standard real estate contracts is?"

"Certainly," answers the guy without making a move, proving that he's an asshole. Ed waits, eyebrows raised. Finally, his eyebrows get tired.

"Well, could you tell me the name, or show me where it is?" he asks Ed.

"May I see your library card?" asks the Asshole.

Oh, great, thinks Ed. "Uh, I forgot it, but it's probably lapsed anyway."

"That's okay, we can find you in the system as long as it was within this lifetime. What's your name?"

Ed rolls his eyes. He's never had a library card. Only the kids have library cards that they never use. "It's Ed Fasouli, but..."

"F, a, s, o, u, l, i?" asks the man, already typing his name.

Leave it to a librarian to know how to spell his name. "Yep, that's it," answers Ed.

"That's Greek," says the man.

"Yep," says Ed. "That's what most people say when I tell them my name: That's Greek to me." He tries to laugh. He can't believe he just repeated his father's lamest joke.

"You're not in the system," pronounces the man without laughing.

"Does that mean you're not going to help me?" asks Ed in astonishment.

"No. It just means you can't check anything out. Kathleen?" he calls towards the back. Four seconds later, the pretty young woman steps out. Oh, he's in luck.

"Yes, Mr. Papadoupolis?"

"Will you get this gentleman the "California Department of Real Estate 2006, Real Estate Law and Regulations of the Real Estate Commissioner with other Pertinent Excerpts from the California Codes" please?

Ed looks at him, and his mouth drops open. The Asshole knows the entire title by heart?

"Why certainly," answers Kathleen McGregor. "Hold on," she says. She turns and lightly steps to a large bookshelf holding many volumes at the back of the reference section. After a moment she returns with a book, six inches thick, and hands it to the Asshole. He passes it over the counter to Ed.

"How do you remember the title?" asks Ed, staring at the man.

"You don't think you're the only person who has been burned in real estate and decides to finally find out what the law is, do you?" he sniffs. "Good luck." He turns, grabs his walker, and shuffles away, the aluminum frame making soft clanking sounds each time it hits the linoleum floor. Ed suddenly feels horribly embarrassed.

As soon as the man has disappeared behind the glass wall of the reference librarian's office at the back, she steps over to him. "You might want to take a glance at this one too," she says in a low voice, handing him another, slightly smaller tome.

Ed feels the weight of the books pull downward on his arms. He looks at the book. It is "California Real Estate Practice."

"It's very good." she says. She leans closer. "People have said that it is really quite more helpful than the other." She smiles.

"Thank you," says Ed, overcome. "Thank you very much."

"And another tip," she says. Is this an act of mercy? Does he look so hapless? "Don't forget to go to the county clerk's website. They have a lot of documents and helpful information there as well."

"You've…" but Ed can't even finish the thought because Kathleen has turned and slipped back to wherever she came from. Ed takes the books and returns to his table. He stares at them, willing them to reveal to him the secret to his dilemma. He's determined to stay till closing time, and it's good knowing that Jayne…Dick, is with Buddy and Meledy. After all, every kid needs a mother. He needs to find the one rusted bolt, rotten washer, or loose wire, the one piece of information that will lead to the solution for his whole, frightening problem. He stares and stares, but the books just sit there. Finally he opens the big one randomly. It falls to a chapter titled "Mandatory Disclosures."

Disclosures. That word has a familiar ring. He reflects back. Tatiana. He remembers Tatiana trying to pronounce the word. Disk louses, it sounded like. Where were they talking? Of course! They were in Cyndee Rohber's office, next to the Golden Toe Spa. It was modern and spartan, remembers Ed. Almost uncomfortable. A few sleek metal chairs, a table and large desk, and a large window with closed blinds. They were signing the papers for the Arvee Street house.

"Now we get into inspections and disclosures," Cyndee had said. And that's when Tat had repeated, 'disk louses?'

He and Cyndee had both snickered. "Disclosures," Ed had repeated, wondering himself exactly what Cyndee meant. He listened.

"As a buyer, you're entitled to know certain things," she had explained to them, "about the property you're going to purchase. These are called disclosures. They're regulated by law."

"Is like fork-loshers?" asked Tatiana.

Cyndee laughed. "No, no! Disclosures just means telling people things. Things like whether an earthquake fault is near the house, or legal stuff, like agency disclosure. I'm only representing you. FB Property Management, who own the house, is representing itself. But technically, I could represent both of you, I'd just have to tell you. The thing that's pertinent here, though," said Cyndee after a slight pause looking directly at Ed, "is that all inspections and disclosures cost money, and someone has to pay for them. It used to be kind of a fifty-fifty arrangement, where the buyer and seller agreed who was going to pay what. But in this market, well..." she trailed off for effect.

"Let me guess," Ed had said, "if I want to write a strong offer, I pay the fees."

"You're a fast learner," said Cyndee.

"So how much?"

"Well, all the inspections, disclosures and closing costs are around $10,000 for this house."

Ed gasped.

"Well, you want the house, don't you," said Cyndee defensively.

"How do I know what all this stuff is for?"

"You'll receive a loan disclosure statement from your broker that will list all them individually. It's standard stuff."

Disclosure statement, thinks Ed. Okay. Where's my disclosure statement for the house on Arvee Street? He looks through the loan documents from Mickey, but doesn't find such a statement. He looks again. So, did Mickey fail to give him something he was entitled to? Ed begins reading the introduction on mandatory disclosures. He doesn't remember Mickey ever telling him anything, and here it says that it even should be "delivered" before an agreement is executed. That must be real estate talk for 'signed.' Well, what about this? "Generally, a seller will not be held liable for an error or inaccuracy on the disclosure form, so long as the seller did not have knowledge of the error or inaccuracy." Intentionally misrepresenting things; that seems to be the MO thinks Ed.

He continues down the page. "The judgments that have been awarded in cases involving violations of the seller disclosure laws include: 1.) Monetary damages to the buyer so that the misrepresented condition can be repaired; 2.) Payment of buyer's attorney's fees; 3.) Rescission of the contract (thereby allowing the buyer to void the transaction)." Ah, this is what he needs: rescission (say that five times fast) of the contract. He's found his leaking valve. Lack of disclosure and intentional misrepresentation could be used for rescission of the contract.

Curious, he now removes all of his loan documents from the bag and spreads them out, one above the other so he can compare them, on the table. If he understood the material correctly, all three of his loans should basically have the same disclosures. He checks the sample disclosure statements in the book again to make sure he's looking for the right thing, and then stares at all the documents. They are so complicated, and there are so many, and they use such obtuse words. How the hell was he supposed to know what was what? He just took Mickey's word for everything. He studies them: Whether it is the agreement with CCM for his home equity loan, or the purchase agreement from FB Property Management, the only thing he finds somewhere on almost all of them is MD LLC. And, he realizes, every one is signed in the same ink. Supposedly different people all signed in the same ink? Ed takes a closer look. That's got to be Mickey's stupid Mont Blanc fountain pen signature. But he thought that Mickey was just the lender, not the seller of the houses? But then, what is FB Property Management, and what is MD LLC? What if...

Somewhere he read that it's easy to look up companies online, so he quickly shuffles his papers together, shoves them back in the bag, and goes to the nearest computer desk. Here he types in "Registry of LLCs in California." Google immediately returns hundreds of hits. The third entry down is titled "California Business Portal." He clicks on it and, indeed, the California Business Portal comes up. There it is, right on the home page. "View the complete name of a limited liability company." This seems pretty easy. Ed types in 'MD LLC.' One second later, an entry appears: 'MD LLC Mickey Schulz and Daisy Schulz, Limited Liability Corporation since 2004.' Ed laughs out loud. Mickey is in business with his incontinent dog! Okay, there's got to be some kind of fraud being perpetuated here.

Next he types in 'FB Property Management, LLC,' and there it is, 'Frank Boy Properties, Limited Liability Corporation, a diversified funds property management company, Mickey Frank Schulz, sole owner.' FB! Fat Boy! They used to call him Fat Boy, so he took his middle name and used Boy! And, 'diversified funds properties,' now that's good. What a scumbag, thinks Ed. That means Mickey knew Ed was buying his dump on Arvee Street when Ed told him the address. Of course. He remembers now. There's got to be a conflict of interest here. In fact, did Mickey ever explicitly say that he owned the house on Mario Drive? Actually, no. He always implied that it belonged to someone else, and Ed…well, Ed never asked, because at that point, he wasn't thinking anymore, period.

Ed sits and watches the red light of sunset drain out of the sky while he ponders the state of his affairs. Finally, he admits that he can't get out of this alone, but he has a chance. What did they say? Lack of disclosures can lead to rescission of a contract. That's what he needs. He needs a lawyer, a really good one. He immediately thinks of the one person who, if he goes with his heart in his hands, will most likely help him out.

Ed gathers up his papers and returns the books to the reference desk. He thanks the Asshole for his help, looks around for the young woman, but she's gone. When he finally steps outside the library into the mild evening, he breathes deeply, enjoying the fresh air, after so many hours of stale books. He goes to his car, pulls out his phone and leans against the side. He hits the speed dial and waits for a connection while he stares at the first stars.

At the Schulz house, Michelle is watching "King Kong" with Sammy in the family room, while Mickey dishes out ice cream in the kitchen. She hears her cell phone ring.

"Hello," she says, warily, looking at the caller ID.

"Hey," says Ed, pausing just a fraction of a second. "Don't say anything, just listen first. I need help, legal help. Please."

*"Self-confidence is like a guarantee that you will end up where
you want to be. But you have to practice it every day. Make it a
goal to feel good about yourself. Remember:
You are who you goal you are."*
Ronald Ace, How to Be Great

18

Mickey is feeling in fine form this morning. It's a beautiful day at
the golf course. The dew is still on the grass where it is shaded by
trees. The sun is high enough that it doesn't make complicating
shadows, but not so high that it feels like it is beating down on
Mickey's bald spot through the thin strands of hair covering it.
He and Tatiana had fabulous sex last night, before he left the
office. The leather swivel chair is getting to be one of his favorite
places. And Tatiana is such an eager learner. He has a reoccurring
fantasy of going into business with her. She could really get
certain kinds of deals clinched.

"I don't know," says Keaton, a local realtor, "it's a substandard
lot, only 900 square feet." They're discussing a property Mickey
would like to sell him, as the group of four walk to the next tee.
The property is in the historical downtown, and has just gone on
the market for two million. The other two players are developers
whom Mickey has met only once.

"It's a perfect opportunity to make a move into commercial
real estate," insists Mickey. "How often does this location open
up? It's a steal!" He's hoping one of the other men will show
some interest as well.

"It's too small," scoffs Keaton.

"Make it look bigger. It's simple."

166

"What do you mean 'look bigger'?" asks Keaton.

Mickey opens his mouth to tell Keaton about an appraiser he likes to work with, but then thinks better of it. Keaton might not approve of some of Mickey's methods. Jealousy is hard to predict, and Mickey makes way more money than Keaton. He wouldn't want to place the appraiser in any jeopardy either. The guy is a real find. He's willing to make any deal work. He can juggle numbers, come up with comps that aren't comparable, blue sky values, you name it. And for a fee, he'll invert a number or two to make a lot appear bigger on paper, but in a way that looks like an honest mistake, if anyone ever notices.

"What about borrowing from one of the adjacent properties? Get an easement. Somebody will give you one, for a price. Everybody has a price. You just have to figure out what it is, and how to obtain it." That's a good line for my seminar, thinks Mickey, as he listens to himself. He makes a mental note. Then, feeling full of himself, he adds, "You know, Keaton, I can't just keep giving you free tips. You should come to one of my seminars."

Keaton ignores that last bit of bragging and says simply, "It seems like a lot of hassle for what it's worth."

"But nobody thinks about what it's worth, Keaton. That's the whole point. As long as you get your commission, what's the problem? You make money on the sale. Later, if it turns out your client can't afford it, oh well. You still might money on the way out too, if you play your cards right."

Mickey pulls out his driver and takes a tee and his ball to the tee box. He sets up his shot. "I just love this market," he says happily. "Whoever had the idea to package up these phony baloney loans with the good ones and then sell them off in shares was a genius. The FDA limits the amount of rat hair in food but no one is counting how many bad loans are mixed in with the good ones."

Keaton listens to him skeptically. He's all for investment income, but the telltale signs of the market imploding are making him feel uneasy. He's just started dabbling in commercial real estate, and he'd really like to see some hefty profits before the whole thing crashes. The thing is, how do you know when to take your cards off the table and get out? But maybe Mickey's right: There are still a lot of people thinking they can get rich in real estate. They are going to do it with or without him. May as well make some money. He watches Mickey as he positions his grip, corrects his stance, and takes his shot.

The ball goes straight, but high, and not very far down the fairway, dropping at about two hundred feet. Almost as if the two incidents had been timed together, Mickey's cell phone starts its insistent digital tone. He decides to answer.

"Yel-low," says Mickey with a self-satisfied air, listening for the voice at the other end. "Hey, Ed! What's up?" he says. "Got some more opportunities up your sleeve?" He motions to Keaton to go ahead with his shot, but of course Keaton doesn't want to take his shot with Mickey yakking. Keaton takes his golf seriously, and he's not about to play with Mickey blabbing in the background.

At the other end of the connection, Ed hears Mickey's voice and leans back against the black leather of his BMW in the parking lot of the County Recorders Office, where he's been ordering copies of various documents, most notably the title to his house—which is not in Ed's name. Ed has a slight smile on his face as he sits in the morning sunshine. He can tell by Mickey's voice that Mickey is expecting him to come crawling. It's the same voice that Mickey always used when he thought he was going to pull a fast one on someone. Ed remembers it from their youth.

"Listen, Mickey," says Ed, making his voice sorrowful, "you know the loan on the house you just sold me? It's only been a month and the payments have already adjusted. That doesn't seem right. Something must have gone haywire. I'm sure you said three month adjustable."

Has it really already been a month, thinks Mickey. His plan is working faster than he thought. "Well, Ed, that was a one-month adjustable. The other one was a three-month. But all you had to do with this one was paint the place and get it back on the market. So you see, I made it a month for a reason. You don't think I can afford to just give you money and let you sit on it."

What a stinking snake, thinks Ed. True to form, as always. When he finally caught up with Mickey about the unknown renters, Mickey had been unsympathetic to his plight. Ed's new lawyer, Adam Sentier, has filed a suit against the Bulkheads, but, like he said, renters are like fungus: hard to get rid of. Ed doesn't want to show his hand yet. He wants to see if there is any tiny, remaining streak of human empathy left in Mickey.

"Well," he says, after a brief pause, "how about the loan for the Arvee Street house? Those construction guys you sent me, international whatever, they tore all the walls out of the house, so now I'm nowhere near getting it back on the market. I thought you'd given me a three-month adjustable, just like the first one. But now, I see that the payment schedule is only a two-month adjustable. I really need a little flexibility here. For old time's sake. I just miscalculated."

Mickey chuckles warmly. "Eddie, Eddie!" he exclaims. He looks to see if Keaton is paying attention to the conversation, but, at that moment, Keaton has bent down to set his ball and all Mickey sees is his ass. Mickey looks at the other two players in their golf pastels. They are watching him. Mickey winks, and they turn quickly away and resume talking to each other in low tones.

"Listen, Ed. I was very generous with you! I can't just change things now because your houses aren't working out the way you expected. What kind of message would that send to my colleagues?"

"Yeah, but Mickey," he says. "We go back a long ways."

"I honor the relationship, Ed," answers Mickey. "But what matters is that you and I signed agreements. Legal agreements. I'm sorry things aren't working out for you," continues Mickey with a note of finality in his voice. He wants to let Ed know that things are going to play out the way he wants them to. The way he has set them up. Not the way Ed thinks he wants them.

Legal, thinks Ed, right. Okay, if that's how you want to play it, I gave you your chance. I may not be at your level of baloney but I'm learning. He was never much of an actor, but now he's going to give Mickey the full monty. He cranks up the self-pitying victim character.

"Come on, Mickey," he almost sobs, "I'm cracking under all the debt, I'm starting to think of suicide..." Ed takes a moment to sniffle, "I don't have a job. The kids. I don't know what to do. I have to sell the house."

Mickey can barely contain himself when he hears this. Yes, indeed! Things are working out faster than he even imagined! "Hey! Come on, buddy! Man-up! It's not so bad. We can work something out. For old time's sake." Mickey pauses as if he's thinking. "I'll tell you what. How about a million five for your old man's place? Would that solve your problems?"

Ed smiles cynically. He's guessed it right: Mickey knows exactly how much Ed's in debt for and he's been gaming for possession of Ed's house. He thinks that by taking ownership of Ed's house, he can tear it down and parcel all that land for condos, then sell them and make a bundle. He doesn't care anything about the neighborhood. "You know how my dad would be turning in his grave, Mickey," answers Ed sorrowfully. "But I don't know what else I can do."

Keaton is still waiting to take his shot. He and the other two golfers are getting impatient. All three sets of eyes are on Mickey. Mickey covers the microphone on his phone and says, in a low voice, more mouthing than vocalizing, "Poor slob." He uncovers the phone and lets his voice fill with empathy. "I'll tell you what, Ed. You come by my office tomorrow at one and we'll get it all straightened out."

Perfect, thinks Ed. That's just enough time to call the DA. "Okay. Thanks, Mickey. I love you man." Ed snaps his phone closed before Mickey can say another word. He sits there with a huge grin on his face. He did it. He's going to get Mickey hook, line, and sinker.

*"I research every detail of the deal I'm thinking of making.
Then, when it is time to move, I move fast because I've done
the background work. So the key to success is, prepare yourself
thoroughly and then, when it's time to move ahead, trump them."*
Ronald Ace, Don't Be A Loser

19

Outside of town, not far down the hill from the sewage treatment plant, is an open space preserve that is part of the river delta. It includes many acres of flat marsh and two large ponds lined with cattails and reeds. It's a favorite spot for birds—especially migrating birds—and other small wildlife, as well as that interesting species known as the 'birdwatcher.' On this particular early summer day, the amateur birdwatchers group is out enjoying a cool late morning walk around the ponds. The mist has cleared and the cattails and grasses are alive with the sounds of small birds. Geese, ducks, a few pelicans and a stray swan glide over the surface of the pond.

Mary Lou, the group's leader, breathes in the tangy air. She is an experienced birdwatcher from way back. She enjoys leading these amateur walkabouts because the people are friendly. She steps sprightly, for her age, along the gravel path, her binoculars swinging easily from her neck. Suddenly she stops. A shrill cry pierces the quiet.

"Listen group," she says in an excited, hushed tone. "It's a tern. They're hardly ever this far inland."

"A fern?!" shouts Oroville, the oldest member of the group. He is dressed in baggy pants and a canvas hat, is seventy-five, and is very hard of hearing. He has a hearing aid but he forgets to turn it on.

"Shhh!" says his wife with annoyance. "A Tern."

The group pauses and listens respectfully.

"Are you sure it's not a plover? I thought terns didn't fly this far inland," says Sandy, an older lady with abundant grey hair and one of the few not wearing a hat. Mary Lou doesn't respond because frankly, she is so engrossed in searching for the tern with her binoculars, the sky could fall and she wouldn't notice it.

"Maybe he's retired. He's trying to get to Hawaii," jokes Jake. Jake tags along with the group mostly just for something to do. He really doesn't care a fig about birds, let alone whether it's a tern or a plover. But he's become rather fond of Mary Lou.

Sandy turns and gives him a disparaging look. Men, she sniffs. Then her nose picks up the scent of something stinky. Good grief, what is it? She looks to her left and then to her right where she sees Oroville. Good grief, again. Is he wearing diapers? She sniffs loudly this time and grimaces.

Grace, Oroville's wife, whose hearing is excellent, is standing slightly in front of Sandy. She hears Sandy's obvious sniffing and turns to give her a dirty look. But then she picks up the scent as well. She looks around her. The smell grows stronger. One by one, the other members of the group notice the smell. They glance sideways at each other and shift from foot to foot.

Sandy is the first to look down. "Oh, my God," she gasps. The pathway is slowly being flooded by sludge oozing from the pond. She looks at her new leather walking shoes, and then up the hill at the sewage treatment plant.

As the group members grasp what is happening, they simultaneously raise their eyes to the hill. "There's a leak," whispers Grace. Only Mary Lou remains oblivious.

Back in town, Ed, who has prepared all night, pulls up to Mickey's building in his red BMW Z4 at exactly a quarter to one. He walks into the building carrying his WholePaychek recyclable grocery bag. Goes through Mickey's door to the reception area. No one is there. Tiffany must still be at lunch. Good, thinks Ed. He glances down the hall. Mickey's door is ajar. Ed quietly opens it. Mickey is at his desk, looking through a stack of papers. His laptop is running. Ed strides right up to the front of Mickey's desk before he says a word. Mickey looks up, startled.

"Hello, Mickey," says Ed. It's twelve-fifty. He's early, on purpose.

Mickey glares at the door Ed has just walked through, quickly turns and hits the 'close' button on his laptop, and then he glances at the clock. "Ed!" he says, pasting a phony smile on his face, a false ring of joviality in his voice. "So early? Let's go into the conference room, shall we?" He scoops up the papers he was working on as he stands up. "Nice briefcase, by the way," says Mickey, looking pointedly at Ed's bag as he rounds the corner of his desk.

"No, no," says Ed, holding up his hand towards Mickey. "Stay. This is fine." And he sits himself firmly down in the chair facing Mickey's desk and places his shopping bag beside him. "Nice hair, by the way." Mickey's got a comb-over. Sucker.

Mickey looks at Ed with narrowed eyes. "Okay, if you insist," he says after a moment's pause. He is annoyed to be upstaged in his own office, but he wants this to go as smoothly and quickly as possible. He sits back down in his leather office chair and quickly separates the pages into two stacks, one he pushes over towards Ed. Then he emits a loud, theatrical sigh.

"I'm really sorry it came to this, Ed. I thought you'd be able to handle it better. But you know, sometimes it's just one of those life lessons. And let's face it, change can be good. So, who's to say whether this is for better or for worse. Do you have a pen?" He holds out one of his Mont Blanc pens for Ed.

"Got my own," says Ed, pulling one from his shirt pocket. "What do you do? Buy those things wholesale?"

Mickey ignores the remark. "So, first: here's the purchase agreement for your old man's house. Like I said, it's a million and a half. You're getting a good price. The market is starting to fall. If you were to put it out there now, you'd be lucky to even get a million. And, this is enough to pay off all your debts—and stop the interest from accruing!—and get a new start somewhere else. At a more moderate standard than you have now, of course, but then modesty has always been one of your strengths."

Mickey finally stops. He gives Ed a sympathetic, expectant smile. Ed stares back. He's seeing the whole fiasco flash through his mind. Tatiana chasing after him. Him asking Mickey for help on a home equity loan to impress her. Mickey sending him that jerk-off construction company who wrecked his house. Him being blinded by lust and agreeing to buy that dump without doing any homework. And then, him running around like a bull in heat, chasing after Tatiana all the time, doing a lousy job at work, a lousy job with his kids, and an even lousier job keeping track of things. Then Mickey fast-talking him into an even worse investment. Him quitting his job to impress Tatiana. The arrogance and idiocy of it all! But it's no excuse for Mickey.

Ed studies Mickey. "Are you really sorry? After all these years of wanting what I had, you think you've finally trumped me, don't you?"

Mickey raises his eyebrows and shrugs neutrally, but inside, he's gloating. It's the coup he's been waiting for.

Ed looks down at the first document on the pile in front of him. It's a computer-generated residential purchase agreement for his house. He really takes me for a fool, thinks Ed. The offer is from FB Property Management LLC, the same company that had to foreclose on the property on Mario Drive. Ed doesn't say anything, just keeps scanning down the document. He's got a plan that he worked out with Michelle and Adam, and he's going to follow through. So far, Mickey doesn't seem to suspect anything. But Ed needs to be very careful. He's an amateur, and Mickey is not only a seasoned professional, he's a scammer: he's got scam radar.

The offer is one and a half million dollars cash, and there is no clause regarding financing. Mickey doesn't need financing. It's impressive that he has this kind of money available, and on such short notice. Michelle was smart to keep track of things.

"Wow, I get forty-five days to vacate the property?" exclaims Ed when he reads that line. "What if I can't find something to move into in that time?"

"Well, I suppose we could figure something out where I can rent it back to you, if you need a little more time," answers Mickey smoothly.

Ed shakes his head. What a guy. He doesn't say anything, just keeps reading, line by line. He's not surprised to see that Mickey has declined a lot of standard things, like inspections.

"Uh, listen, Ed," says Mickey with growing impatience. "This is all just standard stuff like the other deals. I don't have all afternoon here. You asked for help, and I'm offering it."

Ed looks blankly at Mickey, and then makes an exaggerated reach for his phone and checks the time. "It's only one-ten," he says. "You didn't expect me to be finished with all these pages in ten minutes did you?"

"Well, I have another appointment," says Mickey. He's meeting Tatiana at two, and she hates to wait. Ed's plodding approach is getting under his skin and he doesn't want to take any chances. She'd show up at his office if he was late.

Ed flips the page with exaggerated care and begins at the top of page two. A little ways down, he notices that the seller is shown as covering the escrow costs and transfer taxes. Ed also notices that Mickey is taking a commission as both the buying and selling agent. Ed can't help but shake his head. What a guy, he thinks, he never misses a chance to make a buck. He reminds himself to pay close attention to whether or not Mickey has included a dual agency disclosure, like he should have done in the other two deals as well. He casually flips through the rest of the pages. No loan disclosure, no notice of right to cancel, no title report, and most of all, no indication anywhere of who holds the deed to the property! What an idiot! Mickey has still not done a real title search. Ed feels like laughing out loud. Ed isn't even a trustee of the trust!

Finally he comes to the settlement statement. On the

settlement statement, Ed sees that there is a credit of $1,500,000 and a list of impressive fees to MD Financing. There is a $495 processing fee, a $95 tax service fee, a document preparation fee of $400, an appraisal fee of $400, escrow fees of $2,798, title insurance of $3,257 (Where the hell is he getting all these numbers, thinks Ed.), an agent's compensation of $90,000, and finally a loan approval fee of $150,000. A 'loan approval fee.' The old kick-back. Mickey just couldn't resist.

"What the hell!" Ed bursts out. "A loan approval fee?"

"It's my fee," answers Mickey.

"For what?"

"For the cash," says Mickey shrugging nonchalantly.

"So, without my calculator, the bottom line on this agreement is that I get $1,252,555 out of one and a half million dollars? Is that what you're saying?"

"Because you need me."

"That's steep."

"You're still getting a million and a quarter. That's a lot of dough! It ought to last you a week or so." Mickey can't keep the chortling out of his voice now. It feels so good to really sucker somebody into a position where you know they can't move.

"Wow. Is this legal?" asks Ed. Of course he knows that it's dirty play now, but he wants to lull Mickey into calm before he really hits him. Every single one of his loans from Mickey had a kick-back attached.

"Anything is legal, Eddie, to the right people. Caveat emptor...let the buyer beware! You speculated. You wanted easy, free money so you could profit from the real estate market. You assumed you'd be able to do certain things in a certain amount of time and that the market would always stay up. But guess what, Eddie boy? Nothing stays up forever. You lost. Now be a man and take your lumps. There will be other opportunities for you."

"And you make money both ways. Does that seem fair?"

"It's not about fairness," laughs Mickey. "It's about service! I provide a service in a service economy. You used my service. I deserve to be paid."

Ed lets that 'deserve to be paid' hang in the air between them for a moment before he continues. "That may be, Mick, but not when the service is packaged like a product and is fraudulent. You basically sold me a fraudulent product." Before Mickey can answer, Ed reaches down into his shopping bag and pulls out his sheaf of papers and some notes. He pushes Mickey's sale contract aside. Then he dons a concerned expression on his face as he studies his notes.

"Listen, Mick, before I sign this, I have a few concerns that I need to run by you."

"Shoot," says Mickey. He glances at the clock. "Just hurry up." His eyes take on a guarded look. What the hell is going on here? He taps his pen against the desk.

"Well, as I was going through my three loan documents," says Ed, separating one group of paper-clipped pages from the others, "I noticed that there was no loan disclosure statements for any of them." He raises his eyebrows as if to say, what gives?

"Golly gosh," says Mickey, "it must have been an oversight."

"But it's missing on all three of the loans you gave me."

"It's a technicality, Ed. What are you getting at here? I buy lots of errors and omissions insurance, exactly for that reason. It happens. To everyone. Now let's get on with our business and like I said, I have another meeting at two."

Ed hands him the paper clipped pages.

"What the hell is this?"

"It's a loan cancellation on my house and two deeds in lieu on the other two properties. It's illegal to not give disclosures. So I'm giving you back your two crappy houses. And good luck with the folks who've moved in. It is impossible to get rid of renters with today's renter protection legislation."

Mickey looks at Ed speechless. He feels his blood pressure rising. The sun is hitting the window now. "What are you talking about? If you think I'm signing any of these, you're crazy! I'll take you to court for the money and win easily. You OWE me that money. Lack of disclosures is just a technicality."

"Okay, what about this?" says Ed. He reaches down into his bag and pulls out a copy of the title to his house. He dangles it in front of Mickey. "Do you know what this is?" Ed laughs. "My old man thought I was an idiot. So he put the property in a trust and it's never left." He pauses, waiting for a reaction from Mickey. "I can't sell or encumber it because I don't own it. The trust owns the property, and it's executed by a law firm. I'm not even a trustee. So, aside from charging me for title searches…" Ed points at the new documents Mickey had prepared for him, "that you never actually carried through, you don't have any collateral for your loans."

Mickey's mouth drops open. "You had to disclose that," he sputters.

"Well, I am now," says Ed shrugging.

"No!" says Mickey adamantly. "You had to disclose that when you borrowed money from me the first time. The house is the collateral for the loan I gave you!"

"That's what I just indicated. But I pay property taxes every year so I just forgot. If you hadn't been so eager to screw me…"

"Hey, fuck you, small time! You still owe me over a million dollars."

"Well," says Ed looking straight at Mickey, "that depends on who you're talking to, right?" Oh this is good. Mickey's face is getting redder and redder. Ed wants to keep pushing him till he's got his ass is sticking out the other side of the wall.

Mickey rises from his chair. He's about had enough of this. He can get his money another way.

"No wait!" says Ed. "There's more."

Mickey narrows his eyes and sits back down in his chair, waiting.

"There was also no real estate transfer disclosure."

"You noticed that too late. You have three days to claim that, and you didn't, so you lose," Mickey answers.

"What about disclosing that you are selling your own listings. Both those houses were yours."

"Wait a minute. I didn't own the house on Arvee Street and the agent who sold it to you, it was her responsibility to disclose that," insists Mickey. "As for the Mario Drive house, it wasn't even on the market. You were the first person to see it."

"So why was there a lock box on it? And you had no seller financing disclosure on that one either!"

"I'm telling you, I didn't own it. FB properties owned it!" Mickey is clearly flustered now. This whole meeting, which was to be so simple, has veered off in a totally unexpected direction.

"Ah, you're right," says Ed with a friendly smile. "Yes, those 'hard-nosed' LLC's. Loans from MD Financial, not you. Properties owned by DM Properties and FB Property Management, not you. And now, it's not you who is actually buying my house, it's... let's see..." Ed reaches over for the contract Mickey gave him and looks at the bottom line. "Ah yes, here it is! FB Property Management. But isn't MD Financial in the process of foreclosing on FB properties? And let's look at this." Ed folds back the pages in his hand to the yellow sticker, then he takes another sheaf of papers and folds them back to a yellow sticker. Now he places the two documents side by side in front of Mickey. "Look at these signatures! No matter what the business, the signatures all look similar and just happen to be all signed in the exact same colored ink and, judging by the flow of the ink, it looks like your Mont Blanc pen."

"What the hell are you getting at here, Ed? Do you know how many people use Mont Blanc pens?"

"True, but what an amazing coincidence. Country Club Mortgage Company, MD Finance LLC, DM Properties LLC, and FB Property Management LLC all use the same ink and signature. One is a broker, two are real estate holding companies, and the other is a lender. Don't you think it would sound like a conflict of interest, if it were put before a judge? Without disclosure, I mean. And wait!" Ed holds up his hand to stop Mickey from the next string of expletive about to exit his mouth. "I just love this, and I know a court would, too." Ed reaches down into his bag and pulls out three photo copies. "Daisy is your managing partner! How many properties does she owns, Mick? Hey, maybe disclosure rules don't apply to dogs?"

Mickey feels drops of sweat trickling down his temples. His mind is reeling with possibilities, none of them good. He always thinks so fast on his feet, but now his brain is failing him, just in his moment of need. He's frozen! He can't think of anything to say! Then, Mickey's cell phone rings. He reaches to grab it so fast that he almost slips off his chair.

"Hello?" he barks, without looking at the phone number. It's Tatiana, of course.

Ed watches his face closely. He glances at the time. It's two o'clock and he's almost got Mickey where he needs him. They'll be arriving in just a few more minutes.

Mickey glares at Ed as he listens to the voice at the other end of the call. "Listen, I'm caught up in a meeting," he answers. "I know I'm late. I'll try to hurry." He wants to hang up on her, but at the same time, it's an opportunity to try and figure out a way to stall Ed so he can cover up his tracks. But she won't be placated.

"Do you know I paid for this room?!" she shouts into the phone.

"Yes, yes, Tatiana!" Oh, hell! The name slipped out his mouth. "Not now!" he snaps, and shuts his phone. He glares at Ed daring him to say a word, and his face gets another notch redder.

"Oh," says Ed with mild surprise. "So, you are screwing my girlfriend."

"Tough luck," says Mickey spitefully, "She found bigger fish to fry, if you get my meaning. Who put you up to all this anyway? This is way beyond your skill set. I bet Michelle is behind all this."

"So, that's what you think of me? You think I'm just as much of an idiot as my dad. You think nice guys are stupid, don't you?" answers Ed. "Nope. Michelle did not put me up to this. I just finally did what I should have done at the very beginning. So," Ed clears his throat, "where was I? We have no disclosures on anything, including technicalities like real estate transfer, dual agency, seller financing, et cetera. Then we have charging for phony appraisals and title searches. Not nice, but it's small potatoes. The deed to my house is your problem, technically. But you and Daisy loaning money, now THAT is a violation of federal law. And loaning private money outside of your registered mortgage brokerage is a serious violation of the real estate code, and probably illegal as well. And a dog as a property owner and managing partner of an LLC. And, if you signed Daisy's name, we can add forgery. Mickey, you've outdone yourself. But you couldn't stop there. You just had to add your favorite—the kick back loan. That is against the Federal Anti-Predatory Lending Policy and Federal Anti-Kickback Law, didn't you know that?"

Mickey rises up in his chair, his face is now as red as lingerie from Violet's Secret. His fists are held halfway up in the air.

"Oh, wait!" exclaims Ed. "I forgot to mention extortion and tax fraud for stealing money from your own illegal LLC..."

"Why you mousy, sniveling sewer plant worker! Who do you think you are?" shouts Mickey, jumping onto his desk and lunging for Ed. Ed, however, is expecting this and he pops out of his seat and sidesteps Mickey who crashes onto the seat, and onto the floor.

Hearing the crash, Tiffany, who's returned from lunch, comes running. "Oh my God!" she screams. "Is everything all..." she stutters but can't even complete her question, seeing Mickey in a pile with the chair on the floor.

Mickey lurches to his feet and lunges again towards Ed.

"Yeah, come and get me, you dishonest, cheating bag of shit," roars Ed, and he throws himself at Mickey with the full force of all his anger. He shoves that dishonest cheat, who has been responsible for so much misery in his life, right into the wall, head first. Mickey crashes like an overweight dog and sinks to the floor.

"You know what I have to say to you?" says Ed, picking him up by the lapels. He has been waiting to say this ever since he was four years old. "This!" And he lets fly a right-handed fist into Mickey's jaw. "I should've done that to you long ago," he says. He stands up, returns to the desk, scoops his papers into his shopping bag, picks up the bag and steps towards the door.

"You…" growls Mickey. He staggers up from the floor and throws himself at Ed's legs.

Ed had planned on Mickey being on the floor longer. Or, on himself getting out the door faster. When the weight of Mickey catapults into Ed's knees, Ed loses his balance and crashes against the door frame, almost dropping his bag. He kicks against Mickey's chest and shoulder in rhythm with Tiffany's screams and moans from the outer office until Mickey finally loosens his grip. Ed seizes the moment and slips free, jumping over Mickey's prostrate body, and reaches for the one thing in that office that he knows will make Mickey really scream: Mickey's signed, Pete Rose baseball sitting on a small gold pedestal on his desk.

That ball is the beginning of everything Ed really hates about Mickey. Mickey couldn't play baseball worth a nickel, and yet he won the baseball at the Little League Fundraiser. And why did he win it? Because he cheated. Ed saw him cheat. And yet Ed couldn't bring himself to say anything because, frankly, he wanted that ball so badly he would've cheated himself, except he just didn't know how.

Ed strains his arm as far as he can reach. His fingers touch the ball and curl around it. Then he is clasping it in his hand. He pulls it from the pedestal and whips around towards Mickey.

"Eat this, you thief," he spits at Mickey. And he shoves the ball with all his strength at Mickey's surprised and open mouth. Of course it doesn't fit. It's just symbolic. But it's enough to injure his teeth, get some bloodstains on the ball, and slow the action enough so that…

"Mickey Schulz?" booms a loud voice from the doorway.

"If you're going to cheat, cheat huge. Really huge."
Ronald Ace, The Art of Big

20

Mickey hears the voice cutting through his rage like the sound of an approaching freight train. In slow motion, he cradles his Pete Rose baseball in one hand, his mouth in the other, and turns towards the door. A large, imposing figure in a dark suit, with two other dark blue figures like a double shadow behind him, stands blocking the door.

"Oh!" says Ed chirpily. "Look Mick! It's some friends of yours! Your chickens are finally coming home to roost."

Mickey glances at Ed as if he's lost his mind.

"I have a warrant for your arrest," says the tall, elderly figure holding out an ID badge and an envelope. "District Attorney Dinkle here."

"Mickey! It's your friend the district attorney," says Ed with heavy sarcasm. This is the moment he has been working towards for over a week. All those hours in that dusty library, all that time tracking down titles and records, and all that sweat pouring over his loan documents line by line, word by word. And then, putting it all together along with all the information about accounts and deals that Michelle gave him. And now finally: He's got Mickey Schulz.

"Ed?" says a familiar voice.

Now it's Ed's turn to be surprised. There, behind the DA and the two police officers, stands Michelle.

"What are you doing here?" says Ed in surprise. The two

184

policemen step away from the door to let Michelle into Mickey's office, which is getting rather crowded at this point.

"What are you doing here," growls Mickey, glaring at Michelle.

"Oh, I just thought that, before they lock you up, I should at least get the preliminary divorce papers to you. It's all standard stuff," says Michelle, looking from Mickey, to Ed, to the DA to the waiting policemen. "Oh, Mr. Dinkle!" She remembers him from her father's office. "How are you?"

"Fine, fine."

"May I have a moment?"

The DA shrugs. Michelle reaches into her handbag and pulls out a thick manila envelope. She lays it on the desk, opens it and pulls out the pages. "All you have to do is look them through and initial the pages in a few places." She sees Mickey's Mont Blanc pen on the desk and picks it up. Then she pauses. "Or would you rather take the envelope with you and study it while you're in jail?" She looks at Mickey quizzically, pen in hand. "I'll make sure you get Daisy in the settlement, since you two are apparently in business together."

Ed feels like laughing out loud. He feels giddy, exhausted, and thrilled all at the same time. Michelle is divorcing Mickey! He wants to shout at the sky. He looks at Mickey's fuming, red face and longs to say something cutting and witty. But at that moment, yet another figure appears at the door.

In struts Tatiana wearing a new, hot pink suit. "Why you not returning my calls? I call you and call you, but no, you don't answers me, and now…" She stops in mid-sentence, and her glare moves from Mickey to Ed. "Eddie? What are you doing here?"

Ed smiles as the words form in his mind, 'I could ask you the same thing,' but before he can speak them, Tatiana's glare has moved on to the DA. Then she focuses all the intensity of her beam on Michelle.

"Who is this? I know you," she says suspiciously.

"Don't you remember? I'm his wife. We met at the ball park.

Actually, I'm soon to be his ex-wife because Mickey is being divorced."

"Divorce?" It only takes a split second for Tatiana's mind to calculate all the possible functions of this statement. "Oh, Mickey!" she exclaims, stepping towards him and throwing her arms around his neck. "Now we can marry!"

"You Astonian phony," says Ed. This is more unbelievable than he'd ever dreamed. "I should call the INS."

"Oh, shut up, you shit plant worker," says Tatiana, never one to mince words.

Ed laughs. "I wish. I'd love to have my job back and make all this as if it had never happened," he says. But the moment he hears his words, he realizes how wrong that is. He'd still be nobody if all this had never happened. "You two deserve each other," he says looking from Mickey to Tatiana. "In the immortal words of The Ronald: Tatiana? You're cooked! Meet your new boss, The Crook!"

"He's better than you," snaps Tatiana. "He more like The Ronald than you ever be. You make mess of real estate. He's The Mickey!" And with that, she delivers a wet kiss to Mickey's cheek.

The DA stands mesmerized by what is transpiring. He feels like he has fallen into a bad B movie. Like watching people on You-tube who are totally ridiculous, but you just can't stop watching. He glances at his watch. Time is nipping at his heels. He still has to go through all the paperwork with this Schulz guy, and he swore to his wife he would be on time for dinner, for a change. They're going out to the Cormorant for her birthday, and he really doesn't want to mess it up. The boys have invited him to go do a little gambling at Rookie Oaks Casino next month and he thinks it'd be a hoot to go.

"Mickey Schulz, you're going to have to come with us," he says firmly, interrupting Tatiana's little love fest.

"Mickey?" says Tatiana, her expression suddenly very different. Something isn't right here. Now she notices the policemen waiting in the reception area. Now she feels the tension in the room. She frowns at Ed, as if it's his fault. Something is clearly amiss. "You going to jail?" she says looking at Mickey suspiciously. "Humph!" She pulls her shoulders back so her beautiful cleavage gleams between the hot pink lapels of her suit in the overhead lighting of Mickey's office. She shrugs her shoulders. "Don't worry," she says to Mickey. "I have other offer. You always come late anyway." And she turns on her heels, smiles officiously at the gaping group, and struts out the door.

Ed, Mickey, the DA, the policemen, Michelle, and even Tiffany, from the outer office, watch Tatiana's hot pink figure as it disappears out the front door without saying another word. Even Michelle has to admit, that woman sure knows how to make an exit. She turns to the DA.

"Mr. Dinkle?" she says.

Mr. Dinkle tears himself away from the after-image of Tatiana's gorgeous posterior disappearing out the door. "Yes?"

"Can Mickey still be served divorce papers if he's in prison?"

"Oh, absolutely," says Mr. Dinkle, just as a cell phone starts ringing. He pats his coat pocket and pulls out a phone. But it's not his. Michelle digs through her purse, pulls out her phone. But it's silent. Mickey looks at his BlackBerry where it lays on the desk, but it's not ringing. Finally Ed realizes, it's his old Motorola. In all the excitement of the moment, he totally forgot he even owned a phone.

"Sorry folks," he smiles goofily. "Hello?"

"Ed?" says the voice at the other end of the line. "This is Robert Newfield from the sanitary district office. We've got a serious problem down at the plant. Steward really screwed things up, and we need you to come in and fix them. Now."

Nothing could have been further from Ed's mind than the Sump Valley Sewage Treatment Plant at this particular moment in time. But now, it all comes back. Of course! The in-flow and out-flow valves were painted the same color because Steward thought it looked more aesthetic. "I'll be over as soon as I can. I just need to finish off a little business here."

He closes his phone and looks at the expectant faces around him. "Well, folks," he says gallantly. "I'm off to save the Shit Plant! Goodbye and good riddance, Tatiana," he says as he looks at the door where she disappeared. "Can I visit you in prison, Mickey?" Mickey's face has gone from red to white rage. "Michelle," he says turning towards her, "I always loved you, even if you married that bastard instead of me. And finally," he turns to Mr. Dinkle. "Mr. DA, thank you for your help. I've learned so much."

Ed majestically picks up his green recyclable bag and walks to the door. He opens it and steps out into the sunshine.

"Ed! Ed!" calls Michelle running out after him.

Ed stops, turns and looks at her. Her black hair is loose, and she's smiling.

"Yes?" he says hopefully.

"Buddy has a baseball game tonight!"

Ed's face falls. "Oh," he answers. What in the world was he thinking Michelle was going to say? "I am probably going to have to work through the night. Jayne and Montana headed back this morning, so I'm kind of stuck. Do you think…Would you mind, taking care of Meledy and Buddy. Please?"

Michelle rolls her eyes. Somewhere up in the palm tree she hears blackbirds arguing. "You goof," she says, shaking her head. "Of course, I'll take care of them." And she steps towards Ed and throws her arms around his neck and plants a long kiss on his waiting lips.

21

It's late evening at the Sump Valley Sewage Plant. The sun has sunk below the horizon, the big sky overhead is indigo, the first bright stars appear. Somewhere in the dusk, a portable generator starts with a sputter and then sends out a steady grinding hum.

"Okay," shouts a man's voice. "Here it goes." The crew members from the sanitary district, joined by an extra crew from the water district, stop what they're doing and hold their breath for an instant.

The darkness around them is suddenly flooded with light. A rack of high voltage lights, fastened to the top of a hundred-and-fifty foot crane set up between the sediment tanks, and looking like some kind of weird space station, glares down at the scene. A large tank truck parked next to the settling pond starts up its engine again and begins pumping contaminated water out of the pond as fast as it can. A second truck pulls up behind, ready to take over.

Ed stands in the middle of all this action, clipboard in hand, wearing a hardhat, directing crew, equipment, and materials.

"Over there!" he shouts at the driver of a lumber truck as it pulls up in the eerie daylight. "The wood needs to be dropped by the sediment tanks." He turns to Dave. "Has operations gotten the skimmer arm in place and locked down?"

"Sure has, boss," answers Dave.

"Good. Then get Frank to fasten some four-by-fours to the

skimmer arm and we'll use it to support one end of the deck units."

"You mean one deck on each side of the arm?"

"Yeah. That should work. Then we'll set the other end of the decks on the concrete lip of the tank. That should give us a pretty safe platform to work on. Then, get Frank up there to fix up a wooden valve that will fasten to the inside of the tank. He could make it adjustable, to let some of the sludge flow out of the tank. It'll be easier for operations to monitor the flow." Ed keeps his eye closely on the gangway of the primary settling tank where Frank, wearing a hazardous material suit, is trying to install a temporary fitting.

"Do you think it's going to work?" asks Robert Newfield, walking up to Ed. He is also wearing a hard hat and a concerned look on his face.

"I don't know," answers Ed, "but we're certainly going to try our best. It's not going to be cheap. Doug! When Frank's finished up there, hoist Dan up too. This isn't an ideal fix-up, but with any luck the unit should be back on line in three or four hours, and then the trucks can just pump the contaminates from the pond directly into the tank."

"What do you think happened?"

"The relief flow valve froze, plus, the back pressure valve and the flow valve pipes were painted the same color so somebody released the flow valve thinking it was the relief valve. It's a fairly honest mistake. The problem was with the regulation. Steward was not into regulation. He just wanted things to look good."

"Well, he's gone now. I terminated him on the spot. I never did like that little brown-noser. We are hoping that you're going to be willing to come back. With a raise in pay grade, naturally."

"Do I get my own bowl of nuts?" asks Ed.

"You bet," says Robert Newfield, chuckling.

Early the next morning, when the sun is just barely coming up over the horizon on a new day, a disheveled Ed walks into his kitchen. Not much magic happened here, he thinks, looking around at the same old mess. Well, Jayne never was one for housekeeping. Ed takes the coffee pot, rinses it, fills it with water, and prepares himself a fresh pot of coffee. Just as it starts to brew, and the warm, nutty aroma fills the room, Meledy comes padding in, her slippers flapping softly against her heels.

"Dad!"

"Meledy!" says Ed. Meledy walks up to him and he hugs her for a very long time. "Boy, have I missed you. It seems like I haven't seen you in over a month."

"It's only been like a week." Meledy considers him and then reaches up and ruffles his hair. "TG you're not wearing that stupid hair anymore. What'd you do with Mz. Real Estate?"

Ed coughs slightly. "I don't know. Last seen, she was apparently with Mickey." He looks straight into Meledy's eyes. "Listen, beautiful. I'm sorry. I think you've probably suffered most for this. We all make mistakes sometimes, and this was a biggy on my part. But I want to tell you something. I had a friend once who said that even if you fall on your face, you're moving forward." He shrugs. "After years of being so careful that we never moved forward, at least we're finally somewhere else. Look at all that's happened. You got your smart phone with upps. Eventually we'll get the house put back together and it'll be way nicer than before. And, I'm the general manager at the plant now."

"Dad, that's great!" says Meledy, genuinely happy for this news. Then she snickers. "But I can tell you one thing. It'll be a long time before I ever think about getting seriously involved with someone of the opposite sex."

"No!" exclaims Ed. "Don't say that! I want grandchildren."

"Yuck, Dad," answers Meledy, her face blushing.

"Hey, Dad!" says Buddy walking in from the living room, where he had fallen asleep the night before. "You were on the news last night! You saved everybody from contamination in their water! You're a hero!"

"No, go on!" says Ed in disbelief.

"Honest! Michelle TiVo-ed it so you can watch."

"Hey, speaking of Michelle...Who called your mother? Why did she suddenly show up here?"

Meledy looks at Ed. "Dad! You were sinking! Even I could see that. I called Mom. Why would you think Michelle would call her?"

"They're still friends, aren't they?"

Meledy shrugs. "IDK, but I'm the one who said she needed to come and help us quick before something really bad happened."

"Well, thank you, Meledy. I'm glad you took it on yourself to do that. I don't want to get moralistic on you kids, but remember this: Everybody shits and we've all got to pitch in and do our part."

At that moment there is a loud banging on the door. Buddy runs to open it and is greeted by a camera and microphone being shoved towards his face.

"Is this the Feceoli residence?" asks a woman.

"FASOULI residence!!!!" yells Ed. "Get out of here! Shut the door, Buddy!"

Buddy slams the door in her face.

"Just let him cool off," shrugs the woman reporter, turning to the cameraman. "Let's go get coffee and come back in an hour. It is a little early."

The two walk down the path to their van, which they parked on the street directly in front of Ed's Mercedes so that it blocked his driveway. Only now, they are blocked in by a white construction truck parked directly in front of them.

"Wait, turn on the camera!" says the reporter to her cameraman in excitement. "Look!"

The side of the truck is painted with the words, "INePT Construction."

"I'll bet these guys have a story!" she says, rushing forwards towards the three odd-looking men exiting the truck. Before she can reach them, the dark, curly haired man reaches into the back of the truck and pulls out a huge tool box which he swings around to the driveway, knocking the turbaned man to the ground.

The camera man can't stop laughing. "It's the Three Stooges on diversity! I don't believe it!"

"Oh, stop," she says. "What is it that guys have about the Three Stooges?"

But she never finds out what their story is because Ed, noticing them through a new hole in the front room, throws open the front door and screams.

"Get out of here! You're fired! Fired! Fired!"

22

Golf is a beautiful game. But a wedding, if you've looked forward to it for twenty years, is even better. The yard is now beautifully landscaped with native shrubs and flowers. The natural, rock-lined pool shimmers deep blue under the perfectly clear sky. Behind the wedding party, standing on a stone pad built at one end of the pool, where the natural filtration system trickles pleasantly over an artificial stone creek bed lined with reeds, Ed and Michelle give their vows of fidelity and commitment. Michelle found out that she much prefers Ed to her toys, and Ed—well, it turns out Michelle is even more fun than Tatiana and her washing machine. Meledy, Buddy and Sammy beam as they stand beside the happy couple, while Robert and Doug stand with their families among the guests wondering if they too might have overlooked some illegal clause in their loan agreements that could possibly get them out from under the burgeoning debt they owe.

Ed's house, which is now Michelle's house too, sits harmoniously in the landscape, with its new wing and a natural teakwood deck where the caterers have set up the party and are waiting for the ceremony to finish. The musicians are set up over by the hot tub and wait for the cue to break into the final wedding march. In the background, all the way along the back property fence, visible only by an occasional shimmer as the shifting light

194

S. Pareto Rose

hits it, is a tall plexiglass fence. Occasionally, a golf ball pops against it and goes flying back somewhere onto the golf course.

"Do you take this man to be your lawful husband?" intones the pastor, raising his weedy-looking eyebrows.

"Oh, I do!" exclaims Michelle.

"You may kiss the bride," says the old coot, smiling slyly at Ed, and all the guests clap and whistle.

Unbeknownst to the wedding party, Mickey Schulz is having his own moment in the limelight. He is dressed in a bright orange jumpsuit that tends to bring out his rotund form, and yet lends him a certain authority. He stands behind a wooden table at the front of a brightly lit room. There are bars on the windows. Behind him is a carefully painted banner, obviously done by hand, but with an air of legitimacy nevertheless. It reads: 'Future Real Estate Agents of America.'

"Hello, gentlemen," he says jovially. "I'm Mickey-if-you-have-a-pulse-I-can-get-you-a-loan!"

The men in the packed room, dressed in look-alike orange jumpsuits, clap, shout and whistle back. The handful of guards, leaning against the back walls, chuckle.

"Thank you, thank you!" says Mickey, pleased. "Welcome to my seminar on how to make money in real estate. And I can see that you fellas have what it takes to succeed in this business. In today's market, nobody cares how real the assets are. What matters are the risks you're willing to take in order to get the wealth you deserve!"

"Yeah!" the men in the audience hoot and holler. "Tell it like it is, brother Schulz!"

"I'm telling you, now this is absotutely fab'lous opportunity," says Tatiana, leading a group of prospective buyers past the FOR SALE sign and up the walkway towards the front door of a very large, rather new house, on a corner lot surrounded by palm trees.

Trumped

The clutch of miscellaneous people gathering round include an ageless woman with flaming red hair and a tattoo going from her chest up to her neck. A fat lady dressed in a track suit is already perspiring in the morning warmth, while two middle-aged contractor-types keep staring at Tatiana rather than the house. A young man in an off-the-rack business suit looks anxiously around, while a middle-aged real estate woman dressed in apricot is trying to edge past the fat lady to be first through the doorway. At the edge of the group is Jake, a senior citizen, who's come along more for the entertainment than for the business opportunity. All of them have plastic clipboards and pens, provided by CT LLC Foreclosure Tours, with a list of the various houses that they will be visiting this morning during the next three hours. They have shelled out a hundred and fifty dollars for the high-end market tour. It better be good.

Tatiana, dressed in her deeply cut, red linen suit, and also carrying a clipboard and list and a spiral notebook containing flyers for each of the properties should someone in the group wish more information, waves at the white Mercedes van parked at the curb. Cyndee, who's stepped out for a smoke, leans against the outside of the van, partially covering the brand new lettering across the side: 'CT LLC Foreclosure Tours.' Her pin-striped, button-down shirt, with a white collar, and her very short, navy blue skirt gives her a definite professional look. She's taken over the driving and the organizing of the tour route because she can't stand dealing with the stupid questions people ask. She smiles back at Tatiana, licks her glossy lips and winks.

"Now, this almost-brand-new house has also fab'lous pool with hot tub, in addition to four bedrooms, five bathrooms and media room. Is too bad owners had to fork-losh, but is your opportunity." She gives the group a winning smile and unlocks the lockbox, takes the key, and opens the door. She stands holding the door open as the members of the group push like impatient dogs into the house.

"Wait till you see inside," she tells the fat lady as she smiles

196

encouragingly and steps aside to make room for her. "You will understand that this is really house to make dreams for!"

"You sure you don't want flyer?" she says to Jake.

"Na, I'm just here for the fun of it," answers Jake.

The nervous young businessman hurries to catch up with Jake. "I don't get exactly how this buy-in plan works," he says to the older man. "We pay eleven thousand dollars to buy in. Then, they buy the house, and we pay for the upgrading? But who decides about selling the house?"

"Who knows?" says Jake. "But look at it this way: A guy like you. Where are you going to get a chance to buy a house like this for eleven thousand dollars down? Wow, look at this entry, will you," he whistles. The dark green vibrates against the rust colored walls of the room beyond.

One of the contractors, following right behind them, has been listening in on the conversation.

"I mean," he inserts himself into the conversation, "it's a great deal if you get your investment back and make a profit. But I don't get how you control the whole selling thing. Do you get some kind of guarantee that you at least get the remodeling money back?"

"I don't get it either. Look what it says on the flyer here," says the young businessman. He pulls out the CT LLC Foreclosure Tours brochure and turns it over to the back side. Points with his finger and reads. "We guarantee that you will make a profit whenever a property is resold for a profit. Most of our partners make thousands of dollars!"

Tatiana has stopped in the middle of the great room and holds up her hand for quiet. "Now, people," she says, "you will see this house is needing very little remodeling. Almost pure profit in this one. Look," she waves her hand towards the open kitchen. "All new Wolf applinces in the kitchen. Is very good brand. And then, if you go through there, you will see master bedroom suit. Upstairs is bedrooms. If you have any questions, I am here to answer them!" She bestows her most charming smile at the group. "This has big-bucks potential!"

The construction guy in the dark green golf shirt raises his hand.

"Yes?" Tatiana frowns slightly. She prefers the questions one-on-one.

"Who guarantees the selling price on these houses?"

"Ha!" she waves her hand dismissively. "No need to guarantee! House will sell because you gonna do a great job making it resistible. And, if you don't feel confident to do work yourselves, we can provide excellent contractors for you. If you look at last flyer in your clipboard, is information on International Networking Production Technology Construction. Is very reputable company. Also notice that company offers very good financing options if you need help to get buy in." She turns towards the master bedroom before the poor guy can say another word.

He rifles through the papers attached to his clipboard and, there at the back, indeed, he finds a flyer.

INePT
International Networking Production
Technology Construction
Let us take the work out of remodeling.
A subsidiary of **INePT** Financing,
your worldwide partners

"Inept? What kind of bullshit is this?" grumbles the man.

"Let me see," says his partner. He leans over to look at the flyer.

"Miss," says the real estate lady in apricot. "Miss!"

"Yes?" says Tatiana, stopping at the doorway to the bedroom.

"What happens if the market goes down again? I mean, if the value of the property actually goes down in spite of the money we've invested in it, would we still at least get the money we spent on fixing it up?"

"Of course!" says Tatiana full of impatience. She wants to get this tour over with. Cyndee has discovered a listing for an incredible mansion on a hillside surrounded by vineyards. The owners just walked away, leaving everything. Apparently even the towels for the indoor swimming pool and spa. Tatiana can hardly wait. There's no lockbox yet, but Cyndee got a hold of the key from another agent she knows. They are going to have sexy fun tonight! Tatiana always wondered if boys were really what she wanted, and now she knows, nothing can compete with the scent of a woman.

Tatiana looks at the real estate lady and smiles. "Nothing to worry," she reassures the lady. "Government always has bailout."

Bibliography of Works cited in this book
(in order of publication)

The Dream: my life in real estate, by Ronald Ace, 1996, Hapencourt Publishing, Las Vegas.

The Magic of Business, by Ronald Ace, 1997, Spendabuck Publishers, Vacaville, California.

Failure Be Gone!, by Ronald Ace with Vocalis Hrodebert, 1999, Swedish version, printed by Uplifters Books, Los Angeles.

My Life!, by Ronald Ace, 2000, Hapencourt Publishing, Las Vegas.

The Art of Huge, by Ronald Ace, 2000, Spendabuck Publishers, Vacaville, California.

How to Be Great, by Ronald Ace, 2001, Uplifters Books, Los Angeles.

The Art of Big Me, by Ronald Ace, 2002, Hapencourt Publishing, Las Vegas.

Don't Be a Loser, by Ronald Ace, 2005, Uplifter Books, Los Angeles.

The Art of the Resurrection, by Ronald Ace with Lada Ace, 2006, Hapencourt Movie Publications, Culver City.

Also cited in this book:

Broccoli Beef for the Heart, edited by Nyll Esor, 2005, Uplifter Books, Los Angeles.

REmixRag, the magazine for discerning re's. April, 2006. San Francisco.

About the authors

Susan Rose is a writer, editor and translator. She holds a degree in linguistics, spent time at Stanford, and was a long-time member of the Geneva Writers Group and the Bern Writers Workshop. She trained in screenwriting in London.

Thomas Pareto practiced the art of real estate, until opting for a more straight-forward occupation. He holds a degree in Business from Dominican University.

They live in the idyllic town of Petaluma, chained to the natural beauty of a state that's going bankrupt, with their children, dogs, and The Alpha Cat.

Special thanks to Carlos Mencia. If you aren't laughing, you aren't living.

For more updates on this book, go to www.TRUMPEDthenovel. com, or join us on Facebook.

Breinigsville, PA USA
15 April 2010
236237BV00001B/5/P